Francesca

Francesca

a novel

by

ROGER SCRUTON

SINCLAIR-STEVENSON

First published in Great Britain by
Sinclair-Stevenson Limited
7/8 Kendrick Mews
London SW7 3HG, England

Copyright © 1991 by Roger Scruton

All rights reserved. Without limiting the rights under copyright
reserved, no part of this publication may be reproduced, stored in or
introduced into a retrieval system or transmitted, in any form or by any
means (electronic, mechanical, photocopying, recording or otherwise),
without the prior written permission of both the copyright owner and the
above publisher of this book.

The right of Roger Scruton to be identified as author of
this work has been asserted by him in accordance with the
Copyright, Designs and Patents Acts 1988.

British Library Cataloguing in Publication Data
A CIP catalogue record for this book is available from the British Library.
ISBN: 1 85619 048 X

Typeset by Colset Pte. Ltd., Singapore
Printed and bound in Great Britain by
Billings Book Plan Ltd

One

MR FERGUSON, deputy master of Bassington Primary School, sat in sunlight among the papers in his living room, his bird-like eyes alert and glinting in their nests of hair. In his right hand was an old copy of the *New Statesman*, twisted into a cornet, which he banged and clattered against his knee. When his son had pushed himself through the door, and taken up his place in the clearing reserved for accusations, Mr Ferguson, with an impatient gesture, flung the paper away. It struck a pile of *Manchester Guardians*, unfurled itself, and then flopped exhausted against the box of cuttings marked 'Hedgerows'.

'I wanted your help,' Mr Ferguson said, 'and off you go, palely loitering.'

'I was up the hill,' said Colin, in a voice from which he had carefully removed all traces of expression.

'Do I care where you were?'

'Yes, on the whole.'

As the schoolmaster launched into his prepared speech, rehearsing the real and hypothetical crimes for which it was his duty to reprimand his son, Colin let his mind stray towards the future. To be an actor or musician was beyond his powers. He could neither sing, nor play nor paint. According to Mr Kendrew, the English master at Dunsbury Grammar, his writings were ridiculous, for reasons which had been so perfectly expressed by Dr Leavis as to require no further elaboration. All things considered it would be best to start life as a dustman. He would grow strong and angry with the dirt and the lowliness. His friends would treat him with respect, while he would look down on his occupation from heights which secretly distinguished him. As his father continued to address the imaginary jury in the newspapers, Colin moved backwards towards the hallway, fixing his eyes with an expression of beatific detachment on a spot just above the wisp of light-filled hair which haloed Mr Ferguson's head. He reached the threshold without special difficulty. If he left the house now he could catch the six thirty to Paddington. But just as Colin had collected his muscles for the decisive turn, the schoolmaster paused, holding his breath, and widening his eyes in a theatrical gesture.

'Hear that?' he asked, expelling the air from his lungs.

'Hear what?'

'The yellow hammer. Listen. There's another one. Across the valley, answering. Beautiful eh?'

Colin said nothing.

'Off you go now.'

Colin turned towards the kitchen; what was to have been the decisive rebellion had become an act of obedience. So it was with the schoolmaster's ploys.

On the kitchen table he found a shopping bag, containing cheese, pickles, tomatoes, a loaf of white bread and, in a sheet of greaseproof paper, a dripping lardy-cake, stuffed with currants. Colin tipped the objects out, and arranged them in a circle, with the cake in the centre. He filled a kettle from the kitchen tap, and stared for a moment at the wall of the garden. Soon his father appeared, clapping his hands and running across the room towards the window.

'Shoo! Shoo!' he cried. *'Raus, vai, imshi!'*

He threw open the back door, clapped his hands twice more, and then stood still a moment. He sniffed the air, looking from side to side with a faintly puzzled expression. Returning, he caught sight of his son, and said,

'Have you begun the tea?'

'Yes. Are you having some?'

'Not while there is work to do.' He sat at the wooden table

and began to take off his shoes. 'I might just sit down for a moment.'

Leaving his shoes on the kitchen table, the schoolmaster went fidgeting back into the living room to retrieve his paper. He began to read aloud, an old and angry article about the countryside, which blamed the landed classes for waste and desecration.

It was Colin's task to lay the table. The schoolmaster therefore placed his chair on the path to the sideboard, so that Colin had to move gingerly past him, avoiding his stare. Mr Ferguson's face was lined and sunken, and from within the bristling cavities his dark eyes never ceased to keep watch on his son. Colin avoided them, focusing instead on the large red ears, with their translucent edges, or on the thin sour mouth behind which the teeth chomped impatiently, like horses in a stable. As he passed Mr Ferguson's chair for the third time, a large bony hand suddenly reached out and grabbed him by the elbow.

'Leave off will you!'

'Ah,' Mr Ferguson replied, administering a sharp squeeze of fellowship, 'you cannot ignore me forever.'

'I don't see why not.'

Colin's response entitled the schoolmaster to renew his accusations. Mr Ferguson chose, however, to keep this moral advantage in reserve. He spoke in bonhomous tones, holding Colin firmly by the elbow-joint, which he manipulated with sharp prehensile fingers.

'So you had a walk on the hill, dreaming your dreams, planning your plans. Nice place, Offlet Hill, eh?'

Colin tried to free himself without making any sudden movement.

'Did you hear that they are going to build on it?'

Colin grunted. Spoliation was a subject on which he agreed with his father. Mr Ferguson knew this and pressed his advantage home.

'Suburban boxes over fifty acres, each with a concrete drive, a garage, and a sky-blue swimming pool.'

There was a silence. With a gentle tug Colin freed his elbow and stepped quickly out of reach.

'And do you know why? Do you know what that devious old bastard's up to? Do you?'

'Perhaps he needs the money.'

'As though they need money!'

'Well, it's their hill,' said Colin feebly, realising that he was supposed to mount a case for the Wimpoles, in order that his father should triumphantly demolish it. The schoolmaster uttered a loud guffaw.

'And how did they acquire it? Tell me.'

'I expect they inherited it.'

'I mean, how did they first acquire it?'

Colin had reached the table and sat down at his place. He pushed his father's shoes to one side, took a tomato from the plate and bit into it. It was fresh, cool, tickling his nostrils with its greenhouse smell.

'I'll tell you. Careful with those shoes: they're worth their weight in gold. Never, never despise a good shoe. That hill was common land – the earliest map of this region, dating from Richard I, makes it quite clear. It is referred to in the Chronicle as Oflaeta or Oflaetangrund: meaning a relinquished place. A specific ruling in the Manorial Court of John de Bury reaffirms the grant of that hill to the people of Bassington *jusque ad consummationem saeculorum*. Throughout the Black Death and the Peasants' Revolt the land was kept open for grazing, and the records of the Justices of the Peace show that each year for fifty years during the fourteenth and early fifteenth centuries a man was chosen from the village and the surrounding country, whatever its state of depopulation, to report abuses. Watch out with that lardy – nothing ruins a good shoe like pig's fat!'

'Why do you leave them on the table?'

'Are you interested in this argument or not?'

'I don't see it as an argument.'

'Only because your side is so poorly presented. Be that as it may. When the first Lord Shepton was elevated to the peerage, after systematic piracy off the coast of Portugal, and having acquired the neighbouring lands by a deal the details of which James Stuart, the first of England and the fourth of Scotland, refused to disclose even when petitioned by the Lord Chancellor at the request of the Upper House, when this great nobleman spread himself across the country like a plague, driving every living thing before him, naturally he wished to enclose the hill for sheep-farming. A specific judgment of the Court of Star Chamber in favour of the people of Bassington did nothing to deter him, and when his descendants were returned after the interregnum to "their ancient patrimony" as they called it, the hill was surreptitiously included in the petition, described not as Offlet Hill, but as "all that land lying between the stream known as the Ayle and the pastures of Murricombe, to the extent enjoyed by my father, Thomas Wimpole, Lord Shepton of this place". The hill was then planted, to make a pleasure ground for future Wimpoles, and from that moment, as you succinctly put it, the hill has been theirs. Don't touch those shoes, for Christ's sake!'

For two days now Colin had been feeling dizzy. He put down the uneaten slice of lardy cake, and looked across at the window: the world shuddered gently and then stood still. Sunbeams lazed along the garden wall, warming the brick from purple to umber and filling the crevices with shade. Beyond the wall the last three cedars of Lord Shepton's park stood, relaxed and still, leaning their bottom branches on the coping. Colin closed his eyes and thought of the Wimpoles, and of the strange chameleon landscape in which they were dissolved. As the hot afternoons wore on the cedars, elms and copper beeches were stirred by summer breezes; the whole estate would then lose its air of repose as the unprotected trees flung up their branches in a fantastic tarantella. Then Colin, viewing the house across the wild expanse, would believe his father's version. The limestone portico filled with shadows, moving through it like a train of ghosts; the windows, on other days so wide and full and smiling, were now opaque and streaked with pale reflections. And here and there on the balustrade – whether an effect of light or the flitting of doves and house-martens – a strange shifting movement caught his eye, as though something were trapped there and signalling for help. The estate seemed haunted by a fury, pursuing its tenants from age to age in search of expiation. Then the wind would drop, and the empty building would smile again at the tailored countryside, Palladian and public-spirited.

On Fridays the Sheptons would drive up, she in a sports-car, her head bandaged in obliterating scarves, he reclining barely visible, in the back of a whispering Rolls, wrapped in darkness like the creating Word. Three years ago Colin had caught sight of the girl who, gripped by a rigid nanny, had glanced at him over her shoulder with large and static eyes. Yesterday he had spoken to her in Angelo's Coffee Bar, where the sixth-formers from Dunsbury Grammar would gather after school. Today he was to have met her again, in the clearing beside the stream on Offlet Hill. She had not come, and he was half glad, since it made his departure easier.

'Suppose I had stayed up North now,' the schoolmaster was saying, 'working like your uncle in the mill that destroyed my mother and her own mother before her; suppose I had never been to night school, never joined the stampede of the socially mobile: how surprised I'd be by Pickford the estate manager, with his belief in the feudal principle; or by the Rev. Prescott-Haynes, peering at the peasants through spectacles balanced so nicely on his parchment nose. But by some extraordinary contortion of destiny I became a schoolmaster. Only a very junior schoolmaster, because the better positions in our village are reserved for communicant members of the C of E. But all the same, enough of a schoolmaster that I look on this rural order with a certain nostalgia, false consciousness as the master would say. Depressing, don't you think? Or don't you?'

The schoolmaster, after sifting through these peevish

disappointments, began a chapter of his autobiography, describing again his birth and childhood, in the slums of a fictive Manchester. The wire-limbed little Ferguson moved adroitly in that dreadful place, avoiding the man-eating machinery, dodging the hands of jailers, and stopping his ears to the cries of those in chains. By cunning and hard work he reached the Night School, from where he journeyed South, by goods train, carthorse, army truck and bicycle, interviewing knights, trade union leaders, shepherds, Methodists and itinerant salesmen, and forging from their combined advice a new philosophy of man. The epic story, which had been often told, and to which Colin could never listen with his full attention, ended in Bassington, in the ill-favoured cottage by the Hall. Here it was that Mr Ferguson spent his days, tunnelling beneath the edifice of England, so as to bring ruin and confusion to those who had usurped the land of Hamden, Prynne and Morris.

The schoolmaster had taken inspiration from his new surroundings – from the soft green fields, from the hedgerows and copses, from the stone quoins and wooden lintels behind which the gnome-like people of England hid from their oppressors. With what delight he had learned the names and the habits of birds and animals, and how cheerfully he had conscripted them to the socialist cause. Every fruit and flower and fungus, every fidgety and feathered thing joined in the condemnation of injustice, and waited impatiently for the day of its emancipation. And in this tapestry of nature, Colin learned, a human form had been secretly woven. Inconceivable though it was, Colin issued from the womb of a woman, and not from his father's head. But the woman had died, having just enough life to pass on to her infant, and unwilling to adopt the role which Mr Ferguson offered her. In her the schoolmaster lost his hope of respectability. For she was a local girl, daughter of a Dunsbury photographer, a chapel-goer and a giver of tea-parties. After her death it was evident to everyone that the sharp-eyed Northerner – who may not have been from

Manchester at all, and who kept no visible records of his past besides the few smudged photographs of wartime Baghdad – was not a natural addition to Bassington society, and could be entrusted with children only so long as supervised by a colleague more respectable than himself. This colleague was the ageing Miss Spink, with whom Mr Ferguson was not on speaking terms. It was Miss Spink who had revealed to the Parent-Teachers' Association that, in every questionnaire which asked for his religion, the schoolmaster wrote 'ATHEIST' in bold capital letters.

The ruin of his prospects did not matter, however – so declared the autobiography – beside the terrible discovery that the life of the English countryside, the life to which Mr Ferguson had entrusted all his hopes of national resurrection, was no more. He looked around in bewilderment, seeing the wounded land churned open by the machines of Manchester; seeing the zombie-like workmen, crawling half blind from the earth, with those angry proletarian faces which he had wished never to see again; confronting the destruction of ancient things and recognising, at last, that it was better never to have questioned them.

Suddenly, with a piercing shriek, the schoolmaster catapulted from his chair and splayed his face against the window.

'There he goes,' he cried, 'a vole! See, there, in the lettuces, the thieving bastard!' His voice softened. 'Beautiful creatures though, the way they nibble. Quivering all over, like old maids at a tea-party.' His tone changed again, and he added, 'A pity you're so blind to nature. You could have learned a lot from it. Too late now.'

Mr Ferguson suddenly turned from the window and roared with laughter, barking into the space before him as though to ward off a foe.

'Off you go then,' he said, between bursts of merriment. 'Off you go to the promised land!'

So richly absurd was Colin's wish to leave home, that only Biblical phrases could encompass it.

'I thought I'd have tea first,' said Colin.

'Tea? I'm not hungry. Count me out.'

'I hadn't counted you in.'

'Ah,' said the schoolmaster with a sage nod; 'but I might have a bite of lardy.'

He took a knife from the table and ran it across the waxy surface of the cake, dividing it impartially into imaginary slices. Then, without warning, he threw down the knife with a gesture of disgust, and stood back from the table. Bending forward, he became small and concentrated like a gnome; his eyes fixed his son with malevolent intensity.

'So do you know why old Shepton wants to build on Offlet Hill? Do you? No? Then I'll tell you: in order to spite me. In order to punish me for having won the fight against his shopping centre. That's why!'

Colin looked at his father, and felt a wave of pity.

'Do you think so?' he said.

Mr Ferguson spat.

'Of course not. It's just a fantasy.'

He gave a croak of dismal laughter.

'The Sheptons need to augment their substance,' Mr Ferguson continued. 'It stands to reason. "He is deserving of praise and full of divine spirit, whose account books at his death show that he has gained more than he inherited". Cicero. But if you inherit nothing you gain nothing. "Unto him that hath shall be given, and from him that hath not shall be taken away – yea, even that which he hath!"'

The schoolmaster uttered a raucous chuckle, and repeated more softly, 'yea, even that which he hath'. And, shaking his head, he retired into the living room, his eyes fixed on his son in a steady gaze of admonition, his bony fingers reaching out to the dado and guiding him backwards through the door.

Colin's way across the uncut meadow was gay with hawkweed and moon-daisies, and as he went he sang to a mixture of hymn tunes his song of trial and victory.

> Bear it all with fortitude,
> Go down on bended knee;
> Adopt a cringing attitude
> For soon you will be free!

Then he began to quieten, fixing his mind on the bid for freedom that he was about to make. Passing the gates of Bassington Hall, he glanced down towards the house. The windows were walled with the white of fastened shutters, and all was dead and still. Heat and silence pressed each other, wedging in every corner of the world. The gravel path, the hydrangea border, the stock-still rhododendron patch, the scattered soldiery of elms and conifers: all were filmed with expectation. How queer he felt, emptied like a mummy. He wished he could believe in God, to feel this moment as the sign of God's beatitude. But the mocking Mr Ferguson had rampaged through the rows of tender doctrine, and torn up every shoot. Colin's heart, attuned to nothingness, turned inward to protect its void.

His thoughts went back to Francesca Wimpole, and to their meeting in Angelo's. It had been Colin's turn to read; he had chosen a passage from his notebook. His friend Michael shook his tousled rabbi's head; the other members of the Literary Dozen smiled at his gauche uncertain sentences. Looking up, he noticed two girls in the neighbouring alcove. One was an oval-faced beauty, with slender Spanish eyes, who had already caught the attention of Michael's neighbour. Her companion shifted with annoyance at the boy's attentions, and now looked up at Colin as though expecting something. Their glances met, and she began to watch him from a strange, still face in which the eyes scarcely moved. Colin returned to his notebook. But the consciousness of her eyes confused him. He slapped down his hand on the open page.

'That's it,' he said.

Michael began to catalogue Colin's errors: mixed metaphors, disordered images, uncertain rhythms, unhappy words. Colin barely listened; instead he looked across at the girl. She was less beautiful than her companion: her hair was blonde, lustrous, healthy, but somehow detached from her head and disordered like a stage wig. Her complexion was pale, smooth, but just short of that morning freshness which had been the trigger of his first desires. Her eyes too – pebble-grey, solemn, spiritual – lacked the spark of animation, the hint of whim and gaiety which he had coveted in other girls. Her lips were thin, pale, motionless, but with a tense, arrested quality, as though she were seized by secret thoughts, and was trying not to utter them. Only the nose, which was slender and classical, and the rounded chin were truly pretty. Yet for Colin she possessed an advantage over every other girl – namely, that she looked at him with interest and sympathy. Warmed and bewildered, he saw perfection in her face. There was a queer beauty, too, in her astonished eyes, which seemed to stare hopelessly across a void which they themselves created. He got up, made as if to leave, and then went to her table. Only when he stood beside her, and had a view from above of her stringy body, did he recognise the girl whom he had glimpsed three years before, dragged across the gravel by a striding nanny.

'You are Francesca Wimpole,' he said in alarm.

'Ah. I was wondering who I am. Thank you.'

Her voice was soft, barely audible, and she held her left hand close to her eyes as she spoke.

He tried to laugh, but uttered only a thin, disconcerting croak which reminded him of the schoolmaster.

'I liked what you read,' she added.

'Did you really?'

'Yes. Only I don't know much about it.'

'I live next door to you,' he said. 'Perhaps we could meet?'

'Perhaps.'

'Tomorrow, for instance.'

'Here?'

'Not here. Maybe – maybe Offlet Hill.'

And he described the place where she would find him, at

the clearing's edge, where the stream ran over salmon-coloured pebbles, between banks honeycombed by life. She nodded, her eyes, which had neither shifted from his face nor registered any change in the impassable distance between them, now at last relaxed, dismissing him.

Colin's recollections were disturbed by a sound, like a whispering of tiny wings, darting and hovering in the air around him. The ground seemed to sway, and he reached out for the gate-post of the Hall. Above him, a rampant lion tossed its head in disdain. An old red Citroën entered the driveway, scrunching the gravel and setting off at a whisper towards the house. In the back, squeezed between two large men, sat Francesca. She seemed to turn towards Colin, but only with the slightest movement; just as he caught her eye and shot it full of a reproachful sorrow, she adjusted her position, shoved her shoulders against her companions, and then sat rigidly, staring ahead.

He was sure that she had commanded him to follow. But something was wrong with his legs; after a few yards he sat down on a wrought-iron bench that stood beside the gravel path.

He watched a pair of willow-warblers as they streaked the elms with yellow, flicking their tails and whistling in mock astonishment. One of the schoolmaster's favorite lectures concerned the distinction between the willow-warbler and the chiff-chaff. Colin reflected with wonder on this godless man, for whom the world shone with brightest difference, brimful of interest as though it had missed being created only by the smallest fraction of a cause. Whatever happened to Colin, whatever good or evil things should come to pass, he knew that God would not be part of them; the riches of the world had been disclosed to him, their magic dwelt upon and scorned, and where the sacred fount of worship once had stood, he saw only the empty well of curiosity. This at least he would take with him; this at least his father had achieved.

'I *thought* it was you.'

Colin must have slept. He looked up at Francesca, with

no recollection of her footsteps. The pattern of her yellow frock was dimly suggestive of ancient pageantry, and round her neck, falling into the flat hollow of her chest, was a double chain of amber beads, with a golden cross attached to them. The peculiar elegance of this ornament was neutralised by a large gun-metal brooch in the shape of a pig, ridiculously inset with a pearly pink eye. He was struck by a certain disproportion of her cheek bones, which caused her mouth to shift upwards to one side as she smiled, tightening the flesh at the lower corner, and giving to her features a slightly mischievous expression, like a child tempting him to crime. She held her left hand close to her face, ready to veil it.

'Didn't we have a date?' Colin asked.

'I'm not allowed to have *dates*. To be precise, I'm under the age of consent.'

'Surely you can consent to a date? In any case, you did.'

'In a moment of weakness,' she said faintly, bringing her hand closer to her brow.

'Perhaps. But it's a greater weakness, having consented, not to come.'

'I'm sorry.'

For a moment a rapid mime of repentance traversed her features, and she seemed as sorry as any teenage girl could ever be for anything.

'Not that it matters,' he added hastily.

'It does matter. It was very wicked, probably. I expect I'll be punished for it in purgatory, if I get there. One more addition to the heap of sins.'

'Are you serious?'

She looked down at him in vague surprise, as though from some remote oriole window in a castle wall.

'Why shouldn't I be?'

Colin recalled a visit to the new Catholic church in Dunsbury, the smell of incense, the pale-faced altar boys, and the old women for whom this alone was home. Of all the many forms of superstition, Mr Ferguson had said, that of Rome was worst; many times in childhood the Protestant martyrs had been whipped in procession through Colin's thoughts, showing their horrid wounds, and reproving him from stern and outraged faces. His sympathies therefore went out to Rome, as they went out to anyone who tortured those who tortured him. To believe, he believed, was to believe as Catholics did: blindly, submissively, not disturbing God with those awkward questions which the schoolmaster malevolently laid before Him. The wickedness of the Wimpoles, however, had always been painted in Trollopian colours. They had never joined in any feast, service or charity, never been seen in church or chapel, given nothing to any fête, jumble sale or gymkhana. Only an Anglican would have the effrontery to remain aloof from matters of such pressing public concern.

'Are you really Catholics?'

'You mean, are Catholics really Catholics?'

'I mean, is your family Catholic?'

Francesca looked at him curiously.

'Good Lord no,' she said. Her hand passed twice across her face, and then dropped a fraction so that he could catch her words. 'My father's an atheist, my mother's a Jew, and my brother's some kind of Buddhist, except he believes in killing things.'

'But you're a Catholic?'

'Yes. You see I go to a Catholic school, and my best friend's a Catholic. Only I don't believe everything they believe.'

'Such as?'

'Miracles, saints, and – for instance, the immaculate conception.'

The phrase seemed pure, statuesque, like a saint in marble. It was from such phrases, he supposed, that the Catholic faith had been concocted; permanent, untouchable words which stood guardian over the mutable speech of men. He studied Francesca with a vague sense of disappointment. She had a queer, hard, flattened quality, like a cardboard cut-out.

'If I were a Catholic,' he said, 'I think I should believe in that.'

'In what?'

'In the immaculate conception.'

'Would you? I don't think so. Or if you did, it would be because you confused it with the virgin birth.'

'Is that wrong?'

'Very wrong.'

But to Colin it did not seem wrong at all, to confound all the doctrines, and deepen the mystery of each.

'Though not so wrong as me standing you up,' she added, 'when I don't know you and don't know what you'll think.'

Again there was something theatrical in her apology, something almost defiant, as though she were indicating that the Wimpoles had every right, so far as he were concerned, to behave just as they chose, and that it was for them alone to take the consequences, something, moreover, that they were well equipped by breeding to endure.

'Maybe you had something important on your mind,' Colin suggested. He looked at her, attempting a smile. But his sight was blurred, and her features danced before him in a cubist disarray. Only the eyes seemed steady, watching across a distance he would never travel.

'Yes, there was a family meeting; a three-line whip. And I couldn't get hold of you. Actually, I don't know your name.'

'Colin Ferguson.'

Her eyes narrowed.

'Your father must be Mr Ferguson, the schoolteacher.'

'Is that bad news?'

'My father is always rather angry about Mr Ferguson.'

Colin felt a twinge of loyalty.

'My father is always very angry about Lord Shepton.'

'There you are, you see,' she said, as though something in question had at last been proved. Suddenly Colin leaned forward on the seat and, without looking at her, began to speak about his father's worries. It was not right to build on

Offlet Hill; it was not right to spoil Bassington, to wipe away the face of history, to mutilate the gift of nature; if he were not leaving soon, he would join his father in the battle to conserve the place. She too should join; did she not like the country? Did she not feel attached to this place, where she lived, and where her ancestors had lived before her?

'But I don't live here,' she put in. 'I'm at school, near Canterbury.'

'Then why are you here?'

He looked up and saw her reticence.

'Oh, nothing; a sort of illness. Go on about the country. I liked listening to you.'

The evening light crested the rhododendrons, and a slight rustle of breeze set the trees dancing behind her.

'My father is very upset about Offlet Hill,' Colin said, and then hesitated.

'Oh dear. That means he'll get up a petition. My father was so furious about the last one. He called Mr Ferguson a bloody Marxist. What *is* a Marxist?'

'Someone who believes in the ideas of Marx.'

'And what are they?'

'I'm not sure.'

'You must know something, if your father believes in them. My father believes in the "harsh discipline of the market". Which means, so far as I can make out, the survival of the fittest. I am not one of the fittest.'

'My father believes that all men are equal, that it's wrong for some to have everything while others have nothing, and that it's particularly wrong for someone of talent and public spirit to have to put up with a job that is beneath him and to live in a cottage beside a great man's estate. That sort of thing.'

'Don't talk about class; it's so embarrassing. I can't bear it.'

'I don't find it embarrassing,' he said resentfully.

'That's because you don't have to go around feeling apologetic, knowing that people like you for the wrong reasons, and that you're bound to let them down.'

'Do you think I like you for the wrong reasons?'

'I expect so. It hadn't occurred to me. That you like me, I mean.'

'I like you very much.'

He felt a surge of anxiety, as though making a commitment which he could never honour. She gave him a serious look.

'After one meeting? Or one point two meetings? Isn't that a bit – immature?'

'You mean premature.'

'I think I mean immature,' she answered. 'Don't be offended. I'm immature myself.'

'Then perhaps you too can like someone after one point two meetings?'

'I don't know. Perhaps I can.'

Suddenly she raised both hands to her mouth, and pressed them against it, as though stifling a cry.

'I'm so silly!' she said. 'I've got to go back. I'm sorry.'

'So am I.'

'Let's meet tomorrow, on the hill, where you said. Can I call you Colin?'

She turned away, her movements jerky and agitated. Her narrow shoulders seemed to tremble beneath the dress, and she raised one hand to her ear and held it there as though in pain.

'I shall be gone tomorrow.'

She half turned, her face contorted, her thin lips taut and ugly.

'Tomorrow at five,' she said.

'Francesca.'

'Yes. You can call me Francesca. I've got to go.'

Without waiting for his reply she sped down the drive. A cloud covered the sun, chilling the air; swallows began to fly low under the trees, rocking from side to side and darting swiftly past him. He could not move. He looked down the path in the direction she had taken, but saw only the house, decked by the late sun with improbable gold pennants among its still grey stones. His eyes strayed beyond the house, to the side of Offlet Hill, where a clearing of horse-sick pasture held back the line of trees. A heron flapped its slow dark wings above the hidden stream, reached a copse of aspens, and disappeared beneath the canopy of leaves. Had he met her there, he would have enlisted her in the war against the schoolmaster: he would have cast her in some glamourising role, as Lorna Doone or Mélisande, as Rosalind or Albertine. But she had taken the matter from his hands, and rewritten his future in a language of ambiguities. She was not the creature of his fantasies, but an independent being, a will, a life and a sovereign bewilderment. None of the categories through which he had conceived her applied to the reality. She was neither strong, nor cold, nor dignified, nor truly aristocratic. She was neither indifferent to him, nor ready to love; neither anxious to please nor scornful. She was remote from her family, from her background and from the world, and even her religion – which would otherwise have been the perfect defiance of Mr Ferguson's philosophy – was a peculiar discovery of her own, a historical accident, through which she asserted her separateness from all that was expected. Most of all she was frightened – more frightened than he was – but of what he could not tell. The hand which went so quickly to her face, and the eyes which watched so steadily, were on their guard against a disaster which was not merely suspected, but foreseen. He thought of those gestures, and shuddered, as though he too were to suffer from the thing which threatened her. And he knew – with that inexplicable certainty which is also a kind of deep and willing renunciation – that he would contrive to be with her, for just so long as she existed.

The sun had vanished, and homeward-flying ducks shot in pairs across the red-veined sky. A light went on in a remote corner of the Hall. Colin tried to raise himself; but still his legs would not obey him. His head had begun to throb, like a drum softly beaten, and his hands seemed feathery and insubstantial. He called out in alarm; but his voice was a whisper, and no one answered it.

The last train left Dunsbury at half past nine: he must start at once. Colin tried to fix his mind on the future, but nothing occurred to him, save the image of himself as a clerk in a London office. After his suicide his writings would be discovered in a drawer, neatly wrapped in waxy paper. During his weeks of humiliation he would have recorded everything seen and heard, and his employers would be amazed and ashamed to read their portraits. But just how this life, and this death, would constitute a defeat for Mr Ferguson, Colin could not envisage. Perhaps it would be better to postpone things till a better plan of action could be formulated – one in which Francesca could be included. That was it: he would meet her, in the horse-sick field beside the stream, where the water ran over salmon-coloured stones.

But now his head was drooping, a muddiness was thrown across his thoughts like slapstick, and only a few sparse fragments of consciousness grinned through. A silver-blue tube approached through the twilight. He heard voices, confused, feminine, and alert with indignation. He was sure he could answer their charges, if only they would give him time. He was sure he could establish a right to their protection; he was sure he could find the words which they required. 'Please,' he whispered, 'please.' And then all was dark and silent.

Seeing him slumped on the bench, Lady Shepton drove quickly past: Pickford would see to it. And half an hour later Pickford did see to it, carrying the unconscious Colin to the cottage by the Hall.

Two

'HERE,' said Mr Ferguson, 'this letter came for you.' Colin opened his eyes. His father's face was shrivelled like a walnut, the eyes alert and malignant in their lairs. He stooped through a white haze, a white-coated acolyte beside him.
'Where am I?'
'In Dunsbury, of course. Did you expect a private hospital?'
'Hospital?'
Colin fingered the letter. His name had been written carefully, in black italic letters. The postmark was Canterbury.
'Francesca,' he said. He remembered voices, murmurings, short gestures and hurried steps, and somewhere, very faint and faraway, the high, thin, haunting music of a choir.
'How?' he asked.
'He'll come round soon,' said the nurse. Colin looked at her. The skin of her face was tight and shiny, as though clipped somewhere at the back of her head. She wore a starched bonnet, perched like a Christmas decoration in her hair.
'What do you mean?' he asked. 'I'm round already.'
The nurse glanced at the schoolmaster, who looked at her with an expression of knowing distaste.
'You see,' she explained. 'He is always a bit woozy at first. Aren't we, Colin?'
'What's wrong with me?'

'Ah! There's the question,' Mr Ferguson said, rubbing his hands in a distant reference to anxiety. 'They suspected meningitis. Your temperature was consonant with the most romantic speculations. But that was two weeks ago, when Mr Pickford first brought you in. The prognosis is now more sober.'

'When am I coming out?'

'Alas quite soon. I shall have to supervise your convalescence. Can you imagine what hell it is going to be?'

It was odd, but the schoolmaster was crying. The whiteness of the room expanded and absorbed him. For a second Colin enjoyed the radiant nothingness before his eyes. And then he slept.

The morning light swept through the ward, glittering over the bottles, and tinting the sheets with the colour of vanilla ice-cream. The striped patients lay on the mounds like candy bars, sinking slowly. Only by an immense effort of the eyes could he keep them from melting away. Colin tried to sit up, and failed.

'Nurse!'

A rustle of starch traversed the open centre of the ward. And then the sudden photograph of a sympathetic face.

'Yes Colin.'

'That letter. What did you do with it? Where is it?'

'Beside you. Shall I open it?'

Colin nodded, and the ward nodded with him. For a moment all the old men wore flowers for hair, and their teeth seemed like the fragments of glass thermometers. It was not until the next day that, reaching to the table at his side, he was able to hold the letter in his hand. He hoped that his father had not been in to visit him; the schoolmaster would have perused the letter, and perhaps copied it down to be used in evidence.

After a while he was able to read. The handwriting was crisp, precise, adult, with the occasional arty flourish which arbitrarily bridged the gaps between words.

Dear Colin,

I came to the place and waited, and came again the next day, and the next. Eventually I made tactful approaches to Piggy (Mr Pickford to you), because I assumed he had driven you away. I just made a sort of general enquiry, about your father and Offlet Hill, and what Piggy thought of it all, and then he told me how he had found you in the drive and how they suspected meningitis and I nearly died. When I had finished reading the medical dictionary, trying to avoid those positively ghoulish illustrations all of which set you thinking about your own little cuts and swellings, and how they might grow, I went straight to Piggy and said he had got to find out if it was true. He is terrific in a crisis and asks no questions. He came back in an hour and said no, you were alright, a virus or something, but that they were keeping you in Dunsbury. I wanted to write to you straight away but I couldn't think what to say. But now I'm in St. Cat's and expect you're out of hospital it all seems a bit less of a panic, so I thought I'd just write now during prep. and tell you to get well – that's an order – and to write as soon as you feel like it. It is awful here in Canterbury, but I don't suppose you want to hear about it. When I see you, I shall tell you about the German mistress, with whom I'm madly in love. Get well, you must. This is a very silly letter and I shall have to stop writing now and pretend to be doing my maths. You've no idea how upset I was not seeing you again.

Love,
Francesca (Wimpole).

Colin read the letter several times, and then, seeing the schoolmaster fidgeting down the ward, he folded it and pushed it beneath the pillow.

'Ah,' said Mr Ferguson. 'Well again. All credit to the NHS. I suppose you'll be out in a few days. But it would be rather miserable back in the cottage don't you think?'

'I want to come home. I'm not ill any more.'

'Home. Yes, well, you are old enough to leave school at

the end of term: or earlier. Also I think I inspire in you a certain restlessness. Did you know that I have changed my job?'

Colin looked across the ward at Mr Willis, who was sitting up, in bright blue pyjamas, smiling serenely at Colin and mouthing something with his lips. Mr Willis would cry out in the middle of the night, throwing off the bedclothes and fumbling at his throat as though attempting to release himself from the grip of a strangler. Soon the nurses would bear down on him with their trays of surrealist food, causing him to shriek aloud in mock repugnance at the impossible pastel shades and glutinous textures. Colin liked Mr Willis because, although he had been a gardener before his thrombosis, he had found the opportunity to learn all of Shakespeare. Yesterday Mr Willis's neighbour had died, complaining bitterly against a speech of Goneril's with which Mr Willis sought to console him. Mr Willis had abruptly ceased, saying 'Convey my respects to the Bard, Mr Jephson,' and turned in bed with a loud wail of uncanny laughter.

'What are you thinking?' asked Mr Ferguson.

'I am thinking that you make no sense today.'

'I admit, there was a certain impetuosity. Genuine information is difficult to convey. Depending, of course, on the circumstances.'

The schoolmaster rubbed his hands and cackled noiselessly.

'You see,' he explained, 'I have signed on the dotted line. I have conveyed my soul in feoff perpetual to the establishment. I have made the ultimate gesture of capitulation. In short, I am now a communicant member of the Church of England.'

Colin grunted, knowing that his father could not join a church for so simple a reason as that he believed in it.

'Yes,' the schoolmaster continued, 'I have changed my job. I am headmaster elect of Murricombe primary. *Étonnant, n'est-ce pas?*'

Colin watched the nurses approach Mr Willis, with their trolley of tinted exhibits from the slime museum.

'You see,' said Mr Ferguson, 'we had to move. We lost the battle for the hill. What could we do but move? What would you do? Is there a single alternative that occurs to you?'

Colin felt light-headed. He was a bird, suspended above his father's world, and seeing only the flat, vain contours of a landscape that was almost still. One or two words seemed to detach themselves just occasionally, to rise up towards him and then sink back again. The hill: but why connected with communion? Had Francesca been walking there? No doubt Lord Shepton had forbidden her. Francesca was a Catholic. He remembered the golden cross, hanging among the beads in the flat of her chest. And he remembered the pig.

'Does Piggy know?' he asked.

'Does what?'

The schoolmaster shook his head. The wings of the bird were pinned to the sky.

'I think you have not grasped the import of what I am saying.'

'Tell me again. Why have we sold our souls?'

'My dear boy. We have had to move. I had to take the headmastership at Murricombe. A house goes with it. We will be better there, less on top of each other. The doctor thought it would be better so. He even entertained the fiction that your illness might have a nervous origin. I should not tell you that, however; it can only encourage your belief that you have an artistic temperament.'

The schoolmaster laughed and hunched his shoulders. Mr Willis laughed silently with him, tossing a piece of violet hospital jelly into the air. He caught it in his expert mouth, turned and then spat it through the window.

'Mr Willis!' the nurse cried out.

'I am not moving. I want to stay in the cottage.'

'Alas, the cottage is to be sold. Pickford has been negotiating. His lordship wants to demolish it, so as to widen the road. You will appreciate that, with the new houses, there will be far more traffic through the village.'

'What new houses?'

'The houses that they are building, on Offlet Hill.'

'You have made a mistake.'

'Well, let's leave it at that. You will be out soon. I hope to have the house in order. There is not much to be done, on the whole.'

The schoolmaster gave a queer smile, and Mr Willis, noticing it, responded.

'Imagine the colour of my insides,' he shouted across the ward. 'Purple, rose-pink, lime-green, eau-de-nil, no wonder I feel so grotty. I ask you, is it a way to treat a gentleman?'

Mr Ferguson nodded amiably, and then, in a gesture of unusual intimacy, he squeezed his son's hand. Colin withdrew it, and tried to pull himself up in bed.

'Well, I shall be back tomorrow. Is there anything I can do? Any letter, for instance, that I might post?'

'What do you mean?'

'I only wondered. You'll be right as rain in a few days. Pity about your A-levels, of course. But you can always take them next year.'

When the schoolmaster was gone, Colin re-read Francesca's letter. It was clear that he must go to London. He would be a waiter in some fashionable restaurant. While frowning over his pad, he would note down the words and postures of the guests. Francesca would come on some shopping expedition with her mother, and sit down for lunch.

The next day he began to compose a reply.

Dear Francesca,
Your letter was so nice that I don't know what to say. Not seeing you again was the worst consequence of this silly illness. Lying here, I often feel that I am talking to you, and last night I dreamed that I held you by the hand.

In fact he had dreamed of a grave, where dark lizards flopped noiselessly about a coffin. His father lay in it, laughing quietly to himself, his body scattered all over with autumn leaves.

I wish I had some books here, so I could send you a poem. My father brought a textbook of local history, and a copy of a letter that he wrote to *The Times*, which they did not publish. When is your term over? Where will you be? There is something I want to tell you.

He broke off and tore up the letter. After several more attempts he lay back in a feverish doze, listening to the relaxed and routine noises of the ward, and occasionally exchanging a smile with Mr Willis, who had become quite confidential, and would cross the ward to converse with him. When Colin awoke from his doze he was not surprised to find Mr Willis standing beside him.

'I see that you have been trying to write a letter. I always used to find it so difficult writing letters, even to my family. But one day, browsing through the small ads in the *Telegraph*, I came across this chap who advertised a correspondence course in correspondence. Funny idea, but bless me if it wasn't genuine. I wrote off, with my postal order for three and six, and got back a sheet of beginner's notes, with a promise of a similar sheet every week for three months. It began with elementary dos and don'ts, proceeded to etiquette and titles, and ended with some pretty advanced and I should say, looking back on it, rather impertinent stuff, about the style of love-letters, with specific examples. Also, How to avoid an unwanted relative, How to return a present to a mother-in-law, How to insinuate yourself into higher office, and the like. I got quite handy at it, as I could tell from the pseudonymous letters that my friends began to receive. I don't mind saying that some of these missives were rather devastating. In fact the wife of my best friend replied to the address that I had borrowed for the occasion with a letter of quite intemperate passion, in which all her desires were explicitly described. Of course, I burned her letter, and she never found out that it was I who had disappointed her. However, all that is really by way of a preface to my next remark, which is that I am sure I could help you in your present difficulty, and I lay my services freely at your disposal.'

Colin had become so accustomed to Mr Willis that he found nothing to surprise him in this discourse. He pulled himself up on the pillow, and asked Mr Willis kindly if he would care to sit down. With an accomplished bow, Mr Willis drew up the hospital chair, and arranged his limbs meticulously in a posture that perfectly imitated a seated man, while discreetly betraying that it was no such thing. All Mr Willis's gestures had this theatrical quality, and Colin had come to the conclusion that nothing in Mr Willis's life had really happened to him, that everything had passed lightly over the surface of his being, leaving an inner changeless solitude. He felt privileged to know Mr Willis, to be treated as a glancing tangent to this unknowable sphere of loneliness.

'I should be grateful if you could compose a letter to my father,' he said, in his most confidential voice.

'My dear chap, that's as easy as pie. I believe we got to that by lesson five. If you would be so good as to acquaint me with the substance of the projected letter.'

'Well, I am going to run away. And I want him to send the equipment that I shall need.'

'Ah. There's a teaser. What equipment do you consider necessary?'

'I think, a change of clothes, a copy of Horace, and my Post Office account book.'

'May I be so bold as to ask how much your Post Office account contains?'

Colin looked at Mr Willis, whose brown eyes held him fixedly, and who had slightly risen in his chair. It was a rather captivating interpretation of the Family Solicitor.

'Three pounds nine shillings and ninepence.'

'Three pounds nine shillings and ninepence.'

Mr Willis spoke the words slowly, in order to demonstrate the inadequacy of each of them, and the utter futility of the whole.

'Oh, I shall supplement it. I shall work.'

'Work? You have been ill. You need to rest, to restore yourself, to put on flesh.'

Mr Willis rose to illustrate the idea of flesh with large and comprehensive gestures, throwing out the wings of his dressing gown and exposing the bright blue pyjamas, with buttons of yellowing bone. Colin wondered how Mr Willis had lived, or rather imitated the manners of the living. What house, what furniture, what rituals and fetishes surrounded him?

'The money would last a week or two. It is August. I could get a job harvesting, and they would put me up.'

'My dear Mr Ferguson . . .'

Mr Willis resumed the posture of the Family Solicitor. Colin smiled; he had never been called Mr Ferguson before. For some reason he thought of Francesca.

'Well,' he said, with an air of confidence. 'It's my decision. Your role is to compose the letter. If you want to, that is.'

'But you see, I envisage my role as extending just a tiny bit further than that. Just a very tiny bit.'

Mr Willis chuckled, and then called to the nurse.

'Sister! Fetch pen, ink and paper. Or failing those, a syringe.'

Soon he was writing, scratching his head through the thin wisps of hair, and occasionally rising to stroll about the ward. At one point he stopped before a withered face and declaimed:

> A garden is a lovesome thing, God wot!
> Rose plot,
> Fringed pool,
> Ferned grot –

> The veriest school
> Of peace; and yet the fool
> Contends that God is not –
> Not God! In gardens when the eve is cool?

'Mr Fogg, I see that I offend you. Forgive me. I am a gardener by profession. Nevermore shall I see my garden, nevermore shall I work in the sun. For I must die. Do forgive me for interrupting your meditations.'

His tone fell to a hushed whisper as he tiptoed away. He stopped several more times, to converse, declaim or admonish. On his return he reassumed his position at Colin's bedside, and scribbled rapidly on the sheet of paper that the nurse had provided.

'There,' he said, stretching forward with a sigh. 'I think that will do.'

Colin reached out to take the paper, but Mr Willis withheld it.

'I think I had better read it to you,' he said. 'I may be able to correct mistakes and infelicities as I proceed. So, here it is. We were taught to begin Dearest Father, or My Dear Father; however, having in a distant way taken note of your relations, and with due regard to the contents of the letter, I judge that it would be more in keeping to begin Dear Dad. I suggest that you then proceed as follows:

For some time now I have felt that I have been a burden to you. In order to avoid melodrama, and so that you will not think me ungrateful I have decided to take a short holiday. A certain Dr Willis, who toured the wards this morning, came to the conclusion that I am suffering from *morsus conscientiae*, and that I need a change of air. He attributed my condition to a variety of physical causes, but was of the opinion that the air of this district is particularly to be avoided by one in my condition. He has proposed to finance my holiday out of hospital funds, and has booked for me a hotel room in Majorca. I shall be leaving tomorrow, and will probably be in Majorca by the time you receive this letter.

Dr Willis advised that it would be best for me to recover completely before thinking further about family affairs. I hope you are well, and look forward to seeing you on my return.

'How would you end? Love Colin, something like that? Or just Colin? I hardly think that it matters.'
'But why didn't you mention the clothes?'
'Surely you have some clothes with you?'
'Or the Post Office account?'
Mr Willis chuckled.
'Yes. Well that, you see, is the part of the plan which I have yet to reveal to you. Should you like me to do so at once, or have you any further questions concerning the letter?'
'No further questions. No. It is a very good letter.'
'Then let us proceed. I brought with me to the hospital one hundred pounds, which I propose to advance to you. Should you feel inclined to repay it I shall leave you the address where I would live, were I to emerge from here. However, the circumstance is unlikely. I therefore think that you would be extremely foolish to think of repayment. Indeed, you have a certain obligation to remove this money from me, lest I remain too much attached to worldly things.'
Mr Willis had risen, and, interrupting Colin's vague protestations, began a sermon of thanksgiving for the relief of Mafeking. The relevance of this sermon was not immediately apparent to Colin, who lay back on the pillow deep in thought, wondering how he might explain the change in his circumstances to Francesca. His few feeble protests were for the sake of form, and also because he knew that Mr Willis would feel the drama to be incomplete without them.
'. . . and let us raise up our hearts and voices to the Lord in thanks for these mercies, and before all, for our Gracious King and Emperor for whom our many brave sons, husbands, friends, companions have willingly offered their lives, and to whom we again pledge allegiance even unto the death from which God in His mercy has yet chosen to spare us,

and pray that our gracious sovereign may long send us at his bidding and in the pursuance of all that is goodly and done out of sincere and seemly dutifulness to the uttermost parts of the earth, there to deploy our powers and our talents for the glory of the Lord and in accordance with national policy as the King and his ministers shall from time to time determine. In the name of the Father, the Son and the Holy Ghost. Amen. Nurse! Nurse, I say!'

'Oh Mr Willis!'

'Nurse, inspect this man. And if he is fit discharge him at once.'

Mr Willis saluted, wrote an address on the letter which he then dropped onto Colin's bed, and wandered across to his own side of the ward. He took a small briefcase from the bedside cupboard, and, extracting a wad of notes, returned to the chair in which he had been sitting. Very slowly, with Scrooge-like mutterings, he counted the notes onto the bedcover. Reshuffling them like a pack of cards, he counted them again. Handing them to Colin, he stood up, looked away, and said,

'That should see you through. Let me know if you need more.'

He went promptly back to his bed, rolled himself in the blankets, and feigned impenetrable sleep.

Colin copied out the letter to his father, and wrote again to Francesca. He told her about Mr Willis, and about his own plan to come to London. He asked if he could write to her frequently, and, after hesitating, signed 'love, Colin'. He looked again at her letter, and at the envelope which contained it, but could find no address. Eventually he wrote: Francesca Wimpole, St Catherine's School, near Canterbury, and gave both letters to the nurse, asking her to post them.

The next morning Colin crept out of the hospital while the night sister was dozing at her desk. By the time the schoolmaster was fretting in the foyer, he was on his way to London.

Three

TWO YEARS LATER, when Mr Willis died, Colin received another fifty pounds, forwarded to him at the address which he had sent to Dunsbury hospital. It was the remainder of Mr Willis's estate, and Colin lived on it while writing the first volume of his father's autobiography. He worked on the book in his room in the Commercial Road, sustaining himself with cornflakes and black coffee. From the window he watched the traffic, two floors beneath him, and the people as they jostled one another on the pavement. In this part of London people wore a sunken, provisional shape, as though the work of creation were still incomplete. Out in the street he looked away from their faces, and his conversations in the Three Crowns were withdrawn and monosyllabic.

His first lodging had been in North London, in the area below Hampstead that calls itself Hampstead but which in reality has no identity of its own, beyond the fact that unsettled people briefly settle there. The landlady lived further north, at an address which he had found in the window of a grocer's shop. She lived among rococo mirrors and Dresden china, in a low-ceilinged, long-corridored apartment with countless close-fitting, softly-clicking doors, through which she moved swan-like on a carpet of powder-blue. Was he looking for a job? Was he in touch with his parents? Would his mother be visiting? The survivor's instinct led him to answer 'yes' to all her questions, and in reward he found himself climbing the thirty rickety stairs to the cupboard that she had assigned to him, there to fold himself at once, unsheeted, in blankets which stank of cigarettes.

The stairs were populated at every hour. An anaemic woman in a stained amber shawl stood miauling at the front door, as though she wished to be let either out or in – he could never decide which, and in any case the door stood always open. A swollen-eyed man in an airforce greatcoat dripped ash from his cigarette to and from the lavatory on the mezzanine. A cropped sallow girl with the dress and figure of a rag doll continually telephoned on the second landing. And finally there was Anne, who occupied the other cupboard on the final floor.

This top floor seemed like an afterthought. The stairs changed direction before they reached it, and became narrow, steep and shaky, as though they could hardly take seriously the project to ascend so far. The two doors also had a provisional character, fitting very approximately in their frames, and bearing inexplicable mouldings as though they had once belonged to some *piano nobile* in a smart, but demolished, house. Colin often listened to the noises from Anne's room, transmuted by the doors into insect-like scratchings and muffled thumps. They passed each other on the landing, she moving slowly, sleepily, as though still uncertain that the day deserved her consciousness, he running to work, or going out to meander on Primrose Hill. Anne was large, full-breasted, sluttish, complete. She needed nothing, minded nothing. When, during the second week, she stood naked at her door, eyeing him, it was not as though she were motivated by desire. She was propelled by forces of which she was the mute ambassador: forces of transcendent slovenliness which had chosen her as their unresisting envoy. Colin had never seen a naked woman before. The sight amazed him. But he had imagined himself vividly in every masculine role. After two or three awkward failures, he brought his advances to completion, and lay wrapped in the unclean folds of her bedclothes, staring about him at the paperback crime novels, and at the smeared windows on her side of the house, beyond which a row of red chimney stacks slotted into a serrated sky.

Anne and Colin lived, not together, but on the same unswept landing, for over a year. They had little to say to each other, and only once or twice went out to see a film. When he moved he promised to keep in touch, and she smiled at him kindly. He was grateful to her and afterwards remembered many of her gestures with affection. Once, when he had come home from a fight at the brewery, with a gash above his ear, a black eye, and a cracked finger, she had spent her week's rent on taxi-fares to the hospital, and had patiently read to him from *Ulysses*, not understanding a word. He spoke to her about his father, and about Mr Willis. She did not ask what he had done with the hundred pounds, but expressed concern about the schoolmaster, begging Colin to write to him. Anne did not find the world extraordinary; her rhythm was tempered exactly to her circumstances. But when she came across something that had been cast loose from the social order, she acted as though under instructions to bring it in. The same force that had caused her to take exception to Colin's virginity also spoke to her on behalf of Mr Ferguson. She continued to argue the schoolmaster's case in a gentle way until a look from Colin told her that the subject was closed.

As for the hundred pounds, Colin had spent it long before. Clothes and books took half of it; a quarter had been needed for key money to his room; the remaining quarter had kept him through weeks of initial uncertainty. He wrote several times to Francesca; eventually he realised that there would be no reply. Each day he cried on his pillow, and each morning he would start awake believing himself in Bassington, and imagining the rustle of the cedars in the park. It was Mr Willis who finally changed things, replying to Colin's letter with a list of useful addresses: hostels and cheap eating places; charities that provided food and clothing; cinemas with reduced price seats in the afternoons.

He referred to important works in the National Gallery; to convenient corners on which to beg; and finally, in the manner of an afterthought, to factories, breweries and restaurants known for their preference for cheap casual labour. Colin's pride was stung. He felt small-minded, dependent, provincial. That very morning he gathered up the poems on his table, placed them in an envelope marked 'Francesca', and went in search of work.

Jobs were hard to come by, but you could earn a survivor's wage in the brewery, loading the empty bottles into the washing machine. When Colin arrived he would take his card from the rack and insert it behind the clock-face on the machine below. No one told him that if you clocked in more than three minutes late or out more than three minutes early, you lost a quarter of an hour's pay. At the end of his first week he was two and a half hours short, and this embittered him against his workmates. Had he made an effort to communicate with them, they would have responded. But he read throughout the breaks, and had no ready obscenities with which to neutralise the exploratory jokes made against him. While the machines were working the noise was too great and the concentration required to place twelve bottles repeatedly in the twelve vacant holes that incessantly appeared before him made it impossible at first to look up from his task. When at last he did so, it was only briefly, and if he could catch the eye of another worker – as sometimes he caught the eye of the black girl opposite – it seemed that there was time only for that. To venture on a smile was to challenge the machine's authority. The machine demanded super-human qualities of attention, obliterating every human utterance with a violent clatter, like the sound of a thousand orders simultaneously shouted by a thousand angry drill sergeants. Colin would attempt to vary his obedience by placing only eleven bottles in the gaps provided. He would shift the vacant place so as to make each time a different pattern; and for a while this pastime gave him a minimal creative pleasure. However, it angered his neighbour Bill, whose small delight, by contrast, was that of conscientious observance. If Colin continued his diversion, Bill would frantically try to fill his twelve gaps in double time, so as to lean across and insert a spare bottle in the space left by Colin. Bill's sense of duty towards the machine inspired a sense of duty towards Bill; eventually, moved by borrowed compunction, Colin became an obedient slave.

His submissive posture was rewarded after three weeks, just as he was on the point of leaving. He fell into conversation one day with the brewing manager, a lank unhappy man called Mr Simpson, who was impressed by Colin's smattering of education. He was appointed to one of the most coveted jobs in the brewery: that of night supervisor, surveying the fermentation during the long peaceful hours of darkness. The vats gave out a pleasant murmur, and the heady smell of hops reminded him of Bassington, and the scent of hay in the park.

His rapid promotion was resented, and Colin was often forced to justify it with his fists. One day a gang of morons waited for him in the vat house, anxious to readjust his social standing to their own requirements. They leapt out, fists flailing, boots chopping the air. As luck would have it, Colin was carrying the ruler with which he checked the levels in the valves. It had a sharp edge of alloy, and by wielding it in a circle about his head he was able to gash two cheeks, half sever an ear, and poke out a glutinous eye before running for the gate and safety. He did not return to the brewery, but took a job in Fox's Tea Shop in Leadenhall Street. It was no longer possible to live in North London, and besides, Anne had come home one day with a black man, who now lived in her room, playing gramophone, radio and television simultaneously, and bawling spasmodically at the imaginary companions across the landing. Colin took leave of her, and went to live in the Commercial Road. Later, at Bow Street Magistrates' Court, he was found innocent of assault causing actual bodily harm, and looked with pleasure on the ruined faces of his accusers, as they confronted him from the witness box, wilting under the assaults of a barrister who knew all there was to know about the law of self-defence.

Colin's duties at the restaurant were light. He had to clear the dishes from the table, and take them on an aluminium trolley into the kitchen, where they were stacked and washed. For most of the day the restaurant was empty, except for a few quiet ladies who were taking a cup of tea between visits to the bank and the stock exchange. Being below ground, and lit by fluorescent lighting, the restaurant existed in a timeless world of its own, detached from the outer air of commerce: still, solemn and forgotten. The furniture, in stainless steel with red moquette coverings for the stools, was screwed to the floor, and customers had to queue at the metal counter, before five forbidding ladies, each charged with withholding some portion of a meal. There was Doris, who provided insufficient chicken, roast beef or tongue; Phyllis, who was stingy with potatoes and greens; Mavis who curtailed the flow of puddings; Iris who reduced the supply of tea; and Millis who aborted the special orders. They were not violent, but the presence of a helpless male presented an opportunity for malice that only virtue could have resisted. Remarks were made about his accent, his clumsiness, his spoiled and idle manners, his habit of stealing extra food and sometimes cutlery. He chose not to work at the counter, where life was otherwise easy, and to stay clearing dishes from the tables.

Every day, at eleven, one and three thirty, the restaurant swung on its dreaming orbit, into the turbulence of the larger world. The stream of motley secretaries and grey-striped clerks, released from their offices, crammed the narrow entrance, pushing down the steps like the victims of an air-raid. The men were silent, elbowing ahead in the queue as though engaged in some dangerous mission. The girls giggled hilariously, teasing Colin and asking special favours. These were moments of loneliness; sometimes it seemed to him that he looked on the world from a point outside it, and that people passed him – some in silence, some waving – as they pass an animal in a zoo, or a strange painted fish trapped in a bright aquarium.

Sometimes he retired to the kitchen, to play chess with the schizophrenic porter. Colin tried hard to lose, affected by the puzzled concentration of the other's face. What for Colin was a game had the quality, in mad Richard's mind, of an ontological proof. To lose was to fall from existence, to win was to ascend the ladder of reality. On one occasion, angry with himself, with his dreams, and most of all with Francesca who would not come, as he had mentally arranged, with her busy mother, Colin brought the game to a close in seven moves. Richard scratched his head.

'I used to know that trick,' he said, 'but the rules were changed – weren't they changed in 1953, at the international tournament in Paris? I'm positive they were. Probably Dr Nicholson can prove it. Usually he proves things when I don't remember. Still, I wasn't quick enough was I? Hadn't got things together, had I? Shall we play another game?'

Richard's voice was tired and expressionless, beyond despair. Colin rose from the table, and began stacking the dishes from his trolley. Suddenly he wanted conversation. To address Richard in unmeant, mutilated words was now impossible.

'Shall we play? Honestly Colin, I'll try better. Just this head of mine.'

Colin looked at Richard, opened his mouth, but no words came. It was as if a hole had opened in his face at some place unconnected with speech. A great darkness loomed within there, and Colin quickly shut his mouth again, afraid of what Richard might see. He went rapidly to the door, pushing the trolley before him, out into the shadowless white light of the bunker.

He pushed the trolley back and forth, collecting nothing, his eyes fixed rigidly before him. The girls beckoned to him; the men looked away. The tables were beginning to pile high with débris, and in one corner some newcomers had taken the dirty dishes of their predecessors and stacked them roughly on the floor. A half-eaten egg trailed from one of the plates in the dust beneath the table.

Then he saw a man, in starched collar and pin-striped suit, who was reading. Nobody had ever read a book in the restaurant before, and Colin pushed his trolley in the man's direction, ploughing like a tank through the queue before the counter. He stopped by the table, which was against one of the walls, pressing the man into a narrow cavity. He stood for a while, and then blurted out,

'Do you find it difficult?'

'What?'

'To read. In here. Do you find it difficult?'

The man raised a shiny face and astonished piggy eyes.

'I don't know what you mean.'

He turned back to the book. Colin could not read the title: but it had five letters, beginning with F. *Frost*, or *Frump*, or maybe *Faust*. Yes, it must be *Faust*, since it was written in verse – or at least in lines that were decidedly uneven. Colin could not believe his luck.

'I mean, do you find it difficult to read *Faust*? Here, for instance. Take the question of the characters. In the dream of *Walpurgisnacht*, who should appear but Oberon and Titania. Naturally a reference to Shakespeare: but how is it that we have both Puck *and* Ariel? What are we supposed to make of that? I mean, the *Dream* seems to express something familiar, part of me: I don't have to work to understand it. But the *Tempest* – surely this belongs to another order of things, high up on a great spaghetti-junction of ideas, all about you vertiginous drops and no possibility of stopping for a breather. It is a new world, a future world, everything re-made from some angelic specification. Obviously the critics have said a million things about it, and maybe you know what I should read . . .'

Colin was speaking fast, and his breathing was cramped and erratic. He fixed his eyes on the manageress, a handsome woman of thirty, who sat with the account books, by the back door into the alleyway. Something contemptuous in her expression caused him to boil. If he was speaking so much to the piggy-eyed creature beneath him, it was not out of politeness or compassion – though God knows he felt a wave of real pity for this fellow victim – but in order to establish his right to exist. He felt sure that the man would understand this eventually, and offer him some kind of job – not an important job, but one that would enable him to work himself up from clerk to director in a matter of years, maybe even months. He reckoned that an advertising agency would best suit his present needs, though he was not averse to the stock exchange. His maths was good, and he had important connections like Lord Shepton who would provide a reference. He felt certain that the man – Mr Hepworth-Sprigge as Colin impetuously christened him – would extend a welcoming hand. Colin, for his part, did not want pity – God let them fester with their mouldy pity, which was in any case only a way of enjoying their power, as he enjoyed his little power over Mr Hepworth-Sprigge – all he wanted was an opportunity, so that he could show that manageress, with her spiffing good-looks and her laundered life-plans, that he had no need of benefaction.

'Of course, the people here wouldn't stand for me if they knew that I could read,' he continued. 'That's what attracts me to *Faust*. You have to be unnatural, a bit of a ghoul, to begin to see a meaning in it: you have to be somewhere outside the stream of things. We know that the pantheism is a fake, a projection. The real drama doesn't contain heaven or earth or the devil or God. The spirits only appear because Faust is persuaded of their unreality. If they were actual he wouldn't see them. It all occurs in his own stuffy brain. I'm not telling you anything you don't know, but perhaps, while there is time . . .'

Colin continued feverishly. Gradually his mind entered a state of anarchy, and he began digging his finger-nails into his palms. He pushed the aluminium trolley to one side, feeling an impulse to unbutton the white jacket that concealed his tattered pullover, and throw it in the air. Mr Hepworth-Sprigge had said nothing yet, but this was hardly surprising, since he was a well-bred man and was waiting for Colin to conclude his speech, which he was also perhaps enjoying a little. No doubt Colin's words were confused. After all, he lacked education. The schoolmaster, he explained, had made it impossible. But he had kept up with German, and could still quote from *Faust*, not just the famous lines, but even some bits from the choruses in Part II, which no doubt Mr Hepworth-Sprigge would be quite impressed to hear. As he recited, his mind began to wander. It seemed very strange to him that nothing had happened – nothing to speak of – since he had left the house where Anne was living with her black man. Many days had passed. It was winter now, and would soon be spring. Although each of those days was stocked with minutiae, nothing told of his existence. It seemed odd that he had not written again to Francesca. Perhaps his first letters had been lost, or confiscated by a watchful matron. But why had he not written to her at Shepton Hall? Soon he would be nineteen. All his schoolfriends were at university reading sociology, politics, philosophy, or maybe something useful, and he had accomplished nothing. He searched in his memory for someone to blame for this, but there was no one, save possibly the schoolmaster. Of course, Mr Ferguson in his turn would blame the rich, and in particular Lord Shepton. But is Francesca's father to blame for the fact that I am now discoursing about *Faust* to an angry customer in Fox's Tea Shop? Only by some chain of causes too vast and metaphysical to consider. No doubt Mr Hepworth-Sprigge would agree. Of course, he did not have the schoolmaster's disadvantages, and must therefore incline to a greater natural tolerance of fortune. Tolerance is a virtue too. Colin felt laughter welling up from his stomach. He could hardly control it. He was on the point of ringing out, like the bell at Lloyds which sounds when a ship goes down, drawing every eye, changing every movement. He folded his arms across his chest, gripping his biceps with all his strength so as to hold in the sound. Then he noticed out of the corner of his eye that Mr Hepworth-Sprigge was about to speak, and he relaxed at last into a genial posture.

'But there,' he said, letting out a rush of air. 'I have bored you and you must forgive me.'

'I . . . I . . .'

Mr Hepworth-Sprigge averted his eyes. A deep blush had suffused his features; he closed his book and shoved it into an old, soft-leather briefcase, with a brass buckle and a fraying handle.

'I'm afraid I don't know what you are talking about.'

Colin watched in silence as Mr Hepworth-Sprigge wriggled from his chair. The process was long and painful, since Colin blocked the nearest point of exit, making it necessary to move across several seats, each screwed to the floor as close as possible to the formica table. Moreover, the far exit was half blocked by a stainless steel column, in which Colin could see his own face reflected, a grinning mask projected sideways to infinity. He thought he should follow Mr Hepworth-Sprigge and push his pin-striped body through the gap between the column and the table. It was distressing to see how fat the poor gentleman had become, and how many nervous unnecessary movements his body made as it packed itself into the gap provided. His hair was greying behind, and had been smoothed down onto his rough neck with some greasy substance which glistened on his skin. Having wedged him into the impassable gap, Colin stepped back with a friendly smile.

'Look,' he said, barely controlling his panic. 'There's no need to go to unnecessary trouble. Why don't you come out this side? I can move the trolley; I can make room for you. Look! Would you like a lift as far as the door? I expect you are feeling a trifle faint after our conversation. It's also very hot down here.'

Colin continued, imitating the art of imitation, as taught by Mr Willis. Mr Hepworth-Sprigge released himself at last, and scampered to freedom in the upper air. The manageress rose, adjusting the pink paste earrings in her perfect ears, and smoothing the blue tunic over her white camel-hair cardigan. She began to move in his direction, tightening her face in the expression that Colin knew as brain-clenching.

'Yes,' he said loudly, at her approach. 'I am glad you have come. I was just explaining to Mr Hepworth-Sprigge that since this is my last day here I really ought to relax a little and enjoy my surroundings. It will be hard for Richard having no one to play chess with. But come to think of it, you are pretty smart, and there's absolutely no reason why you shouldn't be able to learn, given a bit of application. Tell you what, I'll send you my *Teach Yourself Chess*. I shan't be needing it. No really, any time.'

He walked slowly back to the kitchen, still pushing the trolley, and faintly humming as he sauntered. By the hatch, he cleared a single plate from the last cluttered table, held it up to the light, studied it, and then placed it on the trolley. Richard cried, a small, dry, choking sound, as Colin put on his jacket to go. It was fortunate for Colin that Mr Willis's solicitor chose to send him the cheque at that time. Now he began to write, first stories about the history of Bassington, then the autobiography of his father, and finally a monograph on *Faust*, for the purpose of which he obtained a ticket to the British Library. For a while he was calm, and even began to go out into the world. He joined the Wapping Muslim Society, and each Saturday morning would add his unbelieving prayers to the incantations of Pakistani peasants and proletarian Turks. Sitting in the dark annexe of the mosque, where mint tea was served in glasses, and bearded elders with little English sat grunting on floral-patterned Draylon carpets, he felt alternately peaceful and bold. He began to learn Arabic, in a class of pious enthusiasts. Soon he could write his name, Kulin Furq'sun, in flowing ciphers. He dated a girl from the local hairdresser's, and every Friday she would allow her breasts to be fondled in the ABC cinema. Once, when he had treated her to a Chinese dinner, she sat close against him in the porch of St Anne's, with his hand between her thighs. He made friends with a tramp who lived in the churchyard of St George's at Wapping, and who was an expert on Hawksmoor. And he began an interesting correspondence on London wildflowers with a gentleman from Surrey, who had discovered a wild orchid in a ruined dockyard on the Isle of Dogs, and had written about it to *The Times*.

One day, however, as he emerged from the British Museum with his bundle of papers, a peculiar sensation overcame him. It was a warm spring evening, and the sky trembled slightly through a skin of hazy cloud. The people were moving in the street as though blown by wind, and the traffic stood huddled and immobile against the passing turbulence. Everywhere he felt the press and the commotion of human bodies: but they moved softly, noiselessly about him, like stuffed puppets held above the ground. It was like the day when he had met Francesca: a day in which the physical order was being set aside. He hurried quickly across Oxford Street, past the brass-bound umbrella shop, past the Edwardian theatre in baked rococo, and stopped by the white facade of the Swiss church. It was soothing, nurse-like, promising its sanitary God. He tried to enter, but, finding it locked against him, hurried on. Everywhere in Covent Garden he encountered the same noiseless flutter of people, the same immobile queues of cars. Machines had lost their power in this new dispensation. Their world had been turned against them, and he stood apart from it, shaking out dust from its lifeless inside. On Waterloo Bridge he stopped. The sun was shining on the dome of St Paul's, and the golden cross glittered above the shadow-soaked drum. The slow waters of the Thames slid beneath the bridge, oily and dark, carrying the tributary streams of Dunsbury and Murricombe. There, in the schoolhouse which Colin had never visited, swallowing grief and humiliation, digging still his unproductive garden, lived Mr Ferguson, who at this moment was thinking of his son. A barge passed under the bridge, with painted cabin and a string of washing trailed along its deck. A dog sat in the stern, looking up at the arch of the bridge, and a small neat woman busied herself next to it, peeling potatoes in a green plastic bowl. Colin turned away in fear and misery, and hurried through the city, towards the Commercial Road.

He packed his books and papers in the trunk which he had brought with him, and pushed it to the corner of the room. Mrs Surtees took the key and secreted it in the folds of her cabbage-coloured skirt. She never looked directly at Colin, reluctant to give him the occasion to speak. It was a matter of principle with Mrs Surtees that words should be confined to the minimum, and topics of conversation chosen only from that list of subjects which nature and precedent had shown to be reliable. Colin ventured to remark on the weather, choosing from the four or five descriptions that he knew to be acceptable the one which they might most speedily agree upon.

'A pleasant day, Mrs Surtees.'

He realised at once, however, that if she answered, it would be to prove the impassable distinction between those who were in a position to enjoy pleasant weather and those who were not. The class of landladies, it was to be understood, was particularly oppressed by these arbitrary changes for the better in the fortunes of other people.

'Pleasant is as pleasant feels, Colin.'

Like all of Mrs Surtees's pronouncements, the words had a proverbial flavour. Having digested them, Colin began to search for a way to express himself within the limits of her strict proprieties. Eventually he said:

'This trunk that I brought with me. It's a bit heavy. And I shall probably be coming back to London soon.'

Mrs Surtees sucked in her large cheeks, narrowed her puffy, smoke-inflamed eyes, and scratched her behind in a ruminative manner. These were signs that she would not reply prematurely.

'So I was wondering if you could keep it and let me collect

it later. I shall pay for the – for the space. Also this month's rent.'

Eventually Mrs Surtees sniffed, and said:

'There's them that keeps their money, and them that throws it.'

It was not clear to Colin that these words constituted an acceptance of his offer.

'So maybe if I gave you £5 for the rent, and then, say, another five for the trunk . . .'

'A thing that don't see nothing,' said Mrs Surtees, interrupting him, 'ain't in the way.'

She briefly shifted her focus, so as almost to make contact with Colin's eyes, and then went back to the cupboard with the dark-green door where she lived. There was a rattle of dishes – the signal that conversation was over.

'Thank you,' said Colin, supplying for her use the most optimistic interpretation of their bargain.

He left the house, independent to the tune of twenty-three pounds.

The grocer at the corner had cards in his window, declaring lost or superfluous cats, rooms to let, cars for sale, three-piece suites and two-piece suits as new, imitation leather armchairs, cocktail cabinets (used), and – incongruously – chicken wire and wholesale eggs. Among these announcements were others, advertising Swedish massage, French lessons, and schoolgirls in search of work. He chose one which said, 'Coloured girl seeks driving post. No rush.' The telephone number was local.

Colin found himself on the eighth floor of a modern apartment block. A small black woman in her thirties answered the door. She had thick lips, slow-moving eyes, and a sideways tilt of her head which gave her a look of innocence. Her blouse in a jazzy pattern of parakeet colours concealed two soft breasts hanging down like fruit towards her friendly belly.

'You Colin? I'm Cynthia. Howdedo.'

She smiled pleasantly, and Colin nodded in reply. Already he doubted that the obligation to be wicked would vanquish his natural weakness for virtue. He followed Cynthia into the living room, not sure whether, for propriety's sake, he should pat her shoulders, nibble her ear, or squeeze her bum. In the event he did none of those things, but simply stared mournfully at her buttocks, as they swished from side to side in her puce nylon mini-skirt.

The first thing that caught his eye as they passed out of the dark vestibule was a cocktail bar, a Las Vegas dream in chrome and padded plastic, that looked ready to take off, trailing its festive ribbons through the air. Cocktail-stick holders in the form of monks and madonnas stood on the spotless surface, and a striplight, concealed behind an awning, cast a reddish glow over the polished bottles at the back. The walls of the room were covered in lime-green hydrangeas, and the carpet was patterned with red cartwheels on a luminous orange ground. Through the metal frame of the window the dome of St Paul's was visible, rising above a tall lightless warehouse. Colin took a step forward, hit his head on some hanging bells, and then faltered. A black moquette armchair stood before him. He wondered whether he should sit in it, or whether he should immediately begin their business.

'Speck you's wonderin' about de nex move.'

'Well, I . . .'

'Gawn! Siddown. Make a self a dome.'

Cynthia took a record from a vinyl sheath and placed it on the pink portable gramophone at the back of the bar. Soft, soothing saxophones smoothed the air. Colin lost himself in contemplation of his new surroundings. No room had ever appeared to him so elaborately *soigné*: every detail spoke of domestic pride and wilful self-sufficiency. Along the window-sill polished Mickey Mouses and Donald Ducks in china stood between fragments of airport art: a spindly gazelle in carved teak, a squat ebony fetish, a split rock with pale blue crystalline insides. At the point where the carpet made contact with the skirting ran a strip of stainless alloy, neatly screwed through the carpet to the floor. It looked as though it had just been polished. The walls were adorned with Montmartre posters in gilded rococo frames, and above the bottles behind the bar was a cuckoo-clock with a swinging pendulum of polished brass. The records stood in a white plastic cabinet beside the gramophone; Cynthia polished the top of it with her sleeve as she rose from adjusting the sound.

'Well Colin, wat you's drinking?'

'I don't mind. Sherry perhaps.'

She took a bottle with a South African label from the stack, and poured the yellow liquid into a large shiny schooner.

'You know summin'?' she said, handing the glass across the bar. 'You din' need de normal treetman'. I see dat momen' you come in. Here.'

He got up to take the glass, and she filled another for herself.

'Hee's to us baby.'

They raised their glasses and Colin looked at her shyly.

'I know what you's tinkin' baby. You's tinkin', is de sherry included, or is it extra. Right man?'

'I . . . I wasn't thinking anything.'

Cynthia laughed gaily.

'Comawn!'

She threw the wine into her not unpleasing mouth, and then poured another.

'So baby, you like de way I done dis place? Or maybe you think hee's de real big vulgar Afro package deal? Every dam thing shine an' tinsel an' de ole beads which de mishnries bring?'

'Well, I think it's rather nice actually,' he said, with conviction. 'I mean, I wouldn't want it otherwise'.

'Spoil de picksher baby?'

'Not exactly.'

'Real wicked! Not *exackly*!'

He laughed with her and held out his glass. She filled it, and then came round to the front of the bar.

'You no big sinner Colin, dough maybe you don' live right in accordin' wid de gospel. I see dat.'

'Do you?'

'Like I say; momen' you come in, standin' right dere in de doorway, like you come for firs' communion.'

'I see,' said Colin.

'What you needin', pardon me, is de speshul treetman'. You needin' de real forgiveness, Colin. Dat's what I see.'

The music stopped suddenly, like a shocked heart. Cynthia went slowly across, removed the record, and replaced it with a larger one that sounded just the same.

'Yes baby. Like de good book say, where's dis forgiveness comin' from? Where can man dat's foolish and like a lost sheep go claim his rashun of forgiveness? You think he go to de laundermat?'

'I'm so relieved I came,' Colin responded warmly. 'Who'd have thought I'd find someone just as crazy as I am!'

'Ah'm not fuckin' crazy,' Cynthia replied indignantly. 'It's you dat's crazy man, goin' roun' lookin' for to eksersise dat dere drivin' post, in your condishun!'

'But listen Cynthia, you advertised. I thought . . .'

'Know summin' Colin? Ah see you, an' ah think: ah'm not in de gootime mood.'

'I see.'

'No 'fence. As de book says, dou shalt purge me wid' hyssop, and ah shall be clean; dou shalt wash me, and ah shall be whiter dan snow. Don' reely apply in mah case, but dat no fect' de meanin'. Maybe tahm de Lord take anudder look at dat Bible, see if it can' be updated for de Afros.'

'Shall we sit down?'

She flopped down beside him on a slippery black sofa, and allowed her great brown bosom to slide into his cupped, welcoming hands. For a long moment they sat still, the soft music washing through the room with a soapy swishing sound. Cynthia sometimes hummed with it, sometimes stared silently ahead, not minding him. Colin felt rested. He looked across at the window, dreamed a little, and then dozed off, until the music ended and she rose to fetch another drink.

Cynthia was interested in Tarot cards, and produced a pack to explain them to him. She had joined a circle of enthusiasts who met in a house in Bethnal Green, so as to predict the price of groceries, the fall of governments, and the general influence of the moon. She had a friend called Williamina, and they went together on certain days to Clacton, where the business was good, and you were not pushed into a squalid hotel in a back street, but could take a room on the promenade. She liked the sea, and was particularly fond of shell-fish, although Williamina drew the line at winkles, because their appearance made her queasy. Sometimes when the weather was good they would hire a boat and row out to sea. Williamina would cast for mackerel, while Cynthia, who didn't really like to participate in the death of any living thing, would lie in the boat and stare upwards at the sun. Sometimes it reminded her of home, and then she felt sad.

After a while she glanced at the clock.

'Time for de ole man's homecomin'. Time for de las' farewells.'

Colin restored her breasts to their canopy and stood up, vaguely wondering whether they had finished their transaction. He stood indecisively before her, waiting for his cue.

She laughed, and straightened his shirt collar.

'Maybe you remember dat book of common prayer for de use in churches, and de worship of de common people like you an' me. You know, where it says He is ready to receive us baby, and most willin' to pardon us, if we come unto Him wid faitful repentance. If we submit ourselves unto Him, and from hencefor' walk in His ways; if we will take His easy yoke an' light burden upon us, to follow Him in lowliness pashens and charity. Dis if we do Colin, Christ deliver us from de curse of de law, and many times He'd done dat for me. Also from de extreem mally dikshun which shall light upon dem dat shall be set on de left han', and He will set us on de right han'.'

'You are nice to me,' he said. 'Shall I look in again?'

'Any time baby. You an' me, we make a speshal' rangemen'. Treetman' come in many varieties.'

She slapped his hand as he reached in his pocket.

'What you take me for?' she asked, and laughed uproariously.

It was midnight when Colin arrived in Bassington, having walked from Dunsbury station. He stood in the road, looking at the cottage. It seemed deserted. Why had they not demolished it? The road was unchanged and, on the dark shadow of Offlet Hill, he saw only the outline of the tall still beech trees and the pale ghostly patch of horse-sick pasture. Perhaps Lord Shepton's project was a hoax, a device to humiliate the schoolmaster and drive him from the village. Colin's anxiety came back, like waves of lava welling from underground. He walked over to the drive of Bassington House. It was dark, except for a small window in the attic, from which a yellow light spread over the parapet onto the chimney mount. Colin stared at the light for an hour or more, and then it abruptly went out. Two hours later he was in Murricombe. It was a moonless night, and he could discern nothing of the schoolhouse except the shapes of the gables, and the outlines of the window-frames, which seemed to be made of heavy mullioned stone. Steps led from the walled garden to a porch. From where he stood, the house seemed enormous. Its silence frightened him, as though some death had just occurred. He wrote out his address on a piece of paper, and the words 'Will call again'. As dawn broke, he reached Dunsbury station, and remembered that he no longer had an address.

Four

TWO YEARS later Colin received an answer to his note. It had been forwarded by Mrs Surtees to the address in Notting Hill where he lived in the house of Ken Blakely, the about-to-be-famous television producer. The brown envelope was boldly addressed in his father's hand. But when he opened the letter Colin was taken aback by the thin, trembling quality of the lines. It was from the School House, Murricombe, but had neither end nor beginning, as though sent from no one to no one.

> Since I came out of Dunsbury where your friend Dr Willis died it has been rather hard here, and I have now taken to bed. It seems that I shall in all probability not survive the summer, but since my successor is in no hurry to move in, he has kindly given permission for me to snuff it in this desolate barn. I advise you to arrive soon, since, although the district nurse comes each day, and plies me with painkillers, there is a certain *je ne sais quoi* in her expression that indicates a belief in the brevity of her task. It would be much better if you could be here on the whole, and I hope that you agree. I read a story of yours in some intellectual magazine the other day. My friend Bill Pickford brought it. It was dreadfully cruel, and also rather pointless, I should say, though I'm no expert. The articles in *The Spectator* were more interesting, though extremely reactionary, as I might have expected. I don't suppose any of these things pays you enough to live on. Nevertheless, I imagine you have plenty of free time, and will not be too put

out by the journey to Murricombe. It seems that you already know the way.

Colin fell back onto his bed. He had not expected this, and therefore could not be blamed. Only a month before he had read through his father's autobiography, and, in pangs of self-disgust, had torn it to shreds. He felt better for a while, congratulating himself on his lack of resentment. He had even told Joan Blakely what he had done, explaining how he had emerged at last into a kind of maimed serenity. They sat together over breakfast, Ken having left in his working clothes of orange trousers and bright green shirt. She flushed deeply at his explanation and told him that he was a prig. This was the occasion for a new round of self-disgust, and a new wave of consolation. How vast his self-knowledge momentarily seemed. Eventually he persuaded Joan to look on him with more puzzlement than distaste, and to permit him to publicise his bouts of deft repentance.

Nevertheless, he had not been prepared for this. The schoolmaster's death, like all his gestures, constituted a pre-emptive strike against Colin's defences. This great parcel of reality, dropped right in the middle of his carefully nurtured penitence, blew everything to ruin. Colin lost at a stroke the fragile command over his life that he had pulled so patiently together. Now he must start again, in circumstances which he could hardly imagine. Later he met Ken Blakely on the stairs and explained that he must go home.

'Home, Colin? I thought you had no home?'

Ken's fat lips, which moved slowly in their nest of greying beard, smiled at him their up-and-coming smile.

'Suddenly I have acquired one. It is being vacated for me.'

'We shall miss you,' said Ken. 'Joan especially'll miss you.'

'But I might be back. I mean, I might not stay.'

'Whichever way you look at it,' Ken continued, 'it's a bad deal for us. I mean, who knows what you'll be like when you come back? Who knows where we'll have moved to by then, or whether we shall still be wanting a lodger?'

Ken smiled again, and began to run up the stairs. He never paused for conversation with Colin, who, having come to Ken's attention as a potential script-writer, had since fulfilled none of the producer's expectations. Colin was acutely aware that he offered nothing useful to Ken, and that his habit of pondering the eternal questions both troubled and exasperated someone in full pursuit of nothingness. Ken waved back to him as he reached the head of the stairs.

'Send us a postcard,' he said, cheerfully.

The schoolmaster answered the door. He peered at his son from smouldering sunken eyes, and the grey taut flesh of his face cramped into a spasm that bore some distant relation to a scowl.

'You see,' he declared, in a breathless voice, 'I have the strength to open, and to close, a door.'

But as he turned from the corridor into a room that led from it, he visibly tottered, and Colin stretched forward an arm to hold his father upright. The schoolmaster made an impatient movement, but had not the strength to shake his son away. A bed had been set in one corner of the room, with the old blankets from the cottage, now full of holes, thrown over it. As his father settled down, Colin looked at his new surroundings. There was very little furniture – the oldest desk and bookcase from the cottage, a worn Turkey carpet that seemed to belong to the house, and two battered leather armchairs that stood before the open grate. The walls were panelled to half their height with a pinewood dado, stained to simulate oak, and the giant mullions of the window seemed to divide the light, so that it fell only into the corners of the room, and left an impenetrable darkness in the centre. Beside the bed was a folding table. It carried a glass of water, a jug, and two old newspapers.

'What has been the matter?' Colin asked.

'Decrepitude; death; nothing untoward. Cancer if you must know. They opened me up, whistled, and closed me again. Very considerate, all in all.'

The schoolmaster sobbed, and hid his face in the blanket. Colin sat by the bed.

'You have so much to forgive me,' he said, tonelessly. 'I have meant to come back, many times. Always, at the last minute, something has stood in my way. I was too young. The responsibility frightened me. I was weak . . .'

The crabbed domesticity of their former life had deprived him of endearments. Colin could remember no epithet for 'father' that would sound natural on his lips. He looked at the schoolmaster's small and shrunken form, and flinched as it convulsed beneath his gaze. The face remained hidden in the blanket.

'Shall I make something to eat? Is there something I should do?'

Mr Ferguson flung back the blanket with a violent movement that visibly exhausted him.

'Ah!' he gasped, 'something you should do! Something you should have done!'

'You must forgive me.'

'Must?' The schoolmaster attempted a chuckle. A dry rasping sound issued from his constricted throat. 'There is no must. I have the great anarchic privilege of the nearly dead. Don't come to me with your must!'

He hid himself again. The movements of arms beneath the blankets were slight, but the nervous twitches revealed the stubborn remnants of his character. Mr Ferguson had transformed himself into an obstinate heap of cloth, and now communicated with his son only through the impenetrable signals emitted by the trembling blankets. Colin remembered earlier days, searching for the angry gesture, the moral failing, or the simple mistake which had sundered them. Yet always, it seemed, they had been like this: always there had been the barrier, which made each of them an object of curiosity and horror in the other's eyes, and which had placed between them the traps and the torments which destroyed the hope of peace. Colin began to dream, since in dreaming he was strong and Francesca was there. He could not understand her meaning now; he knew only that she had changed his life for him. It was from her, as much as from his father, that he had run away. And perhaps that was the only genuine action he had ever performed – an action which was at the same time a negation, a refusal. He returned in his thoughts to the heap of blankets, in which a human soul palpitated hopelessly.

'Has someone been looking after you? Surely you can't have stayed here alone?'

The schoolmaster emerged from concealment with a sly expression on his decrepit face.

'Ah there you have it. The National Health again. Not only do they send a nurse twice a day. There are a million extras. I have formed a relationship with the School Health Inspector. It is true she has false teeth. But she also has artistic talent, and her company is soothing. Those are her watercolours on the wall.'

Colin observed two sylvan scenes in execrable good taste.

'I rely on her. Little enough happens in a life like mine. I lack your excellent connections. If I had written poetry, stories, articles, do you think that I could get them published even in the Parish magazine? But then, please do not let me talk like this. You will find the kitchen at the end of the passage. You must be hungry. I asked the Health Inspector to make sure that the fridge contained whatever you, as a creature still healthy, might need.'

'I'm not hungry.'

'You are not hungry. In that case, perhaps you would like to inspect your room.'

Colin went out obediently. The large dark rooms were almost empty. Sometimes he would come across an unpacked trunk, a tea-chest, a cardboard box full of books or china, a heap of clothing still attached to metal hangers. In one room, too, there were the parts of a wardrobe standing beside each other, and his father's iron bed, half assembled, but without a mattress. Another room seemed properly inhabited. After a while he recognised it as his. The bed from the cottage was there, pushed against the wall; so too were the chest of drawers and the roll-topped desk. His books had been unpacked and neatly arranged along one of the walls. There were even some lengths of wood, standing in a corner, as though the schoolmaster had intended to build some shelves and then lost heart. A cupboard set into the wall contained scraps of clothing. The reproduction of a still life by Cézanne, which had been taped to his wall in the cottage, was taped again to the wall in this larger space, looking strange and unhappy, cut off from its former light. Colin went to the window. A garden, overgrown and sprouting opium poppies, marigolds and Russian vine, spread back from the house. Beyond it stood the church-like school in red brick, with stone quoins and architraves, and a steep slate roof. Further still a clump of elms hid the village from view, and on the horizon he could see the slopes of Offlet Hill, treeless on this side, and spotted with Friesian cows. The tears that trickled down his cheeks were difficult to diagnose. Not grief, he decided, since grief bore too much witness to affection. Nor remorse, since that had now been stilled. Only a vast and nameless fear for the future, a sense that henceforth he must stand alone before the void, sole representative of his father's race.

When he looked into the living room the schoolmaster was lying on his side, moaning quietly.

'Are you alright?'

No answer.

He went down the passage to the kitchen. The fridge stood by an old gas cooker, on which he discovered a pan full of black, rancid fat. Inside the fridge there were paper packets containing cheese and sausages, some stale butter, and a tray of rotting vegetables. He closed the door, and decided to sit by his father until the nurse or the Health Inspector came.

The almost white hair fell loosely across the head of Mr Ferguson. When he turned it fell sideways, showing the pate, formerly red, but now white, retaining only a scatter of faded freckles. The skin seemed rough and scratchy.

'Medicine!'

How to obey? Words were short, and explanations outlawed. Colin searched the room, looking into the dusty corners, running his hand along uncluttered shelves, peering over the bed into the pile of boxes behind it.

And then, lifting the blanket, he found that the schoolmaster clutched a bottle in his hand. The grip was taut but feeble; Colin soon released it. 'The Mixture: one teaspoonful when required'. He fetched a spoon from the kitchen and measured the liquid into his father's mouth, which now hung open on a backward-leaning head. The white lips closed over the spoon, and a drop of medicine began its slow progress from mouth to pillow.

'Ah!'

'Better?'

Silence.

Everywhere the same stillness, as though the house had no heart. In the cottage you sensed the pump of hidden arteries, the relentless homely flow of old resentment. But here nothing; the schoolhouse was a realm without a monarch, a place of spectacular loneliness, a stage-set for death. Why did someone not come? For even this desolate place needed tending.

Gradually Colin became aware of permitted rituals. There was that of the commode, that of washing, that of the medicine, and those concerned with the opening and closing of windows and the provision of words. At first words were in smallish quantities, indicative of need. But after the nurse had come and gone, filling the house with reproachful cheerfulness, the conversation flowed more easily. The nurse told Colin that he must expect his father soon to die. All the signs had been completed. Somehow he was to emanate this information, so that the topic of death became redundant. The schoolmaster sensed the change, and began to speak more freely.

At one point he referred to Mrs Ferguson, towards whom

Colin had maintained thoughts of a kind so abstract that at times she seemed no more than one of his father's irritations. Any physical closeness that Colin may once have experienced had since been rigorously expunged from his body, and, try as he might, nothing, not even the vaguest feeling of a forlorn dependence, passed from him to his mother. But now the schoolmaster was insisting on her goodness, her angelic gentleness, on the cruel and uncanny loss that he had experienced, and which had set him on the path of decline.

They had met during the war, in the Army, and he had loved her for her soft blue eyes, for her seeming interest in all his petty ambitions, and all his petty griefs. She was no socialist, and her not quite successful family deeply resented the match. But she listened with interest to his stories of oppression, and had never impeded his lonely defiance of the old ruling class. Abruptly changing his tone to one of scientific exactitude, Mr Ferguson went on to itemise her failings. He was particularly averse to her dainty ways, to her soft-spoken accent, to her habit of saying lunch instead of dinner, to her insistence on the utility of objects which she called sometimes napkins and sometimes serviettes, to her strange and contrary aversion to fried eggs. She was devoid of ideas and immune to their influence. It was not his fault that he had been driven to reading newspapers at table, or button-holing her in the course of the housework so as to embark on political instruction. The schoolmaster summoned up tears with which to authorise his judgement, and then, serenely smiling, fell back on the pillow and snored.

Later he started awake, and called to Colin, who was still brooding over the abstract idea of motherhood. There was a strange solemnity in his father's tone as he whispered to him.

'When *she* died now, she was not afraid. She simply went upstairs and undressed as carefully as usual – although it was the middle of the afternoon – and put up her hair. I came. I asked if she wanted anything. She said, no, only, if you could put Colin where I can see him. I placed your cot in the window, by the bed, and she slowly turned her eyes to look at you. The doctor came, frowned, took a blood sample, prescribed some tablets, and then said he would be back in the morning. It was not in your mother's nature to complain, although she was no longer capable of a smile. When you were fed and sleeping, I came to sit beside her. She stared through me to the dusk beyond the window. There was no sound except her breathing and the cedars in the park. Then I felt tired and got ready for bed. I lifted the bedclothes and got in beside her. It felt as though her flesh had been reconstituted: it didn't move, it hardly breathed now. I had a horror of touching it, and left a gap between our bodies. The gap widened. It became a chasm. But I could still feel, radiating across from her, a kind of raw untouchability. I drifted into sleep, woke, slept again, and then finally came wide awake because you were crying.'

Mr Ferguson paused for breath and his eyes flickered in his head with a sudden emotion.

'By accident, as I stepped from the bed, I brushed my hand against her neck. It was cold, soft, obscene. Like a piece of meat.'

He shuddered, and stared at the ceiling.

Colin tried to shuffle off the sadness that the schoolmaster's words transferred to him. He felt injured by his father's emotion; it presumed on a feeling that he did not possess. It was outrageous, icy, sentimental. And yet, despite himself, he was touched. Was this the real thing, or another subtle counterfeit? As far as the schoolmaster was concerned, the distinction between reality and illusion was no more than an established conspiracy, something which he ironically remarked upon when he chose to, but otherwise passed over in the pursuit of higher aims. Colin looked furtively about him. The dying man filled the house with unseen cobwebs, and if you moved from the bed even a fraction, every living part of you was snared. The schoolmaster resumed his monologue, speaking with longer pauses, and devoid of movement except for the slow plucking of his fingers at the edges of the sheet.

'I am glad you came home in the end. The issue of forgiveness is irrelevant. Why should we trouble to bring order into a relation that never was? No. Let us be frank. You hated me. I behaved in a fashion that has at times seemed arbitrary. I have had to swallow back whatever it was I might naturally have felt for you. But since moving here, and since my encounter with the Health Inspector, who is fortunately past the age of childbearing, I have been able to view my first attempts at domesticity with detachment. I am a wild man, you know Colin, a very wild man.'

'To whom are you saying this?' were the words that Colin did not speak. He murmured, and made an embarrassed movement on the hard wooden chair which had been provided for visitors.

'Of course you doubt all this. Your attitude has been cold and priggish. Even a father is sometimes in a position to notice things. Well, now we shall have to let the matter rest. *Requiescat in pace.* I should not have married, should certainly not have reproduced. No one else of our family betrayed such a weakness. By the way, I hear that the cotton-mill has been demolished. Made way for an ice rink and skittle alley. Perhaps irrelevant. Everywhere the same story. In any case, *I did reproduce*!'

He spoke with sudden ferocity as though Colin might be tempted to deny the fact.

'And having done so, I find a problem of inheritance. I had intended to sell the cottage. Ah! Ah!'

The schoolmaster contorted in pain. His features twisted through ninety degrees, so that his nose hung like a limp tube from his chin, and his eyes arranged themselves along one side of the face, pouring their tears from one to the other and thence to the sodden pillow. Colin cried too, as he wrenched the bottle from the schoolmaster's hands and placed it between the dry white lips. Mr Ferguson swallowed from it copiously, and fell back unconscious.

For two hours, Colin did not move. Then the schoolmaster suddenly threw into his face a fistful of staring eyes, shrieking:

'Yes! I have left the cottage to you! It was not sold! Just imagine! All Bill Pickford's doing! Dismissed, after all, for his socialist opinions! What a laugh!'

A moment's silence.

'Or was it, you think, because he had been messing about with the girl?'

The schoolmaster chuckled a little, and then closed his eyes. Colin held his hands to his face to defend himself. He knew that his father, through unseen channels of insight, had discovered the way to undermine him, and spoke only to this end. There was no defence, except to show that he did not care.

'Really? So what is Mr Pickford doing now?'

'What is he doing?' The schoolmaster looked distractedly towards the window. 'Oh, he got a grant to attend the training college in Dunsbury. He is going to be a teacher. I see him often. He feels that he needs guidance. He has recognised the alienation in which he previously lived. Etcetera. But to tell the truth he is quite a useful man to have around. He is taking over as organiser of the campaign.'

A key turned in the front door and Colin stood up. A robust woman of fifty entered the room, wearing mud-coloured trousers and an ashy kaftan over her drooping curves. Her mouse-grey hair, gathered in a loose bun, was pierced by a bone needle which dangled at the nape of her neck. Her eyes were brown, moist, slowly moving in her mottled, soapy face. It was the Health Inspector, whom Mr Ferguson introduced as Harriet. She at once left the room and crashed along the corridor. A scabby brown mongrel followed her, wagging its shapeless tail, and she spoke to it in an endless patter as she stomped about the kitchen.

'Excellent woman,' said the schoolmaster. 'Quite a discovery. I was buying a chicken in the butchers when she came up and suggested I take one with feet that were less deformed. I followed her into the street but she disappeared.

And then a week later she turned up at the school to inspect the school. And then at the house to inspect the house. And then . . . well, inspection is not the same as cure.'

The Health Inspector came and went several times. She looked at Mr Ferguson with the expression that a businessman reserves for a bad investment, and addressed him, when absolutely necessary, in quiet monosyllables. The schoolmaster, who had never concealed his resentment against all forms of power that were not his own, and who had devoted his life to imposing a wholly original despotism, extended his resentment impartially in this new direction. No residue of recent intimacy penetrated the mask of hatred with which he greeted her, and, if he spoke of her admiringly to his son, it was only to impress on Colin the fact that he had not demeaned himself in mounting her flaccid body.

'I told you I had enough medicine,' he cried. 'Why do you bother me? Of course you must expect to put me in a bad temper. I do not have your robust constitution. For some inconceivable reason I have been unable to dig the garden, unable even to get out into the air. Colin will have to do without fresh vegetables. Perhaps you have the strength to open a tin?'

The Health Inspector snorted and went into the kitchen, where Colin followed her. She looked at him vaguely, as though uncertain as yet whether he were real. Then she set up an easel and placed a stool in front of it. Her canvas bag was open on the floor and brushes, tubes, bottles and chalks spread about inside it.

'I think the view into the hallway is rather staggering,' she said, in an experimental tone. 'I have tried it several times, but can never quite capture the shadows. Or the spaces, coming forward into each other. Like cups. Or pans perhaps. Or dog-snouts.'

She worked with some charcoal at a piece of stiff paper, sniffling as she did so and wiping her nose with the back of one hand.

'Your father does not appreciate this house. He has no real

eye for architecture. If you want my frank opinion, most of his sensibilities remain entirely dormant.'

Colin felt a weight of theory behind these pronouncements; if he were to disturb her it would come tumbling round his ears. He walked past the Health Inspector into the kitchen. The back door opened onto the garden, and seeing the tiny little patch that his father had tried at one stage to dig he felt a constriction in his chest. He returned inside.

'There is food in the fridge,' said the Health Inspector over her shoulder. '*I* don't want any. *He* usually takes some hot consommé out of a tin, or a cup of Horlicks. It doesn't matter which. Usually he sicks it up again. Piss off, will you?'

She kicked the dog away from her bag, and began rubbing at the paper on the easel.

'Poor sod!' she said, with reference to nothing in particular.

During the days that preceded the schoolmaster's death, Colin escaped when he could and walked to the cottage in Bassington. Once he stood in the gateway to the Hall. In the distance, the house had the look of a school in vacation. During one of these walks – when, having left his father in the hands of the Health Inspector, whose remark that she wished to execute an interior in acrylic made him confident that she would remain for several hours – Colin began to debate the problem of Francesca. He wished to assign his feelings to a definite category. Towards an abstract idea he could behave with decorum, inviting it out at mutual convenience, covering it with polite consideration, offering the pleasantest surprises. But this concrete thing demanded other stratagems. He had formed the opinion that he had never really loved. Once, six months before, during a dingy affair that had carried him into the orbit of Ken Blakely, he had toyed with the idea of love. It seemed imperative to justify a circumstance that was so evidently profitable, without referring to the profit. Almost immediately he was overcome by disgust, and, accepting Ken Blakely's offer of a bachelor room, retired from his hasty commitment. He knew that he did not love his father. The proof of this was the pity which now consumed him. Even anger would offer more support to the dying man, who awoke in the night shrieking in protest at the summons, the victim of a cosmic injustice. His father's body as it lay in torment was the utmost frontier of Colin's world. He could go no further towards the soul that once engendered him. From the misery of unfeeling, Colin wished to turn back. But unless he could love, no destination was marked for him.

Francesca therefore became his haven; not because he loved her, but because he could have no relation to her but love. She was the provisional promise of reality. He shrank back from the thought of what she might have done or suffered. No doubt it was nonsense about Pickford. But was it possible that she was alone now, possible that she should have kept a place for him, possible that she should know or wish to know who he was? As he walked through the beeches on Offlet Hill, moving in that mossy, fungus-fermented air, he felt that a little withered soul walked inside him, aping the step of his body, cowed, muttering, with the inconsolable solitude of age. He wanted to breathe, to fill his body with the life that belonged to it, to snuff out the dry tormented ironist and replace it with himself. That evening he wrote to Francesca at Bassington Hall.

Five

WHEN THE answer came, forwarded with useless brochures and cyclostyled letters addressed 'dear Friend', 'dear Colleague' and 'dear Member', the schoolmaster slept the twitching sleep of the unforgiving in the air above Dunsbury crematorium. The Health Inspector had taken Colin's old room at the cottage, for which she paid five pounds a week. Colin took over his father's room, since it commanded a view of the cedars. They sorted through the schoolmaster's correspondence, which was destroyed or handed to the Inspector, according to the ability of its purpose to survive its addressee. Colin left the Inspector drafting her curt replies in the kitchen, and went out into the garden, now overgrown with nettles and brambles. He opened Francesca's letter carefully, after staring for a while at his name on the envelope.

Dear Colin,
What a surprise! How silly to think that I would forget you. Do you think I haven't been following your career? I can't write like you, so I won't commit myself to paper. Only let's meet. I am going to London, to University College, in October, to read German. Could you come to see me at the Hall? It's best to telephone: I'm in most of the time, reading Goethe, and also Henry James.
I really do think it would be nice to meet.
    Francesca.

The village had one telephone box, of the type designed by Sir Giles Gilbert Scott, with a little cast-iron crown above its smoked glass entablature. Colin placed four pennies in the slot, and asked the operator for the number that was embossed on Francesca's writing paper. He leaned against the door, looking down the road towards the hillock on which the old grey church raised its stumpy tower. Suddenly the ringing stopped, and his heart jumped into his mouth. There was a silence. Then with an effort of will, he pressed button A.

'Yes,' said a clipped feminine voice.

'I, I . . . is Francesca Wimpole there?'

'No. Who's that?'

'The name's Colin Ferguson.'

'Who?'

'Colin Ferguson. I wonder, do you have any idea when she'll be back?'

'No.'

The voice was cold, expressionless.

'I see. Could I . . .'

Colin heard a click as the line went dead. Slowly he hung up, and then with trembling hand began to rearrange the interior of the kiosk as though trying to remove every sign of his presence.

He sat down angrily at the desk in his father's room. Now it seemed as though all Francesca's terrors were explained, and he wanted no part of them. He could not forgive her for not being at home: it was as if she had deliberately encouraged him, and then let him fall into the trap which for three years he had been trying to avoid: the grim dark hole of self-doubt and failure in which his father had helplessly thrashed out his life.

He received a rejection slip. The editor added a note, remarking that his story was too long, and the central character unbelievable. Colin began to feel edgy. His few successes had never been of the first significance in his eyes: he thought of them rather as preparations for some vaster design whose contours were still unclear. Now he doubted the existence of that saving project. He was without money, without work, without conviction. He wanted to set forth again, but he had lost all sense of destination. He began to stay late in bed, and to keep to his room, spending hours before blank sheets of paper.

He spoke to the Health Inspector only at mealtimes, and then of impersonal things, such as the nature of Impressionism, or the extraction of sugar from beet. Her conversation was heavy with theories, many of which she would also illustrate in her cooking. There might be brown rice, to illustrate a theory of nutrition; white rice, to illustrate a theory about people who have theories about nutrition; blue, red and mottled fishes, to reprove the English who cannot eat coloured fish on account of unconscious totemism; bowls of fruit illustrating the visual harmony of the English harvest; pieces of meat cut into ovals, rhomboids, cubes and cones according to the principles of constructivist sculpture. Every time the Inspector's mind was penetrated by an idea, some half-digested remnant of it appeared at the table. She paid for the food herself, and often provided a bottle of wine, from which she poured a glass and a half for Colin and four glasses for herself. The dog was fed with a concoction that came from several packets, stirred with milk into a plausible simulacrum of human excrement. 'Eat this shit, you bastard!' she would say, as she thrust it onto the kitchen floor, and always the dog would approach it gingerly as though expecting an explosion.

On the whole Colin did not dislike the Health Inspector. She had moved into the cottage without mentioning the possibility of an objection, settling unilaterally the question of rent. She had a few friends, and the closest of these was Archie, who drove a little horse-drawn covered wagon and who toured the villages collecting saleable remnants. In the back of the wagon he performed useful services like sharpening knives, mending porcelain, and once, with a great shaking of the cart that went unnoticed by the peaceable nag immersed in the study of its nosebag, making some kind of violent addresses to the Health Inspector, who emerged with a tired and dissipated look that remained for several days. Archie sometimes came into the house, but was always a model of politeness when inside, and certainly had no intention of engaging in any domestic act beyond the most generally acceptable, such as helping with the washing up, or sitting down on the cold November evenings with a cup of tea, to enjoy a bit of a natter. This was the only time that the Health Inspector engaged in extended conversation, having, with Archie's agreement, chosen some fairly impersonal topic from the few which they considered acceptable. Corruption in the National Health Service was a favourite, since the Inspector had many impressive details of people who had paid to jump queues, of others who had been refused emergency treatment, and of operations impeded by drunken porters furious for extra pay. Archie liked to hear about human organs exposed on operating tables, and the emendations which they underwent without consent from their unconscious owners. This homely vision of catastrophe caused him to express himself in long judicious whistles of dismay. On less emotional days they would confine their discourse to politics, Archie taking a fairly definite line about people having things too easy, the Inspector entertaining slightly more vague opinions about the rights of the working man, which she would illustrate with arguments from Bernard Shaw. Neither of them considered the matter to be of the highest seriousness, and they would allow the discussion quietly to rock itself into somnolence with no substantial issue being settled. If Colin were present, he would observe their forms as they sunk back in the Edwardian leather armchairs of the living room, their minds released from the burden of cogitation. He wished that the world contained more such harmless creatures, and forgave the Inspector her egregious self-involvement.

He found himself unable to read or write. He would remain awake at night, listening to the rain in the cedars, and the hooting of owls across the park. Obscure feelings of betrayal obsessed him, as though Francesca might be blamed for her failure to materialise, or the schoolmaster likewise for refusing to be wholly dead. The Inspector showed him how to ease his days with harmless occupations. They picked elderberries from which to make wine in the stone vats carried from her previous residence. They bought shallots from Archie – who had an undisclosed source of supply – and pickled them in spicy vinegar. They began to clear the garden, unearthed the remaining tubers and vegetables, and planted bulbs for the spring. They found boletus mushrooms, which they dried, or pickled in oil, according to size. But none of these pursuits could entirely calm his spirits, and every evening, when the Inspector was home, he would walk about the countryside, peering into others' houses, walking over others' property, searching others' faces as they passed him on the road, almost as though he demanded some certificate of existence from this place which his father still haunted.

One moonlit night in December, after a day during which the memory of the schoolmaster had bothered him, so that he felt lacerated with anxiety, he set out from the cottage, telling the Inspector to eat her supper without him. A letter had come from the Blakelys, asking him if he intended to return, since they needed his room and would be grateful to know if they could have it. He had written back, relinquishing whatever right his neglect still allowed him. He would collect the things at the earliest opportunity. Many apologies. Many, many apologies. His footsteps in the cold night air spelt out the rhythm of apology. He had not meant to exist. He was not really to blame. Now that he had freedom, a house of his own, a fiver a week, a housekeeper, he was in a position that he had once coveted. But it needed to be occupied by a definite person, expanding into the corners with an unconscionable sense of self-importance. Colin saw nothing in what he had felt or done but false starts and premature climaxes. His work gave no sign of his actuality;

it did nothing to justify, either his callous rejection of his father, or his nervous obsession with a vanishing girl.

He walked through the park, climbing over walls, and continuing in the direction of Murricombe, across wired fields at the edges of which his clothes and hands were torn. He reached a road that turned off beside a Victorian gothic church, and ascended, between high hedges, to a kind of plateau. The hedges gave way on one side to a wall, and the wall to a gate, from which a gravel path ran among dark Wellingtonias, mounting higher and higher towards a vast pinnacled house which he glimpsed all aglow through the branches of a ruined oak. He began to walk towards it along the winding path, constantly losing and regaining a vision of the moonlit battlements and radiant windows in their pointed frames. Cars passed, cutting the night with their headlights as they took the corners, illuminating ranks of elms and sycamores, a stretch of water, and the balustrade of a stone parterre. Colin pressed back out of sight, and became part of the ivy-covered wall that flanked the lane. He found himself standing on the parterre, and the house majestically unfolded before him, its windows crammed with movement, its high pointed portico bustling with people who had just arrived.

He stood against a tree, looking up at the battlements, behind which rose the buttressed chimneys, moulded at the corners, and below which ran a long fretted cornice, completing and arresting the movements of the window arches of the upper floor. Two spires composed the wings, each buttressed from below, adorned with pinnacles and with tiny ornamental windows in the shape of daggers, exposing the intricate movements of winding stairs. A sound of argument and laughter spread from the portico as a car, arriving at speed, mounted the steps, its occupants jumping in panic from the two back doors. It was a large car, and the double doors of the house would not open wide enough to let it in. It bumped its way back onto the pavement, and reversed at lightning speed through the night towards the place where

Colin stood. It stopped briefly, ejected a slim figure from the front seat, and then roared back towards the house, as though to try again.

'Really!' the figure said, straightening, as the car squealed to a halt before the portico.

It was Francesca. She did not move, for she had seen Colin, and stared at him with eyes that registered no astonishment. She pulled a thin shawl close to her shoulders, which trembled slightly from the cold.

'Golly!' she said at last, 'an apparition.'

Colin sought vainly for some offhand phrase that would both explain his presence and show that she was not the cause of it. Francesca did not smile, but looked at him from her steady grey eyes, as her left hand moved vigilantly to the side of her face. In nothing had she changed, except to become more full in the body.

'If thou hast any sound or use of voice, speak to me.'

'What can I say? After so many failures.'

'I know,' she laughed. 'Are you going to tell me off?'

'What for?'

'For going away last summer. For not replying to your letters of umpteen years ago.'

'So you received them?'

Colin came forward. In a crazy approximation to boldness he took hold of Francesca's arm. She instantly withdrew it, and for a second he almost hated her.

'Of course, they were gibberish,' he said quickly. 'I couldn't expect you to answer.'

She looked closely at him.

'I think you *are* wanting to tell me off.'

Francesca turned, and began slowly to walk towards the house. But she leaned her head in his direction and allowed her right arm to swing freely beside him, as the other pulled the shawl about her shoulders and held itself close to her face. He assumed that he was to follow for a few steps.

'No. I'm just glad to have met you again. Even if the time and the place are so – so unpropitious.'

She stopped, and mumbled something. He made her repeat it.

'Does being a writer make you pompous?'

'Not a writer,' he said with angry conviction. 'Just a hack.'

She looked closely at him.

'That's ridiculous. You must never talk like that. You must work at it, day and night.'

Although she spoke in a whisper, the vehemence of her words surprised him. Something nearer to herself than his own success had prompted her. Some part of her, small but vital, had been mingled with his fortunes, and she seemed to be urging on him the duty to conserve it.

'Francesca . . .'

She swung round and watched the distant figures in the portico.

'And do you know why I didn't reply?'

'But you did reply. You were very nice. It just so happened . . .'

'To your letters years ago, silly.'

'Oh well, since it was years ago, what do I gain by knowing about it?'

'Only the truth. Do you remember – that's what we agreed to share.'

Colin remembered no such thing.

'Of course,' he answered, nevertheless.

'Well, was it so very long ago?'

'Not so very long. But look at you – a grown woman, and – and a beautiful one.'

'Am I?'

Her eyes flashed and then were still. He noticed how often she fell still, with an absolute stillness like a monument. It was as though she testified to something – something eternal and unforgettable, that was nevertheless by everyone and at every time forgot.

'You must know that you are. It makes me feel I should behave as though I didn't know you.'

'Don't you dare. Don't you dare be ordinary.' Again she spoke in vehement whispers, as she set her body in motion. 'You have a duty. Or do you think that's absurd?'

'I don't know. What duty?'

'You see this house? Well, the whole look of it, everything outside and in, makes me sick. This heap of bodies. And me one of them. Maybe your duty is to save me.'

Suddenly she paused, took his arm and began to walk him towards the house.

'Come inside and I'll show you. And don't forget to be really annoyed with me, really angry that I am leading you astray. Is it a deal?'

'It's a deal.'

Colin walked in a daze, elated and confused. At one moment it seemed as though he or she or perhaps both of them had made a definite advance. The next moment it had the aspect of a game, and the adroitness with which she had deflected his curiosity, enlisting him in a venture that was sure to end disastrously, astonished him. But there was no time to hit on a policy, and Francesca, as she pressed ahead with long agile steps, seemed not to require one. As they ascended the stairs, she remarked:

'This house belongs to John Garnsworth; you must be nice to him. He's very stupid,' she added, as though that gave a conclusive reason. 'A lot of people have come from London: I don't know many of them. Somebody's birthday.'

They entered a large open space lit by a many-tiered dusty chandelier, which hung from a stout rod of brass, bolted some thirty feet above them into the apex of a gothic vault. Colin felt her squeeze his arm more tightly, and, looking sideways, he noticed how tense her face had become. Then her expression slowly set again, as though under the hands of an unseen *maquilleuse*. Perceiving a host of people, dressed in every style and fashion, their voices raised in every tone, angry, amorous, magnanimous, disdainful, he held her back.

'Weren't you with someone – I mean some people?'

'We'll join up with them. One of them is a poet, whom you're sure to like.'

'I hope so.'

'You *must*.'

She moved forward before he could reply, and at once they stood together in the long drawing room of the house, where glasses twirled in a hundred hands, and laughter exploded unceasingly. Only in cathedrals had Colin seen such long cold vaults of stone. The ribs rose from a score of clustered shafts, and congregated at the ridge in decorated bosses of red and gold. The spandrels of the arches were bare and white, and the ashlar face of the wall, punctuated only by high lancet windows of leaded glass, descended through twenty feet to a wooden dado, on the panels of which forlorn celtic ladies moped in desolate fields. Here and there a tapestry masked the bareness of the wall, its unravelled borders trailing along the diminutive tables that were ranked against the dado. On the tables were bowls – some silver, some blue and white, some of delicate china, others of brown kitchen ware. By the door stood an old manservant with shaking hand, who dipped a ladle into a silver bowl; further down the hall guests seemed either to help themselves or to be waited on by daughterly girls in billowing paisley-patterned dresses. From two of the central bosses hung great brass chandeliers, but the bulbs in them were dim; more light came from a row of dazzling sconces fixed to the inner wall, where stood a large stone fireplace, with a pointed arch, flanked by crocketed arcades in the manner of a church sedilia. It was towards this place, in which a heap of logs cracked and sizzled, that Francesca steered him.

'Fumsheshk!'

The owner of the voice had extorted this sound from a mouth already oppressed by pastry, and was now brushing the bits of a vol-au-vent from his lips, shutting the rest inside. His blond hair flopped over his face, revealing now one and now the other of two expressionless blue eyes. His maroon smoking jacket with brocaded borders enclosed a soft Byronic collar, and above this his head tilted slightly, for he was very tall. He smiled from Grecian lips with a radiance in which Francesca for a moment visibly bathed.

'Jonathan hello.'

Then, as though remembering some episode with which this name was connected she wilted and looked down quickly, shielding her eyes with her ever vigilant hand. Jonathan seemed not to notice, but stretched out towards her a pair of long arms that might have been expressly designed for the task of displaying whatever they held as ravished by their contact. His strong brown hands latched onto Francesca's arms, the fingers buried themselves in her green satin shawl, and before Colin's believing eyes a terrible ballet took place in which a puppet representing his *bel idéal* was scissored in the air, kissed by lips which flaked its cheeks with pastry, and thrown down beside him, to resume its uncertain life as Francesca Wimpole.

'Jonathan Burridge,' the voice proclaimed.

Colin ordered his hand to stand forth from the dirty trench in which he had concealed it, and grapple with the enemy. Jonathan crumpled the hand quietly and threw it away.

'Yes, this is my neighbour, Colin Ferguson.'

She kept her eyes turned down.

'I thought your neighbours were the Mountfords?'

'My nearest neighbour – the house next door. Although,' she added, turning to Colin, 'now that I think of it, haven't you moved?'

'No. I came back.'

Colin sensed that his logic was faulty, but the noise and the frivolity confused him. The schoolmaster cackled in his memory, full of hatred and despair.

'You came back,' said Francesca.

Her eyes wandered, seemed to smile at someone, and then rested again on Jonathan.

'Fantastic to see you 'Cesca. You look scrumptious in that dress. Wouldn't be surprised if you hadn't filled out a bit since that party of Freddie's.'

'Oh Jonathan!'

'You've got to come racing. I've acquired the most mouth-watering Aston Martin with an engine made from the best of everything. It has a human heart, the kidneys of a horse, and guzzles like a vampire. You'd be swept off your feet.'

'I hate cars.'

'That's what they all say. A virgin's reluctance.'

Colin started to plan his escape. But the route was blocked by a small fat man in evening dress, who held a stout rope, at the end of which a large Alsatian strained powerfully. Its teeth were bared in an immutable snarl.

'Don't mind Pongo,' the man said. 'He's looked like that ever since he broke his jaw on one of Marjorie's biscuits. Nice to see you Jonathan. Mmm darling,' he added, pecking Francesca's cheek. 'Heard your father the other day burbling on about duck shooting in the house. Beautifully soporific. But hardly his line.'

Francesca stood still. She seemed to be holding her breath.

'Peer confesses to elephant gun. Previous encounter with schizophrenic Zulus denied. Ducks to receive Royal Charter. Replicas made available to Council House tenants. Amendment passed. Conservative majority two thousand and six.'

'Liberal.'

'Really? How very extraordinary.'

'I mean my father takes the Liberal whip.'

'Naughty!'

The fat man turned to Colin and held out his free hand.

'My name's de Litham. Nigel de Litham.'

There was a pause.

'Sounds awfully affected doesn't it, the "de"?'

Colin hesitated.

'My great grandfather inserted it.'

Colin looked down the hall, and caught sight of a girl in Harlequin costume doing cartwheels on a recamier couch.

He wanted to draw Francesca's attention to the scene, but she stood apart, as though annoyed.

'Inserted the "de", I mean.'

Jonathan too was standing back, in a manner that suggested only a conditional participation in the dialogue. Suddenly he seemed to curl his body behind Nigel de Litham, in order fervently to invite Francesca to something which caused in her a distinct flush of pleasure, and in Colin a stab of pain. A small, crabbed, elderly thing took up its posture inside him as he listened to the thoroughbred banter of Nigel who, it transpired, was a sort of writer, a peer, and the owner of a considerable independence. These facts were cunningly inserted into a monologue which, while superficially covering every subject from Islamic politics to the shape of a tiger nut, in fact expressed no curiosity about anything except the speaker, and no feeling towards the world other than one of general sexual arousal.

'And now you must tell me what you do, and with whom. I'm most desperately curious. You have such fine eyes, and a most interesting posture.'

'I am a writer,' Colin was about to say, but cancelled the thought. Since it was necessary to pretend, he preferred a catalogue of failures to a manifesto of hope. He told Lord de Litham of his hours in a London tenement, wasted hours of hesitation, aligning words like tin soldiers in preparation for a war that had only imaginary interest. He told of his father's suffering, and of his lonely death, and emphasised that his own refusal of the world was for the sake of childish spite against a destiny that it would be better to forget, and which he could never in any case have altered. He would walk the streets of London, often far into the night, exploring faces, windows, every little human aperture through which he might see but never pass, wondering how he had managed to exclude himself from so much, through what error he had condemned himself to this stance of pitiless observation. Consider the present conversation. Did he have any desire for it? Had he invited it? Had he given the slightest reason to think that he would be interested in the details of an arbitrary fat man's lineage and wealth? Of course not. The whole dismal episode had been brought about against his will, by the stance, the affectation if you like, of the observer, and all that he gained was an increment in his sense of isolation. He did not know what enticed him to these gatherings. Normally he refused – yes, he refused all invitations, all offers of a chance encounter, all gaiety, all normality. Such things didn't interest him. Nothing interested him, or next to nothing. He was a wandering Jew. If he had any taste, it was for Hasidic scholarship.

'You're delicious,' said Lord de Litham, 'I could eat you up. Isn't he delicious, Pongo? When your jaw is better, darling, you can have a really big satisfying bite of his bum – won't that be nice?'

He walked slowly away, muttering endearments, and casting his eyes lustfully from side to side. Colin fell into the hands of a minister's private secretary, who had once (he whispered) been a designer of ladies' underwear. He argued passionately that English upper-class women had become wholly oblivious to pubic semiology: they had no taste for seams and borders, no real grasp of lace or leather, and had fallen well behind the German bourgeoisie in their understanding of elementary fetishism. 'A woman who doesn't appreciate the tragi–comedy of navy-blue, or the lingering sadness of springy pubic hair glimpsed in a frame of pink dentelle – such a woman might as well buy her knickers from Oxfam.' To Colin's grief, the secretary was approached by his minister; his face lengthened to a mournful mask and his words became clipped and ambiguous. Eventually he was led away, holding his hands before him in an attitude of prayer. His place was taken by a woman with protruding teeth who discoursed pleasantly about the history of the house, built by an associate of Salvin who deserved to be better known. She was fierce about the successes of Victorian craftmanship, and had particularly strong views as to the mixing of Early English with Decorated mouldings. Colin enjoyed her line of enquiry. It seemed to him that the world of frothy intimacies would be easier to grasp if it could be approached through the study of so solid and at the same time so pregnant a thing as architecture.

'Architectural historians,' said the buck-toothed woman, 'are the chroniclers of the ruling class, and also their true apologists. We alone are welcome in all their houses.'

Francesca appeared, looking urgent and harassed. She gave the architectural historian a hostile glance, and then led him away.

'That awful woman,' she whispered. 'I've got to introduce you to someone better'.

She pointed to a region of space over which several bodies contended furiously. Eventually one seemed to detach itself and to turn in their direction. The face was white, beautiful, deathly; the hands gestured in a feminine manner, but the firm neck and straight, trousered figure were those of a man.

'Who is it?'

'The poet I told you about. She's called Sarah. I think she's lovely.'

Sarah wore a collarless shirt, loosely tucked into her black satin trousers, leaving unanswered the question of her bust. Her head moved slowly on her strong neck from side to side, the green eyes resting here and there with the grace and condescension of a goddess, but always returning to Francesca, to whom they offered a look of penetrating tenderness.

'Back from your forage, my dear?'

Sarah's voice was slow, deep, and liquid, as though it bubbled up from lungs swamped by some distinguished disease.

'You make me sound like a Valkyrie,' Francesca answered.

Sarah's great green eyes suddenly enlarged and sparkled, and she gestured lugubriously with her painted hands.

'But that is just what you are. A Valkyrie, announcing death. Has she announced *your* death?' she asked, turning to Colin. Her tone was eager, almost greedy.

'Yes, many years ago.'

'Then why aren't you dead? I'll allow that you seem totally wiped out. Vapid even.'

'Oh dear.'

Francesca looked from one to the other, like a frightened child observing a dispute among adults.

'It is kind of you to observe me so closely.'

'You mean why does this fucking bitch who is obviously a freak and a lesbian and ball-crusher take the trouble to shit on me from such a very great height.'

'Now you mention it, it is rather remarkable.'

'Answer: I take an interest in Francesca, and I want to know whether she is going to pick up the kind of man who deserves her. You seem like a snotty child straight out of kindergarten.

'Though I may be wrong,' Sarah added, with as much kindness as her monarchical standpoint allowed. She waved her long amber cigarette holder towards her mouth, sucked on it deeply, and then slowly exhaled the blue fumes into Colin's face. Having completed this ceremony, she made another concession to conversation.

'You have a nice face. I can see why Francesca might fancy you.'

On the whole, Colin thought, the interview was not going too badly.

'I believe you have a mysterious fascination for her. Is that not so, my beautiful angel?'

Sarah kissed Francesca wetly on the mouth. Colin, seeing so many liberties taken with Francesca's flesh, tried to snatch her right hand, which hung limply beside him. It was hastily withdrawn.

'Apparently you are some kind of nonentity from the cottage next door, who stumbled into Francesca's life at the moment of puberty, when the smallest things have the largest repercussions. Also you are a kind of writer. This interests me.'

'Oh?'

'Yes, you see, because I too started life as a complete nonentity, and worked my way up through the exploitation of chance encounters.'

'I expect it helps to be as rude as you are.'

'Do you think so?' she asked with interest. 'I doubt it.'

'Well,' said Francesca, 'at least it makes you seem invulnerable. And then, of course, it is awfully pleasant to find out that you're not. That way you go up a couple of notches, just where others go down.'

It was curious, Colin noticed, that Francesca spoke to Sarah quite loudly, in a tone that was almost relaxed. Sarah spread her hands in a gesture of defeat.

'You win darling. You have ravished me.'

Colin drank copiously from the glass which he noticed had inserted itself between his fingers. It wasn't fair, he exclaimed, this harrowing directness, suitable perhaps among creatures condemned for an eternity to hell, but not at all suitable in conditions where human relations are still more or less tentative. Personally he had never been blind to the purpose of parties, and for the sake of his education he refused invitations as little as possible, and usually only when they coincided. Today as it happened the invitation had come at the last minute. He had looked forward to pleasant, non-committal conversation, of the kind that consists not exactly of lies nor even of half truths, but rather of statements in which only small and publicly digestible fragments of the personality are revealed. He was beginning to understand, however, the regime of truthfulness to which Francesca's friends were subjected; in his own case, he had to confess, he had never been able to separate truthfulness from intimacy . . .

'Off his rocker,' said Sarah. 'Is he going to shut up, or shall I recite him one of my poems?'

And without waiting for an answer she launched out, with the voice of a seaside fat lady wallowing into a dirty-postcard sea.

Good Christ, what a lark, here's a shark
With a spark in the dark of his bark
Like an arc-light, a mark
Of his present incandescence,
His phosphorescent essence
Like the ark, the glowing carc-
ass of the clerk's covenant, the anointed
Death of Mark, the appointment in the park,
The old Kraak-en, the quintessence
The here – now, there – then anointed
Ever onwards like a ghostly cutty sark,
Don't you see it? Can't yer see it? Come an' . . .

'Come and what?'

'Well, obviously, given the reference to Lautréamont, the word I really need is "fuck"; but it doesn't rhyme. I wonder what you think of "fark"?'

'Nothing much,' he said.

'No, nor do I,' said Sarah rather sadly. 'It is an unfinished masterpiece.'

There was a silence, and then,

'You're bored,' she said. 'Don't deny that you're bored.' She looked tenderly at Francesca.

'Haven't I bored him to death darling? Bored him utterly to death with short sharp pungent thrusts?'

'On the whole yes, I think you have.'

Francesca looked sadly at Colin, who walked away, drinking from his glass, and occasionally refilling it at the troughs provided. He recognised many faces, although he knew that he could not know them. And then, in the dark corner next to the sedilia, leaning up against a column which for some reason had been placed there, ashen faced beneath a spray of autumn leaves and bulrushes, was the upright carcass of Mr Hepworth-Sprigge. The little clerk was clearly out of his depth in this company, and in recognition of his inferiority, the guests had cleared a space around him, leaving a distance roughly equivalent to the length of floor into which he might shortly spread himself. His mouth was open, and his head swayed slightly. He looked upwards at the vault in dismay, and his small eyes blinked in lonely tearless spasms.

'Allow me to introduce myself,' said Colin.

'Obliged. Ugh. Pleased. Acquaintance. Make.'

'Colin Ferguson. I think we've met.'

'Poshible. Poshible. Shity? Broking? Boring. All boring. All meaninglesh.'

He stood forward, swaying, and steadied himself against the column with one hand. The autumn spray tottered threateningly.

'Plumptre. Harold Plumptre. Of Plumptre's. Shnot mine. Belongs to fucking brother.'

'Sorry. I confused you with someone else. Man called Hepworth-Sprigge. Works in the city. Don't suppose you know him?'

'Don't know any of the fuckers. Boring all of them. Illiterate bastards.'

Harold Plumptre suddenly seized Colin's arm and steered him into the congregation. He swayed a little, but not so much that Colin could not hold him steady, releasing him only at those moments when, falling heavily sideways, he would do maximum damage. As each successive dowager reared away to wipe punch from her corsage or to restore some maltreated brocade, Mr Plumptre would attempt a courteous bow, at the same time mumbling apologies, visibly embarrassed, and mopping his brow with a sodden handkerchief. Suddenly he pulled himself to a halt, and gave Colin a knowing look.

'Know whosh mosht cultured pershon in shity? Jew really know? Tell you. Be shprized. Mosht cultured pershon in shitty isha waiter. Fox's Coffee Cave, Leadenhall Shtreet. Knowsh all bout Faust, bout Thomash Mann, bout Shtefan George, bout Hegel, Schlegel, Rushkin, Pushkin, Mishkin, Boshkin, Kokoshkin, Soroporogoshkin . . . all of them, the lot. Absholute bloody marvel.' He paused, and pressed Colin's arm with confidential fingers. 'Coursh, he doeshn't let on. Not him. Shept to hish intimates. I'm one of the few, one of the very few. Confidesh in me. Yesh. Confidesh.'

'Extraordinary.'

'Why?' Mr Plumptre eyed him with sudden pig-eyed indignation. 'Why shtroadinary? You think a waiter musht be bloody native? Thatsh your thoughtsh? Shnobbery. Contemptible, emptible shnobbery. Hullo, heresh Sharah. Pretenshioush ol' bag. Hate her guts.'

'Hullo Harold. What are you two discussing?'

'I wash telling Mr . . .'

'Ferguson.'

'Yesh, that's right. Telling him how I hate your guts. Pretenshioush old shlag. Or bag.'

'Many people feel like that. In fact, it is rather original to like me. *He* likes me,' she added, jabbing her finger towards Colin.

This piece of information seemed to have a sobering effect on Mr Plumptre, who backed away and stared at Colin with something like astonishment.

'Jew really?'

'On the whole, I suppose I do,' said Colin glumly. He looked around for Francesca. Sarah and Mr Plumptre fell at once into deep conversation, the former defending, and the latter attacking, the thesis that Sarah had points of considerable interest, not counting the gift of speech and the extraordinary sexual fascination which she exerted, but which, in deference to her purity of soul and because it was pretty old hat anyway, she rarely exploited, over young women with literary ideas. Colin moved slowly away. The noise was deafening, resounding among the impassive stones of the tracery, leaping from vault to vault and re-descending like a hoard of maddened harpies over the rattling heads below. A hand was placed in his, and Francesca's voice said, 'Let's go outside.'

They wandered along a tiled corridor, with a painted ceiling of birds against a mackerel sky. Narrow windows opened onto the parterre, which was white and sparkling in the moonlight. Francesca's high shoes made an unhurried stutter as they walked along. Then, passing one behind the other through a narrow door, they entered a plain, square unornamented room which smelled of dust. In the middle stood a sheeted billiard table, and next to the stone fireplace some large comfortable armchairs. Colin sat down in one of them and closed his eyes.

There came before his mind a picture of the schoolmaster busying himself about the cottage, carrying nails, screws and drill-bits in an old tobacco tin, knocking here and there with a hammer, sawing wood for shelves which were never put up, carrying into the house a roll of chicken wire destined for a run which – on account first of fowl pest and then of the sudden cheapness of eggs – had never been completed. His father had a peculiar way of standing while engaged in these abortive tasks, his mouth full of nails, his hand reaching for a cup of tea which would compete hopelessly with the nails before being returned undrunk to the nearest table. As a rule the sessions lasted two hours, and always a job was chosen that would need three or four hours for its completion; no definite change, therefore, was ever accomplished. The schoolmaster paid particular attention to Colin's 'quarters' as he called them. He had always furnished them rather better than the rest of the house, in order to apologise behind his own back for the poverty which on all other occasions would be paraded before Colin as the essence of their common destiny and the guarantee of their uncorrupted hearts. Colin thought he might finish some of his father's work: the shelves, for instance, above the kitchen sink. Strangely, he wanted to discuss the matter with Francesca.

'Why have you brought me here?' he asked.

'You see,' she whispered triumphantly. 'You have kept your part of the bargain. You are annoyed with me!'

'No I'm not,' he said angrily.

'Well, you could have fooled me. But do you see what I mean?'

'About what?'

He kept his eyes closed, hoping to retain his useful anger.

'About the need to save me.'

'That's all rubbish, and you know it.'

'That only shows how little you know me.'

'It's not for want of trying.'

'There, you see. Look how annoyed you are!'

There was a silence, and then suddenly she spoke in a changed tone, urgent and confidential.

'Please be nice to me Colin. I know I don't deserve it. I am a spoilt child, and a careless one. But I don't want to hurt you. Really I don't. And I am sorry about Sarah: she was dreadful, and I did nothing to stop her.'

He opened his eyes, and looked at her. He felt that he was sitting exactly as his father had sat in his days of hope. How graceful was Francesca's neck beneath the bushy blonde hair, how beautiful her slender body and her shiftless eyes. He had read of the 'consecrated body', lifted from nature and re-worked as a mighty emblem of the soul. This was the task of the Shaman: to place redemption in the flesh. He divined in Francesca's body all the grace and good fortune that he had ever hoped for, and at the same time a voice of warning spoke against her from the depths of his soul.

'Oh, I did like Sarah. Why should you have stopped her from being herself? After all, she's your friend.'

'Yes,' said Francesca simply. Then she smiled. 'I dare say, nevertheless, that you think it's utter hell in there.'

'No – not hell. Purgatory perhaps.'

'The refining fire. That's how I think of it too. But I'm so clumsy.'

'*You?*'

He looked at her in astonishment.

'Haven't you noticed?'

Colin got up quickly, leaned over her, and lightly brushed her hair with his lips. Her smell was delicate, almost absent, like the memory of incense in a disused church. She turned her head down.

'I am worse even than you,' he said, 'and ruder than Sarah. But if I am with you, it doesn't matter. I wish I could explain it.'

'You don't have to explain it.'

Suddenly she lifted his hand to her lips and kissed it. Her lips were cool and moist, and moved hesitantly against his skin. She rose from the chair. Briefly their faces brushed each other, and then moved apart. She pushed him away.

'Well,' she said, 'you cannot imagine a weirder bunch of people. Not just Sarah, and Nigel, but all of them – even when they seem normal it's only an affectation. Do you know what I think?' she went on.

'What do you think?'

'That there are places in the world where God doesn't go. I sometimes think He is as shy as we are.'

'Certainly, he seems to have the same difficulty in making Himself understood.'

'But then, I suppose one shouldn't take too elevated a view. That too is a form of pride – to see mockery as godless. How else should one live?'

He looked at her, his attention captured.

'You tell me.'

'I can't *tell* you: though perhaps one day we'll know.'

She took his hand and led him back to the corridor. Now he was cheerful, and they talked lightly about the guests. Francesca made out a special case for Harold Plumptre, who, she said, was neither a swank nor a teeny bopper, but a good honest drunk of the old school. Colin told her the story of his first encounter with Mr Plumptre, and Francesca stared in amazement, not knowing, she said, whether to laugh or cry.

Jonathan Burridge drove them home, in a black Daimler with detached headlights, wooden running boards, a mahogany dashboard studded with brass-bound dials, and soft leather seats: a sweet-smelling sanctuary, full of an unseen silent power. Sarah and Mr Plumptre were with them. They asked Colin to come with them to London, but showed no regret when he declined. As the car swayed down the country lanes, Mr Plumptre expounded the second *Walpurgisnacht*. Colin recognised the theory as his own, wined and watered down. Sarah, one arm round Francesca, smoked sweet Turkish cigarettes and muttered stanzas from *Don Juan*. Jonathan Burridge looked angry, and asked repeatedly for the road to Bassington as though he had yet to be given a reason for going there.

Mr Plumptre's meditations gradually became theological, centring on such difficult questions as the liquefaction of the blood of St Januarius, the incoherence of the argument from design, and the uncertainty attached to a vision which his charlady claimed to have experienced one Sunday morning, as she placed the flowers on the altar of her local church – a vision in which Christ appeared holding the phallus of her departed husband unintelligibly inscribed in gothic script. The air from the car window had restored Mr Plumptre, who was speaking now more cogently.

'How did she know, I wonder, that it was *his* cock? For apparently Christ said nothing one way or the other.'

Suddenly they drew up at the cottage, and Mr Plumptre stared out at it. A light was burning in the Inspector's room.

'This where you live?'

'Yes.'

'Well I'm buggered. Nearly bought the place myself: must have been two or three years ago. Some cussid bastard of a schoolteacher had it then. Wouldn't sell it. Not even to Bill Pickford. How the devil did you get hold of it?'

'Harold,' said Francesca, 'do shut up.'

'Shan't, so there! Bill Pickford turned out to be a bad hat as well. I expect they conspired about it – Pickford, I mean, and the schoolteacher, keeping the house off the market. But how did *you* get hold of it?'

'I sort of borrowed it really,' said Colin.

'Here,' said Mr Plumptre. 'What did you say your name was? Here's my card. I want to have lunch with you. Soon. Somewhere in the city. I know a good place. Wednesdays are best. Fascinating conversation. Fascinating. Funny, you remind me of someone.'

Colin was standing in the road, waiting to say goodbye. Then Francesca too got out from the other side.

'I'm tired,' she said. 'I'll stay at home.'

'Home?'

For a second he could not grasp her meaning.

'Yes. My parents are away. There's only Mr Jacob and old Felicity. Maybe you could walk up with me?'

'To the Hall?'

'It isn't far.'

She ran back to the car, kissed Jonathan lightly, and then leaned into the back, where she pressed her mouth against the taut white mouth of Sarah.

'Oh, and Sarah,' she said, as she stepped back again.

'Yes darling?'

'Will I see you tomorrow?'

'I don't see why not. Do you envisage some impediment? Pluto perhaps?'

'His name's Paluto.'

'Pluto, Paluto, what's in a name?'

'Will you be at the flat?'

Francesca sounded anxious.

'I don't see why not.'

'Then I'll see you.'

'You'll see me. Are you sure it's Paluto?'

'Sarah!'

'Funny. I could have sworn he bore the name of a deity.'

Francesca stamped her foot and closed the door of the car, which drew away. The road swung inward towards the park and then ran parallel to the wall. Colin looked at Francesca, his mind full of questions, but she took his arm with tense, clutching fingers and steered him in silence towards the Hall. By the gate stood a clump of elms, and he pulled her towards it.

'What do you want?' she asked. Her eyes were motionless, blank. He covered them with kisses, which she did not resist, but received as a monument might receive the kisses of a pilgrim. He stood back, and her eyes slowly focused on him.

'Don't come up with me,' she said.
'I thought you wanted me to come?'
'No. Not now. Not beyond the gate.'
'If you insist.'
'I insist.'
Her teeth chattered with cold. He put his arm round her.
'I can manage. Please.'
He took off his jacket and held it out to her.
'Are you sure?' she asked distantly.
'Yes. You can give it back – when we meet.'
'Tomorrow. I'll come down. In the morning. Can I?'
Colin hesitated.
'I could come up.'
'No, that would be too much trouble.'
Her tone suggested that the trouble would be hers. Without another word she turned and walked quickly towards the house.

'Goodnight,' he called.
She did not look round.

Six

'I HEARD you pacing about all night.'
The Health Inspector pointed to the canister of coffee on the Aga. Her preference for canisters belonged with her khaki clothes, her lack of belongings, and her ability to dress all organic matter in the form of something edible: they expressed a deeply military outlook, a rough survivor's solipsism. She wandered in the jungle of the world with no knowledge as to whether her side had lost or won, or whether the cause which once enlisted her was still somewhere believed in. He felt that his occasional dispatches ought to be brief and optimistic.

'That's because I was pacing about all night.'

'Ah,' she replied, with a note of relief. 'I thought so. Your father used to pace about all night. I put it down to guilt. It was one of the things that he never talked about.'

'What else did he never talk about?'

'Beethoven. Cucumber sandwiches. The stock exchange. Quite a few things really. Also disease. That was his greatest weakness.'

Colin sat at the table and surveyed his surroundings. The table, now that he observed it, was not so bad; its heavy top of deeply stained elmwood sorted quite well with the whitewashed walls, and it was with relief that Colin took in the fact that the Inspector, who shifted slightly in the rocking chair as she turned the pages of *The Guardian*, had not hung her pictures here. Mrs Ferguson's old spode plates had been fixed to the wall beside the door. But there was no other sign, that he could notice, of a woman's absence. The cottage was his father's tomb, in which the vacated symbols of a life were slowly crumbling. Colin looked at the Inspector, relic of a flippant intimacy in which both she and the schoolmaster had acted solitary, animal roles.

'I've sometimes thought,' she said, 'that the rhythm here doesn't suit you.'

'What rhythm?'

'The rhythm of life. Too full of shadows. I like shadows. Especially I like the Prussian blue under trees.'

After a pause, Colin said:

'Are you working today?'

The Inspector nodded. This meant that, at some hour which remained indeterminate until it was upon them, she would thrust down her brushes in a jamjar of murky turpentine and, without further preparation, grab the canvas bag which lay always in readiness behind the door, and jump onto the moped which stood parked beside the dustbins in the garden. While the time of her departure was uncertain, her return at six o'clock was always punctual. It was characteristic of the Inspector to grant these little offerings of predictability. On the whole, they made her even more enigmatic.

'What I mean,' she continued, 'is that there is no contact with the vast and changing world, the world of mass communication to which the majority of people belong. No telephone, for instance. No television. Television is becoming an important influence in the development of the human personality. It may or may not be a good thing. Where's that fucking animal?'

'On my bed.'

'Ah. So *he* slept at least.'

'After his fashion.'

'Did he fart much?'

'Not very much. I hardly noticed.'

'Good. I was beginning to worry about his ulcers.'

Colin drank some coffee, which had a sour chicory taste.

'I wonder whether you shouldn't really be in London. You need society, colour, violence. I once knew a man, a near neighbour, who lived down here as a gardener on a large estate. He was highly educated and somewhat sad. Once, after a pint or two, he confessed that he had always wanted to be a writer, and that he had come here to be alone and embark on a literary career. He had dried up almost instantly. Poor bugger never published a thing. Never even wrote a letter.'

'What happened to him?' Colin was mildly curious.

'Oh he died. Two or three years ago. Had a dicky ticker. Long time in hospital. Would have been better off living it up in town, silly sod – and he could have afforded it too. But scared stiff, that was the trouble. Scared of life, scared of death. Scared of life *because* scared of death. Scared, in short, of Nothing with a capital N – with a trail of capital Ns. An entrail.'

'I wish you didn't have so many theories.'

'Can't help it. It's my way of maintaining contact with reality. What shall we have for supper? I saw some wholesome-looking . . .'

'Oh buy what you like.'

'Yes. I was intending to. Do you think you will be going to London?'

Colin was beginning to find the Inspector's line of thought rather tiresome.

'I might. When I have finished the piece I am working on.'

The Inspector carefully folded the newspaper and stuck it on the window-sill, between a porcelain jug and a heap of Agatha Christies. Then she moved slowly into the hall.

'Was his name Willis?'

'Who?'

'The would-be writer.'

'Oh yes. Old Willis. Silly bugger. I must do some work before going.'

She dropped out of sight into the living room. He heard

the easel being shifted and the zip of brushes as she wiped them on bits of newspaper. Colin made a mental resolution not to end like Mr Willis, not to give way to an interest in youth, as the ordinariness of life is at last triumphant. The events of the previous evening had yet to be interpreted. On the whole, however, they did not promise much. He followed the Inspector into the living room, from where he could keep watch over the front path, and intercept Francesca, should she come. He had a sudden dread of her meeting the Inspector, whose brown shapeless form, draped over a stool before the easel, had a curious air of something past, like a ghost keeping vigil over the place of its undoing. She made a movement, and a dab of bright vermilion suddenly appeared amid the grey-green shapes before her. Colin, looking over her shoulder, studied the painting for a moment. He recognised the view from the window. The church spire, Pickford's cottage, the wooded tail of Offlet Hill. But it was as though they had been caught up in a tornado flecked with the discordant feathers of tropical birds, and whisked aloft over England. It was like a vision of judgement, in which he expected to see himself, his father's ghost, and the Inspector too, in her potato-coloured kaftan, swept unresisting towards their final end.

'Your father never appreciated colour,' the Inspector said. 'He would have preferred it if the world had been engraved.'

Colin thought of his father dying in the camp bed in Murricombe, protesting at the summons which had caught him unawares. Once, just before the end, the schoolmaster had tried to apologise for the Inspector.

'You see, Colin,' he had said, rising up on one elbow, and pointing to the light that just made its way through the rose-clad windows of the schoolhouse, 'she is a comfortable woman. She comes from outside. It was only natural that I should feel some sympathy for her. Besides she believes in me, believes in what I am, what I might have been.'

Recalling his father's words, which made so little contact with the reality, Colin felt a spasm of grief.

'He perceived,' the Inspector continued, 'only the outlines of things, though I grant you he was very good at that.'

Colin felt that he had not known his father, and was invariably interested by the Inspector's observations, which seemed to correspond to nothing in his own experience. He asked her what she meant, and listened as she developed a critical analysis of the schoolmaster's obsession with the countryside and conservation, which betokened, she suggested, too great a desire that the shapes of things remain unaltered, and too little awareness that life requires them to change, and that life will always triumph in a cascade of colour. As she spoke the dog came scratching down the stairs and into the living room. Pricking up its ears, it began suddenly to bark.

'Shut up you filthy cur!' the Inspector shouted. 'How often do I have to tell you not to interrupt?'

She squeezed chrome yellow from a tube onto the piece of newspaper which served as her palette, and began to work at it with a palette knife. Her large body hardly stirred within the kaftan, and only the soft white neck trembled slightly as her hand pressed the knife handle and moved slowly from side to side. Her lips were pale, rounded and slightly apart, like a child's, and her head, as it slowly turned towards him, seemed detached and eerie, like a doll's.

'But your father did have public spirit. No one can deny that. In a way, it shows how dangerous public spirit is.'

Each discussion ended this way, with a proof that, after all, Mr Ferguson's virtues were of only ambiguous worth. Yet there was admiration in her tone, and the frequency of her references to him showed that the Inspector had been deeply struck by the schoolmaster. If she spoke to Colin of other things, it was generally in order to add weight and variety to the thoughts which Mr Ferguson inspired. At night she sat smoking a pipe, writing notes in pencil, and from time to time repeating the story of his last months, sometimes embellishing, but mostly content to relate in a monotone the central episodes of his death and cremation.

She had been particularly struck by the enormous curiosity which came over him concerning the world of politics. He asked for his newspapers and cuttings – which had been transported in disarray to Murricombe, and which he attempted time and again to re-order, but always in vain, and with mounting grief and anger. When the Inspector took over from Colin at the bedside, the schoolmaster would begin to speak, exhausting himself in speeches to the House of Commons and letters to *The Times*. He advised her, she said, to take notes of all that he said, since the opportunity would soon arise to make use of it, the Inspector being strong enough to suffer the preliminary trials of politics, and to carry his message into action. He perceived a sudden change for the worse in the prospects of the country. Nothing short of a moral revival could now save England – but a revival without creeds, without class or character, without authorities. The schoolmaster's last hours with the Inspector were devoted to the question of how such a thing was possible; as he wrestled with the problem, she said, he stared at her with a novel quality of anger, as though she were to blame that his words were not already law, and his plans no more than lonely fantasies.

'Public spirit is a virtue only in those with power. Shut up, you filthy cur!' she added to the dog, who was barking again. Colin noticed a tapping on the back door, and the sound of the latch being lifted. He ran back quickly to the little dining room, hoping to guide Francesca away from the house. But it was too late. She stood already by the pinewood table, wearing jeans, a man's shirt of Bombay stripes, and large gold cufflinks which protruded from the sleeves of a cashmere cardigan. Not a trace of the previous evening's anxiety seemed to remain as she smiled, and handed him his jacket with a warm glancing kiss.

'What an adorable place!'

Her eyes wandered everywhere; the dog, who had scampered in from the living room, ceased to bark and sniffed the air in front of her. She patted the shapeless, breedless, colourless creature, and its tattered jaws stretched into a hideous grin, while its tail, of an irregular notched design, executed two or three tired arabesques of salutation. Perhaps, he thought, the schoolmaster's taste had not been so very bad. There was something simple, masculine and unassuming about the furniture, and, if you had no knowledge of the presence that had once so dismally haunted it, the cottage did indeed have charm. He liked the plain white walls, the ground glass lampshades, and the rough black boards on the floor. The wooden staircase was rather pretty from this angle, where the corner caught the light from the tiny oriole window, and you could see the polished knob of oak surmounting the newell post. He supposed that the carved elmwood chest which contained his father's papers was rather appealing; just possibly the old blue and brown carpet on which it stood was genuinely oriental. Even the Inspector's picture of an oily duckpond, set in a Victorian frame of painted gesso, did not seem too bad, as long as the lights were off, and you did not look at it too closely.

'I'll make you some tea,' he said, and beckoned her forward.

'Can I do it? I want to see your sordid masculine kitchen, and to extract the cups from a sinkful of greasy water, full of drowned rats and spiders.'

'That might have been the case, except that you see, there is a woman in the house.'

He watched her, as she smiled, giving the dog another comradely pat.

'What's his name?'

'Who? Oh, the dog. I don't know. He doesn't belong to me.'

'Ah, he belongs to the woman,' she said. 'Now what do we make of that, Watson? Wait, let me see. He lives with a woman, on terms which cannot be very intimate since she presumably knows the name of this dog, while he does not. But then, she runs the house, and cleans the kitchen, so, unless she's a servant – and he couldn't afford a servant –

she must be someone whom he gets along with quite well. That means she must be unattractive, since anything else would lead to friction, of one kind or another. She must be good natured, and also a little distant, if she can live so closely to someone who finds her unattractive. She must certainly have a life of her own and yet' (they were in the kitchen, and Francesca was picking up oddments and looking here and there into cupboards and drawers) 'she has no possessions to speak of, all these things being far too obviously accumulated over a lifetime here. Unless of course she keeps her stuff in one room – but then she would not be the type who takes an interest in the house. She works for a living, since he wouldn't be able to stand her around all day, and oh yes, look at these, she paints in her spare time, and would probably have made pots if it weren't for the fact that she doesn't like the kind of people who make pots. I put her age at around forty; she wears clothes like potato sacking, has nice fresh white skin, and theories about nutrition. She does something optimistic, like social work. I expect she's a kind of PG, quiet, undemanding, a bit narcissistic – well, I've looked at about everything I *can* look at. So, am I right?'

'Approximately,' said the Inspector from the hallway. 'But I am nearer fifty than forty. I also regard my job as an expression of pessimism – though I admit I have a very peculiar character, and others might take a more cheerful approach.'

'I hope I haven't said anything offensive.' Francesca came forward. 'If I have, you must blame it on Colin, for misleading me about his lifestyle.'

'How did I do that?'

'Oh, in a thousand ways. Anyway, I'm Francesca Wimpole. How do you do?'

She held out her hand which the Inspector, coming forward with a jamjar and a pair of paintbrushes, waved to one side.

'I'm Harriet. Oh bugger! I'm dripping paint.'

She stooped abundantly and rubbed the floor with the

inside of her kaftan. Then she looked at Francesca.

'I didn't mean to disturb you. I'm just going out. You know my friend Bill Pickford.'

'Piggy! Oh yes.' Her tone changed, and she added, 'Poor Piggy. I suppose his life is very different now.'

'I don't know what it was like before. He's at St Margaret's. You wouldn't know the school. But they like him there. He has a good heart.'

'Unlike his successor. But you won't have noticed Mr Jacob. You can tell he's around only because the world suddenly closes in on you, with some frightening and non-negotiable plan. Apart from that, he is more or less invisible.'

Colin stood dumb and awkward, confused by Francesca's transformation. She made tea, moving about the kitchen with the quick exuberant movements of an inquisitive child, peering into jars and saucepans, opening cupboards, and finding cause for comment in everything. She fingered the rough old cutlery, and studied it with as much interest as she might a service of silver-gilt. She held the plain white mugs to the light as though the cracks on their sides had been subtly inscribed there by a famous master. She entertained the Inspector with a stream of questions, about her life, her work, her opinions, her hopes, and the Inspector, in whose personality nobody had hitherto taken any serious interest, became emotional and confused, looking at Francesca with eyes that seemed to glow with admiration.

Francesca produced the tea pot, a faint ribbon of steam curling from its spout.

'Where shall I put it?'

'On the table.' Obeying the schoolmaster's orders, he slipped a mat beneath the china.

'One of the really bad things about me,' said Francesca, 'is that I get all human relations in the wrong order: everything is jumbled up, and now I feel dreadful for not having said a thing about your father. Someone told me he died; I meant to write; not having written, I meant to speak;

not having spoken, I meant to forget. And now, the way you put the mat down reminds me I must mention him.'

Her eyes met Colin's; they seemed innocent, yet distant, as though viewing a total stranger. Embarrassed, he began to poor out the tea, and the Inspector said:

'Of course you shouldn't mention him. There's no point in discussing the dead.'

She took the tea and sat down. Someone had once loved the Inspector, had brought her into the world, had drained from the stream of her own blood the foetus-measure of red life, had held the flimsy sack of fluid in hopeful arms, fed it the sour milk of humankindness, washed its dirty buttocks and wiped with tender hand the snot from its little nose. Some remnant of that mother love had survived in the tubes, streams and cataracts that filled the Inspector's massive body, had lazily swirled in some hidden whirlpool, and been glimpsed by the schoolmaster in the act of love. Colin contemplated these facts with amazement, and studied the Inspector as she guiltlessly swallowed her steaming tea. She put down the mug and got up at once.

'Good. I must be off now. Goodbye Colin. If you don't go to London, I'll see you this evening. In any case, I thought we would have ham and carrots, with madeira sauce.'

She nodded enthusiastically at Francesca, and then kicked the dog.

'What a cow!' said Francesca, as the door closed behind her. 'Or shouldn't I say that?'

'You can say it. But it isn't true. She knew my father intimately, which gives her a right to exasperation.'

Francesca moved closer to him. He smelled her almost no smell, and started back.

'You should tell me about your father – if you want to.' She spoke quietly and her eyes searched his face.

He showed her the cottage, explaining Mr Ferguson's life as a village radical. He told her the story of his mother's death, as the schoolmaster had recounted it. And then, since it was a sunny day and the hoar frost had melted, they went out into the garden.

'My father had many qualities,' Colin said. 'He spoke to plants as though they were children. He looked at buildings as though he shared secrets with them. He would stand on a hilltop with his eyes like beacons, sending out important messages which had been relayed to him from centuries before. He did not love me.'

'You are obviously wrong.'

He corrected himself effortlessly.

'He did not love me well. But he loved this place, he loved England, and even if he was destructive of everything personal, that doesn't alter the main fact, which was that he held things together. He took special responsibility for this little corner of England, working to improve its moral countenance. He wanted Bassington to frown with puritanical dignity. He wanted it to speak for the common people, unfriendly to power, haughty towards rank and wealth, well-ordered like a private garden, and didactical as a Methodist sermon.'

They had left the garden and were walking now by the wall of the park. Colin described the wall in his father's language, praising the freestone coping, and the solid foundation work. He explained the merits of English and Flemish bonding, and demonstrated the articulation of the wall space, by means of plinth and coping stone. Panelling and buttressing were also important as protections against the weather, and in giving vertical emphasis. He pointed to the dentilation – a stylistic favourite of the Victorian builders working out of Dunsbury – to the careful pointing, and to the pattern work, now barely discernible in bricks so rubbed by time. The schoolmaster was not really a Marxist. His socialism came out of Morris and Ruskin, and was never so fervent as his love of a job well done, and done for ever. He hated all that was cheap, expendable and made for power and profit. If he resented landowners in general and Lord Shepton in particular it was because they had so frivolously neglected the charge which history had laid on them – which was to maintain and embellish the good works of honest men. In building, the morality of the world acquires form and substance. Obedience is indeed a virtue; but obedience to a higher law, and not to the will of power. In good building you see the obedience of free men, who love the matter they handle, imprinting their desire for permanence, and eliciting an image of their own abundant life.

All life, other than the life of lords and businessmen, had been sacred to Mr Ferguson. He knew the names of trees, plants and birds. He knew the virtues of roots, weeds and mushrooms; on autumn mornings he would scavenge on the village green, plucking the mossy ink-caps from their bed of grass, while baffled schoolboys swung their satchels, watching him. They called him the Wizard, and his class would look with awe and consternation, as he brought to them each morning the discoveries of sunrise. Once he tended an otter, binding its broken leg, feeding it on muddy minnows, and finally setting it free in the stream watched by his excited children. In all this he had a townsman's scholarly interest – and his children discovered through him what their own parents, stupefied by television, lacked the interest to tell.

Francesca listened carefully. For her Bassington was simply the Hall, its park, and the secret places which she had made her own. The Hall was a clearing in the jungle of outside: a place where thoughts and actions of the public world pushed aside the work of nature, and where her father moved softly and powerfully like a king. To love it was impossible; to relate it to the secret life of plants and animals would be to set aside its rule of law. In the West Wing her father had destroyed the Georgian mouldings, ripped out the panelled doors, and smoothed over the bumps and cracks of centuries. Now it was a great white open space, lit by spotlights on steel runners, with modernistic furniture in plastic, and white lambswool rugs on which you walked hampered and observed as in a dream. It was a place of dread: an illuminated chamber, where the harsh light of inquisition extinguished all uncertainties. They entered the park. The rhododendrons had been cleared, and some of the trees had been felled. Soon it would be neat and angular like a tennis court. Mr Jacob had instructions to slice the park into clean comprehensible parcels, and to remove any muddle where unauthorised life might grow.

'Then my father was right,' said Colin.

'About what?'

'About the motive for these obsessive improvements.'

'And what is the motive?'

'First, of course, the need for profit. But more importantly, the need for power: power over ordinariness, over nature, over life.'

'Do you think that's fair?'

'No,' he conceded instantly. 'But I was trying to follow your mood.'

'You mean, if it comes from me, I am bound to agree with it?'

'Something like that.'

They became aware of a man walking slowly towards them from behind the house; he wore a brown checked jacket and waterproof trousers of camouflage-green. There was something distinctly odd in his slow, careful gait; his head sat motionless on his shoulders, as though dexterously carried towards them on a butler's tray.

'That's Mr Jacob,' Francesca said quietly. 'Don't say anything, and he'll go away.'

Mr Jacob altered course slightly, and Colin saw that he was making towards them. His head slowly turned as he approached, probing the space between them like the turret of a tank. When the small perturbations of movement had entirely ceased, his large liquid brown eyes settled on Francesca, and his mouth hung slightly open. He was a man of forty-five, small, robust, with slightly withered skin. His lips had the texture of moist pink worms. The faint expression on his face suggested the last ripple from a remote and unapproachable core of being.

'Ah,' he said at last, 'Miss Francesca.'

There was a silence, during which Colin stared at the Hall and the distant sky, and then back to Mr Jacob, trying to see these things in a clear relation. The great sash windows of the *piano nobile*, separated by ionic pilasters of portland stone, and crowned by cornice and attic storey, were reflecting the blue of the sky, and smiling emptily, serenely, onto the winter landscape. Beneath the cornice, leaden rain-water heads, decorated with cherubs and swags, guided the water from the gutter above; climbing towards them, twisting here and there across mouldings, sills, pilasters and window frames, was a single trail of ivy, which grew from a vast decorated iron bowl that stood beside the door. Colin wondered who had trained it to laugh so lightly at the solemn order of the long facade: some timid, rebellious, feminine spirit had been quietly signalling its distaste for the Wimpole discipline, and if Mr Jacob looked sternly at Francesca, it was perhaps because he believed she was to blame.

'Yes Mr Jacob.'

'His lordship is home. Been asking for you.'

Mr Jacob's voice was slow but somehow cunning, as though it concealed more meaning than it was politic to display. Observing his large still eyes, Colin saw, immersed in them, the drowning image of Francesca, cut off from any help that he could offer.

'I had better go,' she said, quietly. 'Any idea what it's about?'

'Couldn't rightly say, miss.'

'Will you be speaking to him?'

'Wasn't planning to. Got to see to that elm.'

Mr Jacob slowly set his body in motion, starting with a rhythmical, stationary clomping of his boots. He followed this with a swaying of the hips, then a forward movement of one arm, and finally a steady champing of the jaws, which was the signal for the whole body to start off across the park.

Francesca raised her hand to her face, and began to walk

quickly towards the house. Her complexion had instantly changed from pink to grey, and she was once more an anxious, whispering thing. It seemed an enormous concession to Colin's reality that she suddenly paused, turned, and, blinking slightly, asked him to follow her.

'But would your father mind?'

'Oh no.' Then she added, 'There's no need to meet him.'

They hurried sideways, scuffing the grass like football-playing children. At the door of a slate-roofed outbuilding they stopped, jostled, touched unmeaningly, and confusedly went in, to a place smelling of bran, soap, wax and curds. She swept over the flagstone floor, brushed the corner of a large deal table, and stopped beside a dresser, where rows of patterned plates and dishes, matching soup-tureens and ladles, sugar bowls and sauce boats, a museum piece of everything, placed her on display. Then she disappeared into another room. He followed her, and caught her hand. They were standing by an Aga, closed, cold, unused, and above it a frowsty picture of a sheep dog in sepia, set in a black lacquered frame. She let him kiss her, and even touched him through his pullover, tapping fingertip apologies on his breast and shoulder.

'Perhaps I should go back home?'

'No,' she whispered. 'Wait for me. Wait in the drawing room.'

They entered a corridor of white plaster and polished boards, punctuated with dark-wood furniture that had been rubbed into a thousand glimmery eyes. A long paisley carpet preceded them towards the door which stood half open at the end. He glimpsed the open whiteness of a vestibule, hugely illuminated, with shadowy cornices, marble columns, ornate fireplaces, and gilded mirrors. Then, guided through a panelled door which closed quietly behind him, he found himself at the front of the house, in a long tall room which he occupied alone. The yellow sunlight, softened by carpets of buff and blue, sloped across the floor and over the little tables, made a pool of shadow by a giant leather armchair, and drew his attention outwards from the coffered windows to the cold outside.

Along the bright path of oat-coloured gravel were gathered winter shades of black and green and silver grey. Clouds were forming westwards; a little wind stirred the scant brushes at the edge of the lawn, with a rustle that faintly sounded through the window. A grandfather clock ticked, picking at the rope of hours. Colin noticed a bright canary yellow ball on the polished mantelpiece, resting under the portrait of a gloomy ancestor. He held it in his hands. It was a clock, made of plastic, with a hood that opened; inside was a screen upon which, at the press of a button, luminous numbers appeared. Playing with the buttons he could change the hours, minutes, years and days, but always, after a discreet moment, the numbers would vanish and give way to the actual time. Twelve thirty-four, on the 2nd December. He stood for a moment, lost in reflection as to the cause and meaning of this ugly thing. Francesca entered quickly and closed with a click of softened brass the slowly swinging door.

'Isn't it fun?' she asked.

'This thing? It's hideous!'

'I think it's lovely.'

Francesca turned down the corners of her mouth. Colin was beginning to recognise these little warnings. Across the minefields which surrounded Francesca there were only uncharted paths. Perhaps it was for his sake that she so often waved him back; perhaps one day there would be a well-marked road to her, at the end of which she would greet him happily with open arms.

'What is it?' he asked. 'I mean, apart from a clock.'

'It's a million things. It can add, divide, and multiply like the seed of Abraham. It also tells your fortune and predicts the eclipses of the sun and moon. I gave it to Daddy for his birthday.'

Colin replaced it with simulated reverence.

'Daddy says I'm to give you a drink. All is well.'

'What is well?'

'I am.'

She stood against the light, motionless and enigmatic.

'What funny things you say.'

'One day, perhaps, I'll speak like a grown-up. I mean that I'm better than I was. Better than a minute ago. Do you want a drink?'

'Why not?' he said.

'Do you think I'm falling in love with you?'

She looked candidly at him.

'I don't see why you should.'

'No, nor do I. But the trouble is, I don't see why I shouldn't. Let's have this drink.'

They returned to the flagstone scullery, where Francesca took from an old refrigerator a long green flute of wine. She began to open it at the side-table, on a barman's corkscrew of nickel-plated brass.

Brusquely and clumsily the door was pushed ajar. A large bald man in short red dressing gown and velvet slippers strode on bare legs towards them, rolled his large grey eyes, raised his hand to his face, and halted abruptly.

'Who's this?'

'I told you, Daddy. It's Colin Ferguson.'

'Oh yes. Make a pims 'Cesca.'

She placed the bottle unopened beside the corkscrew and went again to the refrigerator. Lord Shepton shook slightly his handsome head and then focused on Colin. His eyes registered no emotion, and his lips were entirely without the suggestion of a smile. Then, raising his eyes, he spoke in loud and measured tones, as though addressing an audience.

'Bien fort, avec deux glaçons, et une tranche très mince de concombre.'

'Yes Daddy.'

Lord Shepton looked around him, strolled a little, stared at the window, and then noticed the bottle on the side table.

'What's this she's giving you?'

'I don't know.'

'My question was rhetorical. It's a Gewürztraminer. Shouldn't be too bad. You'd better give me your opinion. Never know with Alsace whether to drink it young or old.'

His tone invited no response, but on the contrary conveyed the impression that anything Colin might say would prove superfluous. Colin imitated a sagacious nod. Lord Shepton continued to stare at him, his form motionless and monumental.

'Who first introduced income tax?' he asked suddenly.

It was an example which the schoolmaster always gave, when illustrating the subtle perfidy of the ruling class.

'William Pitt,' Colin replied.

'Correct. Give me that pims.'

Lord Shepton swallowed from the glass, half closing his eyes, and then held it at arm's length before him, studying its contents.

'Mon Dieu! On dirait de l'extrait de senne, aspergé de pipi.'

'What's wrong with it?'

'Everything. *Sers bien le jeune homme. Il n'a pas l'air tout-à-fait bête.*'

Lord Shepton retired from the room, sipping as he went. Francesca opened the bottle in silence.

'I hope you don't mind the scullery,' she said at last. 'It's the safest place, you see.'

Colin did not see. But he put his arm around her shoulder as she sat down, and touched the electric perimeter of tension. She moved slightly away from him, and he became conscious of his hand, which he could neither abandon nor remove.

'The essential,' she said, 'is not to go on squirming and squirming on the end of his line. But if I bite through it, I live forever with that hook inside.'

Colin was silent, uncomfortable. A cloud passed, darkening the room; then quick warm sunlight ran again into the far corner and danced there. Francesca got up quickly. Her ozone smell rose with her, mingling with the fragrance of the wine she poured.

'Alright now. I've forgotten him. He's a good man really. You wouldn't believe it, but he's terribly shy.' She paused. 'Would you like some food?'

Without waiting for an answer she opened the door of a long windowed cupboard, on the slatted shelves of which were tins and vegetables, a basket of eggs, and several large stone jars. The produce was heaped artistically like a harvest festival, giving a theatrical impression of surfeit.

'How many of you are there?' asked Colin in astonishment.

'Oh just my parents. And my brother sometimes.'

'What's your brother like?'

'His existence is more or less hypothetical. There is an apparition who was originally introduced to me as my brother. He is sometimes manifest on Saturdays, surveying his expectations in a rather gloomy way. But I can't say that I know him personally. Nobody knows him personally, he doesn't even know himself personally.'

'What does he do, this apparition?'

'He appears. In various places. Here. A place in Yorkshire. Also sometimes in the city, Harold Plumptre says. Once he joined a group of Buddhist dropouts; but it didn't last.'

'So who eats all this food?'

'Nobody. But there's a kind of special life permitted in the kitchen. Old retainers come to chew carrots. Do you eat eggs?'

'I eat anything.'

This proved to be inaccurate. He picked at the omelette which she made; its ochre colour disgusted him; he imagined in its crinkly contours the tracks of tiny animals, the churned-up corners of fields, the mucky outposts of cattle-farms and sheep-pits. Francesca also did not eat, and left her wine untasted.

'You're not drinking,' he said.

'You're not talking.'

Colin stood up in his imagination and delivered a political

speech to the Ladies of Dunsbury, who greeted with warm applause his simulated sentiments on abortion, crime and immigration. He alerted them to the threat from the left – not the moderate left, that well-meaning Fabianism, offshoot of the Oxford establishment, landed and successful, directing its efforts towards the social improvement of a class that it would never understand. No. They were a dying breed, and their hour was almost come. Already they were retiring to their cottages and country houses, composing their memoirs, lying supine on the couches of fashionable drawing rooms, or glowing with graceful bonhomie on the nation's television screens. He referred to that other, secret force, that desperate undercurrent of resentment, rising here and there to articulacy in the mouth of some ill-used schoolmaster, some ambitious shop-steward, some trustless outcast in a cellar or a garret – small, dark, ambient souls that have only to encounter each other to enter into deep enduring conspiracy, whose loyalty to a cause is as unswerving as their pursuit of it, and whose war is without pity since it is on behalf of pity that it is waged.

'I can't speak,' he said.

She looked at him in silence. And then, very slowly, she lowered her eyes, pushed away her plate, and placed her hands beneath her chin.

'Well,' she said, 'we're in a pickle.'

'Did I ever tell you about my Uncle Steve?'

She shook her head. The stiff bunches of her hair lifted and settled again. Colin was beginning to panic. He was walking in a state of drunkenness through a room where china people sat speechless at china tables, and sometimes there fell from their lifeless hands a tempting glass of crystal. Should he save it, or should he let it fall?

'Look!' said Francesca, pointing. Two cock pheasants whirred past the window, flashing their feathers, and shaking their tails.

'I was about to tell you about my Uncle Steve.'

'Go on, please. Don't mind. There's something the

matter with me.'

'Uncle Steve had several peculiarities. He was light-headed without being daft; undernourished without being starved; greedy, but with a taste (which he rarely indulged) for moderation; irascible but given to prolonged fits of universal benevolence; filthy in his personal habits but always meticulously dressed and manicured. In short, a chameleon from most points of view. But he was a romantic in his relations to women. I might as well add that he was a small-town solicitor, who looked after the financial arrangements of elderly widows, and who cultivated fastidious bachelor habits, such as piano-playing, watercress, bird-spotting, collecting insects in jamjars, and peeing in a well-formed arc from the top of the fire-escape into the leaves of his landlady's tulip tree. It was this last habit that finally secured him that love of a good woman for which he had always yearned.'

'What a foolish thing to yearn for.'

'I am speaking about my Uncle Steve. It might have been different had you asked me to refer directly to myself. What *is* the matter with you?'

'Nothing. Go on.'

'It was one evening, after he had carefully arranged the stamps for Trinidad and Tobago in the new album, and was about to replace it behind the glass doors of the walnut cabinet. Suddenly he heard a step on the stair, and, thinking it to be his wife, climbed from the drawing room, no, sitting room, onto the fire-escape, through the window that had been thoughtfully provided by the Edwardian architect for that purpose. In addition to its standard purpose, of letting light in, or out, according to taste and the time of the day. No sooner had he emerged onto the cast-iron platform . . .'

'I thought you said he wasn't married.'

'I said he had bachelor habits. Are you going to tell me that forbids the presence, or even, come to think of it, the absence, of a wife?'

'Go on.'

Francesca was looking at him, with that immobile expression which he now realised she had inherited from her father, but which in her case created an air of penetrating directness – an appeal for absolute trust in her, which fostered his distrust.

'Yes. He had emerged onto the cast-iron platform. This was in some ways an achievement. He lacked an arm, and had spent many months learning how to vault through a window without it. But in other ways it was a defeat. It should not be necessary, hearing one's mistress ascend the stairs, immediately to cease what one is doing – whether it be arranging stamps, listening to a symphony, speculating or peculating – so as to vault through a window onto a fire-escape. Wife, I mean, not mistress, though you understand that in the case of Uncle Steve, such particulars are not of the first importance. She was a schizophrenic of an amiable variety, judged from the point of view of an outsider (which was the point of view adopted by Uncle Steve). Her hallucinations corresponded, on the whole, with the opinions Uncle Steve wished on her, and when, as happened, their worlds entered into collision, it was only to soften at the point of contact, making a smooth sticky slime of nothingness from which each would extract a meaning suited to his present situation. These collisions took place in bed, infrequently, and were usually followed by sleep. Her tiny body was perfect in every detail, and not spoiled but on the contrary embellished by the surprising crops of hair that flourished in her armpits, her chest, her belly and at the base of her spine, and which he would periodically harvest with shears kept for that purpose. You must have divined, however, that Auntie Kate – her name was rarely used – was not so valuable an asset as this would seem to imply. Her hair, even when collected in the quantities which with her were habitual, fetched a very poor return on the open market, being judged too brittle for the upholsterer, too fine for the brush-maker, and for the manufacturer of cyanide entirely second-rate. Of course, any source of income was welcome at a period when

Stanley Gibbons were revising their catalogue almost every week, and on the whole Uncle Steve decided that it would be better not to disturb Auntie Kate by any rash or sudden action. He therefore hid from her, as best he could, the repugnance with which he greeted her presence after hours in his living room. It was out of delicacy, in addition to the natural promptings of self-interest, that on the occasion mentioned, he took to the fire-escape, only to find that it had been hacked off at the second floor, and that he could not make his exit through the garden. After an hour or so of indecision, during which he heard Auntie Kate rummaging in the walnut cupboard and uttering howls of rage and derision, he was taken short, and began to relieve himself in his usual manner, in the leaves of the tulip tree which he could almost touch with his toes from the severed tip of the fire-escape.'

Colin introduced the landlady's niece, who took pity on Uncle Steve's predicament as she observed him from the other side of the garden. Francesca smiled as she recognised herself. Tenderly, sadly, he reconstructed their first meeting as Uncle Steve, hastily buttoning himself, conversed from the height of the fire-escape with the girl who promised faithfully to rescue him, swearing on the gun-metal pig, with pink pearly eye, which she wore on her breast. Colin began to believe firmly in the existence of Uncle Steve. He was profoundly impressed by Uncle Steve's opinions on the subjects of opera and horse-breeding. In his quiet but eccentric way, Steve led a life that was little short of exemplary. He troubled no one. He exploited no one. His inclination was to submit impassively to the workings of destiny, and to trust, up to the point dictated by prudence, in the mercifulness of God. This was why his discovery of true love had been such an extraordinary experience. Why had *he* been singled out, who had done nothing to deserve this benefit, or punishment, according to your point of view? The very arbitrariness of the thing forced him to accept it. They must have their reasons, he thought, and good reasons too – don't they always make sure that their reasons are good? Had they not established offices for the manufacture of irrebuttable reasons for all the things which they took it into their heads to do? Colin was buying time, for time was the dimension in which they shifted towards each other. He moved along its rough unfriendly surfaces, edging about its awful abysses, towards that moment when their fingers touched across the table and she said, with the solemn directness that constantly deceived and undeceived him,

'I think that I actually love you.'

Colin took her hand, which became rigid, and gripped him like a claw.

'Does it embarrass you?' she asked.

'Not that you love me. Although, if you only *think* that you love me, then yes. You see, I have always loved you.'

'Always? From the first?'

Colin felt reckless.

'From the first time I saw you.'

'Are you sure it began only then?'

'What do you mean?'

'Nothing. Silly.'

They kissed, clumsily, across the table. She drew away, hardly smiling.

'Why had you always loved me? I've been horrid.'

'Not to me.'

'Especially to you. Whatever little opportunity I had, leading you into traps and then pushing you into them, did you not see how I took it?'

'Are you serious?'

She ran her left hand through his hair, then quickly withdrew it.

'As serious as you are. You see, I believed in you. Knowing nothing about you, except that you are really real.'

'Scarcely a distinguishing attribute.'

'You don't know. You don't know what it is to live – down there.'

'You mean where *you* are? I think I do.'

'How do you know?'

'Because, even when I have you in my hands, you are running from me.'

She came round to him, and hugged his body so tightly that the breath was squeezed out of it, and he had at last to force her away. She had been crying, and did not bother to dry her eyes.

'You see,' she said, 'I really want someone to do that to me. For ever and ever.'

'Well, only God can do that for ever.'

'Then perhaps it is God I want.'

She took him across the park. She was leading him, as one child leads another, into a world where by conspiracy nature's laws are partially suspended, where words have double meanings designed to entrance the hearer and to lead him astray, where beneath the blameless exterior of things, a secret life perpetuates itself in accordance with its own amoral purposes. Francesca's was a world that had to be personally unlocked for every visitor. Some who were allowed in would never be permitted to leave again, while others would slip readily across to the normality that waited on the other side. Colin belonged to the first category and was treated with ceremony, as becomes a sacrificial victim. They walked through the dusk, towards the wall of the place that she needed him to see. Francesca carried a key, which she had snatched from a shelf in the gunroom, and with this key she opened a heavy wooden door in an arch of stone. They were among rushes, on a little path, she just out of touch. It was a law of the place that things stood and moved always just outside one another's reach: it was a place of isolated things, juxtaposed in unrelation. And then they looked at the water of a pond as it lazily moved under the distant light. Another law was that things should be always diminishing, shrinking into their essences and sleeping there. The light slid up and down on the tiny swell, sank a little way out, appeared again, shivered into fragments, and then gathered in the centre of the pond where it faded into nothingness. Francesca did not look at him. Her few words were whispered; often he could barely overhear them, as though she were talking to herself. The trees had proper names, and by the bare-armed larch which she called Alan there was a rhododendron patch, and a bench on which she used to dream. She had interpreted their meeting in a manner of her own, according to laws and symbols which he did not know. He was baptised anew, and the name Colin, in the language of this place, had quite another meaning, just as their encounter, re-enacted here, denied the years of interpretation with which he had overlaid it. Here was order, but not the order of political beings; safety, but not the safety of things still living; remoteness, but not the remoteness of the unfamiliar; love even, but not the love of the flesh. Everything was unearthly, still, without fulfilment or redemption. He could not affirm it; he could not deny it. Like Francesca, it was and was not, in equal and conflicting measure.

But when, having closed the door, she stepped forward a determinate number of steps, turned to him, and stopped his mouth with a kiss that grew until his whole face seemed drained of life, he saw that there was no turning back. They walked in silence to the house. 'I will see you tomorrow,' she said, but nothing more. As he left her she looked at him in a kind of alarm, her left hand pressed against her cheek, her eyes wide and motionless. He knew then that everything was ruined for him, and that he wanted it so.

Seven

'YES,' SAID the Inspector, in a tone that was as near to anger as her nature allowed, 'you will be going to London soon. Unless you prefer me to leave.'

It was another clear day, and Colin, who had not slept, blinked at the light in the kitchen window. Except at the edge of the pane, frost had melted to droplets, which scattered the rays of the sun.

'I must finish this article. It is inconceivable that I am in your way.'

'You do not know my way. You have never wanted to know.'

'True.'

Colin helped himself to the kedgeree, which the Inspector had prepared in a metal canister on the Aga. He finished eating and, to his own surprise, began to sing. Often the schoolmaster had hummed beneath his breath – sentimental tunes by Balfe and Ketelby. Colin chose Mozart – Leporello's catalogue of his master's conquests.

'Stop that braying. I am unmusical.'

'True.'

'I should prefer not to leave,' she continued, 'all things considered. It suits me here. I have become attached to the place. The only serious inconvenience, although at my age it could be considered a major one, is the abstinence. I would probably feel different after a really good fuck. Two really good fucks.'

Colin's imagination laboured to hoist her into the

necessary appliances. He felt no disgust, but only a kind of pity, which turned out, on examination, to be directed towards his father. The Inspector was right to draw his attention to these matters. It was obvious that he should concede her inheritance. He began to observe his surroundings with amazement.

'Harriet,' he said, 'you must have Archie or someone to live with you. You belong here.'

She became tearful. Although this did not suit her, it was a useful ploy, since it arrested the conversation at the point most favourable to her projects. Disquieted, Colin left the room, imitating the stride and posture of a decisive man.

He walked on Offlet Hill, but the path was blocked by a yellow excavator. He had the idea of going straight to the Hall and knocking there. Alternatively, he could go to London, revisit the places he had known, watch the barges of waste-paper as they passed by Wapping water, and join the restless workless men at the doors of betting shops, squandering time. There was much to do, much to acknowledge, in answer to the experiences he hadn't had. There was a formidable absence to record.

He saw no one on the drive that joined the crested gateposts to the house. The low sun pointed the pebbles, separating them one from another, unweaving and then weaving again the long scarf of gravel. He placed a foot on the frost-locked margin of the drive. It manifestly did not belong there. The gravel formed around it with reluctance, refusing to accommodate the outline of his shoe. It was, however, a normal shoe, or nearly so. True, it had not been cleaned since the Inspector had tried to change its colour from brown to black by using the wrong polish. But here and there a bit of shine remained; it fitted against the creaseless trousers in a manner neither coy nor beggarly. The uncharitable quality of the gravel was not explained by it. He tried with the other foot. For a while it seemed to fit more comfortably into its surroundings, and he decided to appoint it to the office of the next and decisive step. Then he noticed that the shoe touched against an imprint. A large car tyre had pressed its royal seal in continuous self-affirmation from house to gate, clouding the frost into troubled patterns.

He walked quickly up to the Hall. As he reached the grey oval, where the drive forked before circling round to the house, Mr Jacob appeared with his black and white sheepdog, crunching the gravel in a leisurely manner as the turret of his head swivelled steadily from side to side.

'I was wondering if you could help me.'

Mr Jacob did not stop, nor did he proceed. He seemed to stay walking in one place, as though it were the rest of nature and not he that had caused the apparent motion. His silence had a cosmic meaning. Colin decided to adopt a Newtonian standpoint.

'I am certain that you can help me.'

Still Mr Jacob did not reply. The sheepdog now turned in its course and prodded his nose into the air that Colin had vacated. He swallowed a portion of it, and then expelled it in a furious bark. Colin also barked. Relative to the place where the dog and Colin contended, Mr Jacob began to move along a straight line. Colin strode after the grey-green hacking jacket, which he seized by its leather elbow.

'Is Miss Francesca at home?' he shouted.

Mr Jacob continued to adjust his coordinates in a regular manner. Opening his mouth as if to speak, he thought better of it, and with his right hand freed his left elbow from Colin's grasp. For some while they moved together across the front of the house, which slid gently backwards, bearing a large white waving figure in one of its attic windows. The dog ran towards the bushes. Mr Jacob called to it, turning as he did so to Colin.

'Miss Francesca left this morning with his lordship.'

He spoke the words slowly and distinctly, but seemed to establish no link between them. Colin rearranged them in contrasting sequences. The one he preferred was 'His Francesca mis-left this mourning lordship.' He returned Mr Jacob's solemn stare, mouthed a question, and followed patiently as Mr Jacob walked on. A robin settled on the gravel and then hopped into the sun. The dog had fallen silent. Mr Jacob said,

'I don't know who you are.'

'Nor do I.'

Colin felt he might be getting somewhere. Mr Jacob seemed to embark on a process of silent reflection.

'Sometimes Miss Francesca's here. Sometimes she's not. It's the same with his lordship.'

The thought was exactly Colin's. He greeted it with incredulity.

'She was here yesterday,' he said, as though this constituted a decisive refutation.

'Could be. That would explain her leaving.'

Mr Jacob took a pipe from his pocket and studied its charred interior as they walked.

'But where? London? Do you think it was London?'

'Might be London. They weren't got up for the bleeding tropics.'

Mr Jacob called again to the dog, and began to walk more briskly. Colin allowed himself to be out-distanced, and then turned back in the direction of the tropics, which he envisaged swamped in blood.

'Where do you think they live?' he asked the Inspector. She was slowly stirring eggs into melted butter, and frowned in concentration.

'You mean our neighbours.'

'Of course.'

Colin stood in the kitchen, his rucksack swung on one arm.

'An impossible question. You had better hit the road. Perhaps you'll find out.'

'Where? How?'

'Your father was equally impatient. Bugger! Look what you've made me do.'

Colin went up to the room that had been his father's and

surveyed it conscientiously. Books and magazines, mostly the schoolmaster's, lined the walls. A delicate filigree of frost sealed the little window panes. Memories of Mr Ferguson addressed him from every corner. He wanted to fix them in his spirit and gradually compress them. To return here would never again be possible. It was only fair, therefore, that the place should furnish an unshakeable motive for departure.

On the chest beside the window his father's maps were piled where he had left them. Once or twice Colin had touched the maps; their stiff canvas, obedient to the same imperatives of stability as the land they described, resisted any movement that was not their own. The schoolmaster had pencilled his own paths on the Ordnance Survey. Certain fields, houses and monuments were circled with the light red pencil that he carried in his pocket for marking schoolwork. Most of the maps were of Bassington, Murricombe and the surrounding countryside. Their pencilled additions spoke of terrible loneliness, of an attachment to time and place that was effected only at one remove, by a private exercise in cartography.

Beside the maps stood four old medicine bottles, dug from the garden and opalised with age. Colin did not know why the schoolmaster had kept them or why he had retained, as the one memorial to Mrs Ferguson, the doily of yellowing lace surmounted by a bowl of lalique glass. This horrid object stood on the little mantelpiece, blatant in its aimlessness. Other things were more explicable: the books of history and socialist thought, the boxed cuttings from newspapers and magazines, the parts of a fishing rod and the chest of rusty tools. But one object stood out from all the rest, and served as a kind of pivot about which the schoolmaster's world could be swung entirely, to reveal its shocking underside. Above the bed was a Hogarth frame, in which the schoolmaster had mounted a reproduction of an autumn scene by Nash. One evening Colin had slipped the wooden backing from its clips, and found that the picture hid another, a mezzotint of Bassington Hall, showing the house as once it had been, with a crenellated turret, since demolished, that clashed hideously with the Georgian Order. Colin did not know how his father had acquired this picture, or why he had suffered it to remain concealed beneath his favourite painting. But it was the detail that was needed to complete the schoolmaster's monument. The whole of Bassington was contained in the tiny room. As Colin left he felt, for a moment, what it was to love and bury the being to whom one's life is owed.

When she opened the door to him Judith Blakely appeared shabby and undone. Her blank eyes were set in an artificial smile, and she flapped her arms, embracing him.

'Fancy it being you.'

She was openly confessing to him that her life was ruined. Colin sought for an excuse, but found none. His homelessness was too absolute not to be apparent.

'I was wondering . . .'

'Stop wondering and come in.'

They shuffled, first one, and then the other, towards the open kitchen, with its glow of white enamel and litter of plastic toys. A round wall-clock in a pinewood frame ticked on the wall. Colin remembered snatched embarrassed breakfasts, and Ken Blakely's bearded face rising from behind *The Guardian* with an expression of goodwill so abstract as to imply that, if Colin were included in it, this was not to be taken as a sign of personal merit. It was obvious now that Ken had gone. The kitchen was dirtier, the toys more disordered, and the washing-machine piled high with unwashed clothes. Even the clock seemed to tick on torpidly as though time no longer signified.

The mug of instant coffee infused with bitterness the sentiments she spoke. Colin received Judith Blakely's suffering as an outrage. In moving back to his room he would be doing her a favour. It was monstrous to be trapped into generosity after contemplating only ruthless deeds. For a moment, as he watched the shaking of her tear-stained face, he was tempted to refuse what he had come to beg. He wished to benefit no one. Without the flow of love, Judith's domesticity was stagnant. She was beginning to dissolve in the ordinariness in which she moved, like a dilapidated houseboat in a muddy backwater.

Later, as he unpacked, he thought of Ken Blakely with curiosity. To have married, that was one thing. To have left, that was another. Between those two events, both ineluctable in the laws that govern Blakelys, a line was strung of flapping intimacies and drab obligations. They made a spectacle more definite than any Colin could generate. He had sought neither this nor any other banner to the world. Now Ken was stringing up some new row of pennants in another garden. Judith would wait and wait, knowing by degrees that there was nothing to wait for. Already the encroachments of a mortal lethargy disfigured her movements, so that her arms and fingers snatched at the air in jerky paroxysms, fighting the urge to collapse. As he thought of the Blakelys, Colin's outrage turned to alarm. Had Francesca made him so pitiless? Or was it some other ghost? He went out into the yellow air of Notting Hill, and walked in agitation towards the town.

At University College he was told that Miss Wimpole did not come in, that they did not know her address, and that in any case they could not give information to strangers. The House of Lords had the same instructions. The telephone book had none.

Then he remembered Harold Plumptre. He found the card in his breast pocket, where papers accumulated from week to week. A secretary told him that Mr Plumptre was in a meeting. It was dark when finally he got through. By then he knew the inside of the telephone box in the way that a man buried alive knows the contours of his coffin.

'Whosat? What? Colin Ferguson? Do I know you? Have to remind me where we, how we . . .'

Colin reminded him.

'Sounds frightfully plausible. Was I pissed?'
'A little. We all were.'
'Always happens to me. End up drunk and incompetent, scattering cards around like birdseed. Nuisance. I mean, how are you? How are things?'
'Fine. I want to meet you. If that's possible.'
'Don't see why not. Good idea even. Perhaps. Thursday?'
'I mean now. There's something I want to ask you.'
'Careful now. Is this blackmail?'
'No. I think you can help me.'
'Help you? Well I'm buggered. El Vino's at six? Yes? Good Lord.'

Colin's hand trembled as he replaced the receiver. He could not believe that words meant anything when severed from the face which uttered them. He turned to the girl who had been pressing her nose against the glass for several seconds.

'Francesca!'

But it was not her. Sitting across from Penney, at the formica table that bore their coffee cups, he ceased to perceive the resemblance. She told him about John, whom she hardly dared to telephone, lest his wife should be home; he told her about Francesca, whom he could not find. They agreed on the tragic quality of their cases, and exchanged addresses. Colin kissed her as he left, and thought about her, in a vagrant, softened way, as he sat in the tube.

Hurrying down Chancery Lane, the stiff-collared clerks sweeping past him with the washed-out expressions of early evening, Colin began to revise the plot of his forthcoming life. In a way, he thought, it was a relief that he had put a toe into Francesca's world, even if it had affected him like a bath of acid. Everything that he feared in her could now be explained. He believed that each social class has its own source of suffering, just as it has its own manners, and sports, its own way of speech and means of livelihood. Even solitude came in a variety of forms, according to the class of the recipient. In Francesca's case it was a luxury package, a

Pandora's box of glittering insults, each designed to dazzle her into silence and submission. The same solitude had been administered to Lord Shepton when a boy, and no doubt also to Lord Shepton's son, who hovered like a ghost on the perimeter of his own inheritance, not daring to take it up. Almost certainly there was a spell here that could be broken, and he hurried onwards cheerfully, believing that it was up to him to find her and to wave the magic wand. His own solitude, so sad and defeated to those who had no knowledge of it, contained a thousand useful secrets, a thousand ways of living like a worm in the darkness, invisible, malignant and full of a gratifying power.

Mr Plumptre was deep in conversation at one of the tables, a bottle of wine half empty before him. He looked up after a while and peered over his glass, his eyes watery with drink.

'Are you he?'

He spoke very slowly and distinctly, as though expressing a difficult thought.

'I think so.'

'I think so too. I kept a glass for you. May I fill it? This, by the way,' he added, gesturing across the table, 'is Cranmoor Bunce. Peculiar name.'

A small dark man offered his hand, and peered intently into Colin's face as though certain that they must have met before. Mr Plumptre remarked, 'I am beginning to remember you,' in a tone of intense nostalgia.

Colin glanced round at the loud Edwardian room, with its flushed, prosperous faces, and the shine of spilt wine on the mahogany counter. Fingering his neck, he discovered a tie, and was pleased again at his secret capacity for survival.

'Or I'm ceasing to forget you. There are always at least two ways of looking at any fact. If it is a fact.'

Mr Bunce abruptly got up.

'Got to go,' he said, in a choked, startled voice.

Mr Plumptre looked at him.

'Home. Nice . . . Nice drink. Many thanks.'

He went, ducking beneath the elbows that jousted in the door.

'Gone. Home,' Mr Plumptre meditated. 'Pleasure of domestic life. Dusting, sweeping, washing, airing, eating, acts of public digestion, private defecation, partly public, partly private mingling in localities that do not bear to be named. Yes. A nice life.'

There was a pause. Colin drank from his glass, looked at the label on the bottle – which said Chablis Bougrots in mock medieval script – and then filled his glass again. He felt immensely cheerful, as Mr Plumptre called for another bottle.

'Glad you like it,' he said. 'The tipple of the intellectual. We were talking about Rilke.'

'About domestic life.'

'No, that was an interlude. I was giving way. To a weakness.'

'What else do you . . . does one give way to?'

Mr Plumptre roared ferociously.

'To passion.' He paused and looked thoughtful. 'Also to panic, and to oncoming traffic from the left.'

The noise was increasing, and figures packed themselves through the door as though expecting infinite space. Mr Plumptre sank lower in his chair and began to discourse sadly about the Duino Elegies. He was fairly clear about number one, but after that the meaning eluded him. Sometimes he regretted that he had not been to university, but that was the trouble coming from a family with a firm. You are born into the firm. Every act, feeling and perception belong to the firm. You cannot escape its divine displeasure, nor can you feel assuaged by its spasmodic warmth. Everywhere you see the traces of the firm; you hesitate to step further into it, just as you hesitate to withdraw. And so *hier bleiben wir, und nehmen immer Abschied.* Mr Plumptre lapsed gently into his chair, and began to mingle his reflections with tips for the stock exchange and vague offers of a job.

Someone knocked against the table. Mr Plumptre looked

up blearily. It was Mr Bunce, who stared at them for a moment in wild-eyed agitation. His thin mouth twitched, and his dark forehead pulsated as though the skin were pinched by a spiteful interior hand.

'Harold. That money. I must have it now.'

'Is it Cranmoor Bunce? I thought you had gone home. I imagined you already at home. I was gaining considerable satisfaction from the thought of you at home, peacefully reclining beside the domestic hearth. It really is rather beastly of you not to be at home.'

'Harold, please be serious. I bumped into Hugo. He told me.'

'Told you? I thought that you knew.'

'Yes, but I did not know that *he* knows.'

'This is boring my guest. How much do you need?'

'Two thousand.'

'I am kind hearted on the surface, I think you'll find.'

An air of deliberation had entered Mr Plumptre's manner. He appeared entirely sober, even as he filled his glass, raised it quickly to his lips, and drank from it, slapping his lips.

'I have never doubted it, Harold.'

'Very kind hearted, to those whom I like. Of course, you'll say that I don't like many people, and that too would be true. Colin Ferguson - that's the name isn't it? Well, there's someone I like. That harpie who writes poetry - Sarah Germ. I like her too.'

Mr Plumptre had extracted his cheque book, and, talking to himself in a tone of quiet rumination, he wrote out, using an old marbled fountain pen, 'The sum of Two Thousand Pounds', in a slow, fine italic script. He signed the cheque.

'To whom should I make it out?' he enquired absently.

'Oh, Biddle and Company would do. Or C. Bunce, Second Account. It's all the same.'

'Biddle. Funny name that. Almost as funny as the other one you mentioned.'

Colin looked down at the table, acutely ashamed of Mr

Plumptre. Always, in Francesca's world, the good things gave way immediately to a terrifying play of power.

'I have a better idea. I shall put "Colin Ferguson" instead. It has a pleasant rhythm to it, and see – the "F" looks very good, with a nice flourish reaching across to the "n". On the whole a nice-looking cheque, I should say. Almost a work of art. Now I am beginning to be grateful to you, my dear Cranmoor. If you had not returned, if you had gone home to fester at the fireside, why – a moment of pure inspiration would have been denied me. The world would have been poorer for it. Very much poorer.'

Colin and Mr Bunce remained speechless as Mr Plumptre detached the cheque and carefully inserted it between the table top and the base of Colin's glass. Mr Plumptre leaned across the table and peered into Colin's eyes.

'You're not going to refuse. You cannot deny that you need it.'

Colin was silent. He tried to apply his mind to the problem of what he might do with so much money, but fell into a swoon of self-distrust. Money played no part in the plot that he envisaged, and seemed only to postpone its climax. Mr Plumptre began tunelessly to whistle, and sat back in his chair with averted face. Mr Bunce stood, his jaw working as though in pursuit of words, but finding none adequate to his desolation. Colin's disgust extended to include him. It was intolerable that, having discovered himself to be a victim, the man did not immediately vanish. He did not cringe, he did not whine or supplicate. He simply stood by the table, moving only when pushed by a passing customer, an upright corpse that they would have to bury in its city uniform.

'Of course this is a joke,' said Colin.

Mr Plumptre looked round.

'Ha!' he said. 'Ha. Ha. No. Let me try again. Ha ha ha! No luck. It doesn't *seem* like a joke.'

Mr Bunce took a step back from the table, but then was pushed forward more firmly by a wedge of pin-striped bodies. Colin tried not to look at the cheque, which prevented him from lifting his glass, and so made speech the only refuge from embarrassment.

'The reason I wanted to see you,' he said, 'apart from the fact of your company . . .'

'That's a good one! Hear that, Cranmoor? My company! My brother's fucking company.'

'I mean, apart from seeing you and talking about – about what we've been talking about . . .'

Colin faltered.

'Yes?' said Mr Plumptre kindly.

'. . . was to ask how I could get hold of Francesca Wimpole. I seem to have . . . to have mislaid . . .'

'Mislaid! That's a good one!'

'The address.'

'Address – ah! Cranmoor here will tell you. Know her well, don't you Cranmoor?'

Mr Bunce seemed to take command of himself. His hands tightened about the edge of the table, and his eyes did not so much come into focus as begin to move slowly together as though bolted from behind by a rigid bar. The gaze shifted gradually from Colin to Mr Plumptre and back again.

'Well,' he said. 'I see how it stands. I am sorry to have troubled you Harold. Sorry to have formed these expectations.'

'For God's sake, Cranmoor. You sound too Victorian. Are you planning to haunt me, or would you be content with a sudden reversal which throws me lamenting from the wheel of fortune?'

Mr Bunce's tone was venomous.

'I take the point, Harold. You are quite within your rights. But it is unworthy of you to mention Francesca. Most unworthy.'

'I didn't mention her,' Mr Plumptre remarked in a melancholy tone. 'This young man is to blame,' and he gestured lassitudinously towards Colin, who looked away in distress. Colin remembered Pluto – was it Paluto? – the deity who had crowned Francesca's image with a halo of negation. No trace of cheerfulness remained, and his plot was utterly in ruins. He searched for the idea of a substitute – Penney, for instance. But these vagrant emotions were no longer possible. He must join Francesca in her solitude. Nothing else was permissible. Colin looked up, to see Mr Bunce disappearing into the clamour of Fleet Street, and Mr Plumptre staring at the half-empty bottle.

'Curious,' Mr Plumptre said at last, 'that one can be cruel in quite that way. Very curious. For I am not a cruel man. Really. I shall regret it. But from the scientific point of view the future regret is far less interesting than the present cruelty. Have another.'

He filled their glasses with movements which seemed suddenly drunken and uncontrolled.

'Oh and by the way – Francesca. The poor bugger was quite crazy about her. Didn't come to anything. Wish you better luck. Only, she'll suck you in, you know.'

'What do you mean?'

'Nothing in particular. The number is the same as Sarah Germ's. I've got it here.'

He brought out an address book, and copied a number slowly and shakily onto a scrap of loose paper.

'What she lacks in education she amply makes up for in style. And such a sting to her! Quite floored that bugger with the silly name who was in here asking for a couple of thou. Why are you going? Here, wait a minute, you've forgotten something. And I want your address. Very anxious to continue our conversation about Trakl.'

Mr Plumptre extracted the cheque and waved it in the air. Colin wrote Judith Blakely's address in Mr Plumptre's address book, took the wine-stained cheque and went out into the street. He walked steadily at first, and breathed the night air in the manner of one who has made an important decision. But at the first telephone booth he began to shiver, and after dialling the three letters and the first three digits of Francesca's number, he stopped, looking distractedly before him. He replaced the receiver, and walked back along Fleet Street, intending to return the cheque to Harold Plumptre. Soon he found himself standing before the rigid figure of Mr Bunce.

'Frightfully embarrassed. Terribly sorry.'

The words squeezed their way through pale fixed lips.

Colin looked up at the clock of St Dunstan's. It was already eight. His fingers were cold, tense, hungry for human flesh. He studied his companion's neck, but without conviction.

'Oh, Harold, you know,' he remarked pleasantly, 'is terribly shy. He compensates by getting drunk.'

'Irresponsible,' said Mr Bunce. Colin wondered whether this word signified agreement or some peculiarly absolute mode of dissent. The noise of the traffic had diminished, and the dry winter wind cleared the pavements. Circumstances could not have been more favourable to conversation.

'So you know Francesca Wimpole.'

Mr Bunce flinched slightly.

'I do know her. But not well you understand. Not well. Poor girl.'

'Poor girl? Oh, you mean her father.'

'Her father? Certainly not. The one good person in her beastly life, I should say.'

Colin was mildly astonished.

'Pluto?'

'I beg your pardon?'

'Nothing. I think it must be the name of a dog.'

'Could be,' said Mr Bunce stiffly.

'I suppose you were waiting for me.'

'Waiting? I have been agitating. I have been out of my mind.'

'Yes. It is certainly a day for confessions.'

'That was not a confession.' He paused, and then took a step sideways as though preparing to move away. 'You could say it was a request.'

'Request? Oh, you mean the money.'

'The money.'

'The best thing is for me to take it to a bank – if they'll cash it.'

'They'll cash it. No cheque of Harold's ever bounces.'

'And then . . . then . . .'

Suddenly Colin began to laugh. He convulsed, roared, and shook from head to toe, so that the whole of London seemed to be laughing with him, with the exception, he noticed, of Mr Bunce, whose pale, stiff face was propped on its pole in the midst of universal hilarity like an unmoved street-sign vainly issuing its commands.

'I don't see the joke.'

At last Colin regained possession of his voice.

'The joke is, that I shall then give you the money.'

'Give? A loan is all I require.'

Mr Bunce looked as though he were taking a stand. If so, however, Colin was sure it was not on a matter of principle.

'I said give. But I need your address.'

'Mr Ferguson, here is my card. I am speechless.'

'Good,' said Colin, who took the slip of paper and walked on. The encounter had fortified him to such an extent that he was able to complete the dialling of Francesca's number. The telephone was answered immediately, and the voice was Sarah's.

'Is Francesca there?'

'Who's speaking?'

'Colin Ferguson.'

'Greetings. She was talking about you. Round about you, I should say. Do you want me out of the way when you come?'

'Yes please. If I'm invited.'

'Shall I give you some advice?' Sarah did not wait for his answer. 'Go for what you want. Make it painless. And get out quick. Hang on, here is the dear girl.'

Francesca's voice was faint and hesitant. There was nothing in her tone to negate Sarah's warning, and Colin found himself stuttering out his own name as though unsure that he was entitled to it.

'Oh, Colin. I'm sorry.'

'Why?'

'Why did I go?'

'No. Yes.'

'It was Daddy. I . . . and things here. Come round can you? Please?'

The plea was urgent, telegraphic, from an outpost that would soon be overrun.

'But where? When?'

'Now,' and she named an address in Islington.

Colin arrived in the street, cheerless and afraid. The seered trees cluttered his path like military entrapments. The houses were frosty, their windows lifeless and blank. Their cold grandeur mocked his cringing advances, and as he passed them the ancient petition of the Fergusons was held aloft and ridiculed. Colin felt the shadow of the schoolmaster beside him, rehearsing grievances, meticulously defining the points of history and politics which justified his bleak despair. Suddenly the large stucco houses gave way to a row of cottages. The first of them, raised on a little plinth of brickwork, was hers. Colin opened the gate, and left his father's path for ever.

Eight

ONE MORNING two weeks later, when they had been lovers for a fortnight, Francesca woke him lightly with a touch on his brow. She was dressed and smiling, sitting across his body. Cold morning air entered the bedroom from the window which she had opened.

'Weren't we ridiculous,' she was saying.
'What are you referring to?'
'Those hesitations. I was trying not to fulfil my promise.'
'What promise?'
'The one I made to you, all those years ago, how many – seven?'
'Something like that.'

Francesca's belief that she had promised always to tell the truth, was so fundamental to her vision of Colin, that he never openly questioned it. It was a guarantee of his importance, and his title to her love.

He pulled her towards him. Always, when he kissed her, Francesca's eyes would shift at the moment of contact and look away. It was one of the many little gestures by which her body contradicted the tenderness which she had lavished on him. She sat up stiffly.

'Do you remember how it was when you found me here?'
'Of course.'

It was a habit of Francesca's constantly to reinforce the idea of Colin as her rescuer. It did not worry him, that she had constructed her love out of stories which might at any moment be disproved. On the contrary, he entered the spirit of them, and joyfully accepted his role. For him too, narrative was more soothing, more replete with possibilities, than fact.

On the occasion to which Francesca referred, Sarah had conducted him to the living room, pushing open the door with a wave of the arm that directed his eyes first upwards to the cornice, then downwards to the wooden floor, and finally sideways to the half-closed partition. 'Watch out,' she said, 'it bites.' Colin pushed open the partition; Francesca sat in an armchair, staring fixedly at him, her mouth set in a kind of principled negation of a smile. She did not rise; nor did she greet him, and when he went to take her hands, she held them out slowly and tremulously, as though they had been severely burned and even the air caused her pain. He touched them as softly as he could, kissed her brow, and knelt beside her. To none of his questions would she give an answer. But suddenly, just as he began to think that he must run from the house and never come back to her, she reached out hesitantly to touch his lips, and said, 'I want you.'

She allowed herself to be carried towards a bedroom, and, as he pushed the door behind him, he heard Sarah go out into the street. Only two hours later did he learn that the bed in which they lay was Sarah's.

Everything had passed as though rehearsed to the smallest detail. Even in the greatest intimacy, Francesca was absent from her body, watching it with that look of penetrating stillness which seemed so near to honesty, but which, he knew, was no such simple thing.

'Wasn't it peculiar, the way we seemed already to belong to each other?'

'Yes,' he said, because this was the answer which the story required. But it had not been at all peculiar. When everything that they did was preceded by its own narrative, how could it not be accomplished without a sense of *déjà-vu*? Colin sat up and took her hand. It was strangely rough and broken, like the hand of a labourer.

'Shall we resume our conversation?' he suggested.

'Oh yes.'

Their conversation centred first on the schoolmaster, and secondly on Lord Shepton. Those were the main subjects; but there were a thousand subsidiary motifs, all of them lighter and more readily intertwined. There was the problem of Sarah: was she good or bad, beautiful or ugly, a blessing or a curse? There was the conundrum of Francesca's 'identikit', as she called it. What would define her, what would give her sense and life? She wished to be poor and unprotected like Colin, who in turn wished to be rich and spoiled like her. In truth, however, each was solitary in his own peculiar way. Even more pleasant was the question of their life: who should do the cooking, and who should buy the food? Where should Colin stay and how often should he visit her? Were they to share their friends, or should they inhabit separate spheres, coming together by their own natural gravity in a periodic shower of sparks?

The conversation began on this first morning, and was soon to assume overriding importance, as the true substance of the bond between them. Colin and Francesca were characters in a cooperative fiction, which they embellished each day with the impetuous garrulousness of children. It was already light when he awoke on that fateful morning, in her bedroom now, overlooking the garden with its creeper-covered walls. Francesca had turned from him, her left arm dangling from the bed. She had not moved or made a sound since falling asleep eight hours before; but when he touched her, she took his hand and squeezed it gently. The room was awash with clothes. They were scattered about the floor, hung over the backs of chairs, and dripped from drawers, cupboards and window-sills. All of them seemed expensive, tasteful, and the object of a kind of obsessional neglect. Books retreated from them against the wall: novels, poetry, the Loeb classics, some ageing fashion magazines. A collection of little boxes, in bronze, stone and plaster, was neatly arranged on an old oyster-patterned chest of drawers, beside which there stood an ebony column, bearing a Chinese bowl in red and gold.

Something emerged from the bowl that seemed like the plumage of a golden pheasant. He went to look at it more closely, and Francesca immediately sat up.

'You will want some tea,' she said, and then studied him curiously as he fingered the object, made of exotic feathers mounted on a moving frame of ivory. 'Why do you like me?'

'I don't just like you, Francesca. Perhaps I don't like you at all.'

'What is it then?'

'Love. Perhaps you'll give me time to discover what the word means. Or do you plan to run away?'

'I can't: this is my lair. You've run me to earth. You wouldn't believe it, but that's neither a fan nor a head-dress, but a puppet.'

'What does it represent?'

'It came without instructions, just as I did. Perhaps it represents me.'

She hid from him. When he saw her again, she was standing in the window, dressed in a blue silk gown, putting back the hair from her neck with her hands. Her expression was serious.

'At least,' she said, 'you can't be pursuing me for some irrelevant motive. That would be in breach of our agreement.'

'Depends what you consider to be irrelevant.'

'Money, for example. An ancient name and title.'

'Shall I tell you a secret? I am fascinated by those things. But they fascinate me less than you do. On the other hand, you couldn't be what you are without them.'

'I *am* serious,' she said.

'Do you think I am not?'

Francesca quickly left the room, and returned a few minutes later with two bowls of milky tea.

'Well,' she said, 'we had better talk about it. Bit by bit I shall persuade you to see me as something other than my father's daughter. Maybe you can persuade me that you are something more than your father's son.'

And so sipping from their bowls like feasting soldiers, they rehearsed the story of their past campaigns. Already, however, Colin was less interested in the great theme of Lord Shepton than in the chosen particulars of Francesca's life. He was fascinated by Sarah, who greeted his presence with an indifference bordering on contempt. As time wore on, the enigma of Sarah seemed to intensify, and since Francesca herself seemed to possess no special information about her friend, Colin began to observe the girl more closely. On the morning of his third day Sarah, who was standing in the kitchen, snorting quietly as he prepared Francesca's breakfast, suddenly turned to him.

'I don't suppose you wish to know what I'm proposing to do with myself today,' she announced.

'Not particularly,' he replied, believing that Sarah despised all attempts at politeness.

'No, but I am going to tell you anyway, 'cause you be needin' 'struction man. I get out of this place see and I'm on a real high, jay-walking through the dust-storms in a jesserant of silver-plated dreams, knocking the riders off apocalyptic horses, and blowing the minds of street bums like dandelion seed to say she loves me she loves me not.'

'That's very interesting.'

'Wait, I haven't got to the interesting part. I arrest my movements, or better, my movements are arrested, in the Fisher's Arms, a pub that you wouldn't know, but which at midday gives a beautiful spectacle of human hair pressed against cut-glass windows saying fuck me. There I encounter, by previous arrangement, a Most Important Person, closely connected with the synod of the C of E, who wishes me to revise one of the new liturgies for the use of acid-heads and coke-sniffers. I am to become official methologist to the established church. He will buy me a drink, and I shall offer him samples of my work – knitting, failed evening-class pots, plants that were never watered and which died in interesting contortions – and then he'll want to screw me, like these vicars always do, and there's the first problem of the day. Yes or no? In Lambeth Palace or St Pancras Hotel? Not here, in any case, since Little Angel doesn't like that kind of thing and drops great pre-Raphaelite tears down her lily cheeks. So what do I do? My next appointment is at four, *thé dansant* at the Ritz with the manager of the Moscow State Circus . . .'

'I see there is a dilemma.'

'Then the answer is a lemma.'

She moved into the hall, pausing before the mirror by the door, where she adorned her face with green mascara, and, pulling down the pouches of her eyes, said 'ugh!' at the blood-streaked murky whites that lolled beneath them.

'You know Ferguson old man, this house has a very strange atmosphere all of its own. You must be prepared for some surprises. *I* don't mind it, because I float in the air, buoyed up by poetry. All the arrows fall short of me, and return spent towards the lower regions. But you!'

'What about me?'

'You are sort of decent, uncouth, humble. You inhabit those lower regions. Arrows come to you not spent but purchased, for hard moral cash, and you receive them into your flesh like a dutiful Sebastian. She will hurt you, because you are innocent. Oh, I'm innocent too, but not the way *you* are. You progress through the world in a bovine way, you absorb yourself in pleasant, seemly tasks, you make ends meet, you have that about you which makes one think of *settling down*. I dare say you even have a regular job.'

'That's not true!' he cried, as though it were the most important point to establish in his favour. But then he reflected that he had applied for a job with a weekly which had advertised the post of assistant literary editor.

'In a way it is true. You've taken on Little Angel as a regular job. It will be full time, and you'll be paid nothing. But you'll do it all the same.'

Sarah lost no opportunity to remind him that he had something to learn from her, something which she was not quite disclosing, and which perhaps could not be expressed using the ordinary resources of their language. Sometimes she would make this clear with a look – and she had infinite ways of seeming startled into recognition – sometimes with a chance remark, or even an isolated word, chosen from her armoury of fashionable slang.

As Francesca sat across his body, letting him toy with her cuffs, it was again the subject of Sarah that occupied her. There was a kind of exhilaration for Colin in defending Sarah, in speaking fairly and reasonably of someone who clearly wished him dead. Francesca was beginning to feel that Sarah poisoned her new endeavours. It was as though every experience with which she sought to fill the void of life had already been anticipated and pre-empted by her friend.

'But why get rid of her?' he asked. 'I thought you loved her? At least, you told me that *I* had to love her.'

'Yes. That was your first test.'

'Did I pass?'

'I think so. You tried, at least.'

'I have tried to *like* her. But I can't love her, except as my neighbour, and therefore as myself. Which is not very encouraging.'

'That's too sophisticated. Almost as sophisticated as Sarah. You know we've been lovers since schooldays?'

She looked away as she said it, and he gripped her hand.

'I'm not so stupid that I haven't seen,' he replied. 'But I hope it's over.'

'No. I mean, of course, the physical side is over: but not that sense of her presence beside me, plucking at my mask.'

'You mean, you still love her – enough to feel the force of her judgement – and therefore you want her to go?'

'Oh God, I suppose that is it. And I can feel your dismay, anticipating that I shall prove my love for you in just the same way. But you know there is no comparison. This is the real thing: the thing which makes me neither my father's daughter, nor the mischievous Francesca Wimpole, but simply me. Do you see? Oh Colin, please tell me you see.'

This was a surprising turn in the story, since it was accompanied by a flood of tears. Nevertheless, he uttered the words required of him, and embraced her according to the rules. As he walked to his room at Judith Blakely's house, he wondered just how much this real Francesca, the heroine of their little drama, was the product of *nostalgie de la boue*. For certainly, he was a dull, awkward creature beside Sarah, and one who fitted well to Sarah's bleak description of him. But then, he too had a part in the drama, and he remembered this with gratitude. It was for his sake that Francesca urged him into the narrative, and maybe she was right to believe in those possibilities which he had doubted for so long. After all, he could yet become an assistant literary editor. He was even writing again. In his room at Judith's house he sat quietly, composing an essay on domestic ornament, and sketching a story about the cheque which he had taken on behalf of Mr Bunce from Harold Plumptre.

He worked well. After an hour or so, he felt confident that, in the matter of domestic ornament, his recent experiences in Francesca's world were not devoid of value. He looked on the objects by which she was surrounded with his father's moralising eye for detail. The schoolmaster hated those styles which spoke of power and servitude; for him, there could be no legitimate decoration which was not also a form of utility – a way of making things to last. All the same, Mr Ferguson had never been happy, as the Inspector was happy, with the new, plain, functional styles. Previously man had assumed the right to give to those objects nearest to him a human form. He had empowered himself, mortal though he was, to impose on objects the imprint of *his* life, to make objects participants in a great spectacle, in which the continuity of the species was to be perpetually celebrated. And that ambition, Colin argued, justified just as fully the flamboyant silverware of Bassington Hall as the quoins and coping-stones of the Dunsbury builders. The minimalist, earthy and electronic styles of the twentieth century, on the other hand, express the vengeance of objects. Now it is no longer things which are in the service of man, but man who is in the service of things. Objects have risen triumphantly from means to ends, and wear towards humanity the condescending smile that men once wore towards them. Every object is complete in itself, deriving its logic from a material, or from a technological symbolism which secretly offers the crown to instruments. Each knife, or glass, or cup refuses the claim of human life to constitute its true significance. And that is why modernist objects remind us so horribly and so excitingly of death, and at the same time trivialise death, by showing it to be no greater disaster than the collapse of an organism. Objects of the older school were kinder to us, since they showed us that their indestructible materiality, their insentient obstinacy, would be a means to our ends. It would be used to fix for ever what we are, and would obey beyond the grave our last call to order. Insofar as they spoke to us of death, the old objects also consoled us with the image of our spiritual survival. That was the true meaning of Bassington Hall and its miraculous interior; and of the outrage committed by Lord Shepton, which Francesca, in her fugitive way, had encouraged through her gift of the orange clock.

Colin put down his pen. It was clear that he was much more in need of her love than she of his. What persuaded him was not the Hall itself, but her garden. The pond, the trees, the light on the water, the untouchable surface of those rarely visited things, all seemed to start back from him in his memory with just the same quick refusing movement that prefaced her fondest gestures. A small alert forbidding hand was raised in front of all of them. She belonged there, and, in the outer world, sought not love but a kind of distant and metaphysical protection. She sought it from him because he was poor, inept, and yet determined to survive by his own devices. She was looking for his secret wound, so that, by a tender blackmail, she could secure his protection, convincing herself and the world that she stood by her own devices, and had nothing significant to lose. He did not mind this blackmail. On the contrary, he looked for the ways in which he might join her in a mutual fraud, from which the strangest, loneliest gentleness might grow.

He reflected for a while on the nature of fraud. There is the fraud of deceit, which demands protective measures. You remember to distrust all gestures which symbolise their own generosity. 'I am generous,' says Harold Plumptre's hand as it writes the cheque. You stab the hand, and its owner's eyes will suddenly meet yours. Then there is the fraud of bewilderment. You do not wish Sarah to understand you, to move around you, to trap you with a sudden smile. So you adopt an aimlessness which will make you seem superfluous. This is a weakness which benefits no one. Then there is the peculiar fraud of honesty, the adoption of truthfulness as the sole standard of good behaviour, the whole cement of a relation: the soul lurks untroubled in the darkness which this light conceals. Her eyes would stare back at him, innocent mirrors which returned his love in a frame of absolute truth. If only he could trap her into deceiving him, then he could see through at last to her soul. Colin picked up his pen again, and wrote out the first flimsy paragraph of the tale of Mr Bunce.

Then the telephone rang and, after a moment, Judith Blakely put in her head at the door. Her manner was heavy and furtive, as though there were something that he ought to know – about his right to be there, about his attitude to her, about her own dreadful circumstances – which she was not going to reveal, but which he ought to have discovered for himself. He was offended by her orange dress, crossed with canary-yellow zigzags. Even now, when he had no need of her cooperation, he could feel no pity for Judith, and stared up at her mournful face with a look of unconcealed hostility.

'You are wanted,' she said. 'Someone called Francesca Wimpole.'

'Francesca!'

Judith winced disapprovingly.

'She sounds distraught.'

Judith turned away, making room for him as he ran past her to the phone.

'It's me,' said the small occluded voice. There was a confused background noise of shouting and laughter, and the throbbing of a bass guitar. 'I just wanted to hear you. What are you doing? Why aren't you here? I wish I could see you.'

'Where's here?'

'A place you wouldn't like. I don't want to be here. Why aren't we together?'

'Why indeed.'

He wanted to say 'darling', but no endearments had graced the cottage table and he could not use the untouchable fripperies of the salon. A great barrier seemed suddenly to erect itself, and he shouted across to Francesca uncertain that he would be heard.

'But what's the matter? Why don't you come home?'

There was a silence.

'Who are you with?' he asked more gently.

'Oh. Sarah. And people.'

Her tone was distant.

'What people? Do you need to see them?'

'I'm fed up.' Her voice was so faint that, when he heard the words 'I miss you', he could not be sure that she had really spoken them.

'Well,' he said after a pause. 'I'll come and join you.'

'Oh no.' Her tone now was urgent, full-voiced. 'Don't do that. I'll see you back home. Is that possible? In half an hour? Please. Oh, thank you Colin. Thank you.'

Colin knocked on the door of Judith's room, where sometimes she sat at a desk, doing something that seemed to require a great amount of brown paper. She did not get up as he entered, and for a while he watched her, moving slowly and painfully, shifting things from one side of the desk to the other, opening and closing drawers. Then she reached out to dust the leaves of a rubber plant that stood on the desk in a ray of sunlight. Suddenly her gestures, which seemed to have no other purpose than to leave things unchanged, touched him with sorrow. He remembered the schoolmaster, fidgeting through his maps and papers, and the same absence that had stepped from those rude gestures of survival now invaded Judith's room, and accused him of the heartlessness which he had once desired.

'Judith, I'm sorry. I am really sorry.'

'Why should you be sorry?'

'About everything. The way I talk to you, for instance.'

'Forget it. At least you talk to me.'

Colin admitted, however, that he did not want to. That was the whole truth of the matter. He acknowledged that the fault was his, implored her to forgive him, and made many protestations about a source of confusion in his life which, despite her curiosity, he was reluctant to specify. It was nothing to do with Judith. He liked her, admired her, respected her; he knew that her life was difficult. He wished he could do something to help, and he didn't mind admitting that it was partly the sense that he could not help that made him so uneasy. It was true that he had once complained about the wallpaper, but it had been a child's room, and of course he liked the children too . . .

Judith interrupted him: 'You make it sound as though I am preventing you from going. But as a matter of fact, I hadn't realised that you wanted to.'

She got up, and her dolorous shoulders drooped lower as she approached the table between them. A cornet of white tissue enclosed some flowers there: withered, drying snowdrops that he had given her the day before, and which had been left where she first put them down. He looked at the brownish flowers, and then at her dead face.

'I am dreadful company,' she continued. 'Since you want to go, I think you should. But there is one thing I want to say first.'

Colin stood to attention, because he had found that this had been the most certain way to avoid the schoolmaster's homilies, not by refusing to hear them, but by dissolving them in a secretion of indifference. He stared before him, at a loud red abstract painting in a brushed steel frame, and tried to imitate its self-important emptiness. Judith spoke of the time when Colin had first come to their house, after a party at which he and Ken had discussed many things together, in particular Goethe's *Elective Affinities*, which Ken wanted to adapt for television. She knew that Colin did a line in Goethe; it was one of those things he could be sincere about, and which therefore attracted people to him. So he was right to trot it out in company and when there was something to be gained. It had always been supposed that she didn't understand such things. That was Ken's view, and she had learned to share it. After all, she had housework and children to occupy her, and besides it was very important for Ken to appear well-informed and exceptionally on top of things besides her, and it would be quite wrong to compete. That was why it had been Ken who took the decision to ask Colin to stay, as a sort of paying guest, although of course things had soon passed the stage when the transaction could be conceived in monetary terms, but that too was fine by her, since it was to be supposed that the boy was a screwed-up genius who would blossom out with a bit of kindness and education, and through getting to know the kind of people who would be useful to him, and to whom he in his turn could be useful, people like Ken for instance . . .

Colin broke his pose and made to interrupt her, but she reached out her hand and silenced him.

'Don't worry, I'm not saying you used us. I'm saying just the opposite. Ever since that second evening, when you told us the story of your father and of Mr Whatshisname – Willis – who helped you out of hospital, I felt that having you around would be good for all of us. I felt sorry for you; at the same time, I saw that you were moving in no direction. Ken was all direction, rushing too fast away from everything that really mattered. I thought you would soften his ambition, or at least cause him to hesitate. But of course, after that first occasion, when you had established your claim, you retired to your room, and hardly spoke to us thereafter. Maybe you were bored; maybe you took a dislike to Ken's upward mobility, his ultimate indifference to everything that didn't serve his goals. Maybe you couldn't face the tensions that were developing between us. I wish the word "us" didn't keep coming back to me, but it does. And that is part of what I wanted to say. You depended on us, even if your thoughts were elsewhere. I came to care for you, Colin, just because you were so dependent. It gave a purpose to this "us" that I keep referring to, that Ken had brought you here, and that I had to look after you. You were by far the most palatable by-product of his career, or at any rate the one least likely to take him away from me. I don't expect gratitude. But this story has a point. About two years ago, you remember, you were very ill with something like glandular fever. I was alone here looking after you; you wouldn't let me tell your father, even though the doctor was worried. Nevertheless the news must have got around, because one day the telephone rang, and you were asleep, not to say delirious. When this girl asked after you I said I couldn't possibly disturb you. She replied in the strangest tone that she had no desire to disturb you, but wanted only to know what was wrong with you. Naturally I was curious to know her identity. "Francesca Wimpole," she said. Her voice was exactly as it was on the phone today: sepulchral, eerie, like a voice from the grave.'

Colin's attention had now focused entirely on Judith's face, into which life had been transferred by a miracle which for him happened daily, but which never ceased to surprise. His dread at his sudden insignificance made Judith seem fully in command of him, archepiscopal as she traced the contours of his sin.

'What did she say?'

'She said that I had *got* to look after you, that you *must* get well, and that she would pray for you. And she made me promise not to tell you she had rung. I asked her if there was any special reason and she said, in that peculiar spectral tone, yes, there is a special reason, I cannot see him now, I cannot see him ever. I feel him thinking about me. And he mustn't. Now those are funny words, and this girl is clearly a funny girl. And don't deny it because it is written all over your face, you are going to live with her. I should say, you are going to try to live with her. I mention this because I think that, all things considered, you may be making a terrible mistake.'

Colin stood for a moment, and then cried out:

'Why are you telling me this? What's it to do with you?'

Judith was calm, and stared at him with the unmoved authority of a woman in despair.

'I thought you should know.' She turned round slowly to resume her occupations at the desk. 'Besides, perhaps it will be easier for you to leave, if you think that I have imposed on your feelings.'

Colin stole the bottle of whisky that Judith had left on the table in the hall. On Primrose Hill, he drank half of it, and observed the swimming bulks of people, as they passed his bench. They were dressed in their winter outfits of padded waterproofs, their heads creased and lop-sided with sorrows that impertinently refused to be his. Once a girl returned his gaze, and he debated whether to follow her. He thought of Penney, and of Anne. He sank unhindered into his ancient mood, the mood of Hamlet's nutshell, into which he crept, diminished almost to a nothing, and counting himself king of infinite space. He peered out over London with the malignant cunning of the outcast, who saw to the ends of things and saw that they were futile.

The dogs intrigued him, and one in particular, carving out a passage through the winter air with meticulous sideways movements of the nose, prompted him to get up and follow. It had a white coat, with dirty smears of a greyish colour that made the pattern of a ship on its broad flat back. Its legs were short, but whether because Colin followed it, barking softly, or whether because of some private business of its own, it began to move quite fast towards some trees. When Colin fell down at last, and lay quietly staring at the sky, the dog had already disappeared over the top of the hill, proceeding with urgent movements in the direction of Hampstead. Someone stood above him; he could not tell whether it was a man or woman, but he did not mind which, since the winter clothing made the figure soft and springy as he jumped upon it. He threw his punches wildly and eagerly into the woolly mass. As the two locked figures rolled together, mildly protesting at the injustice of this encounter, Colin's bruised and reddened face stared with a kind of raw fellow-feeling into the half-closed eyes of his antagonist.

Nine

'YES MISS,' the policeman was saying, 'but he has to be brought before the justices tomorrow.'

Colin, who had taken a fancy to the nautical moustaches, the trim fringe and the large voluted ears of Constable Bottomley, smiled with pleasure. There was something about the word 'justices' which he particularly liked: it was authoritative, old-fashioned, upright, and yet also a trifle absurd in its implication that so abstract and singular a thing as justice could be more than one.

Francesca knitted her brow, looking pert and pasteurised in her clean white frock and sailor jacket. He could not understand why he had been so angry with her, although two hours before he had been carrying her pummelled spirit in his arms, accusing her of the most horrible offences.

'You see, angel,' Colin said, continuing a conversation which had begun before she arrived, 'the whole thing began entirely without your agreement. It has to take its course.'

That was the word he needed – 'angel'. Classless but stylish, expressing not love but a moral idea of love. As an endearment it was anodyne and theoretical, and he did not mind the fact that Sarah had thrown this word to him from those crazy upper regions where she snorted like the tempest on her winged imaginary horse. Colin knew he wasn't drunk, because he could count the panes in the leaded windows, could follow with his eye the grey-stone mouldings that rippled around them, could blink with exemplary innocence at the white canopy of plastic which covered the bulb above the pinewood desk.

A ledger lay open, in which his details had been entered. His whole case had been worked into presentable form, and Constable Bottomley was visibly satisfied with the statement of facts. He felt that a lawyer was unnecessary, although Colin was entitled to call for one. As they drank the tea which another officer in shirt-sleeves had brought from the back room, Bottomley rehearsed the arguments against legal representation in cases of drunkenness and common assault. 'The problem,' he said, 'is the ABH factor. Had it been GBH I wouldn't have hesitated, but with ABH it could go either way.' He meditated, sitting on the desk with his legs swinging into the central opening.

Before Francesca's arrival, Constable Bottomley had entertained Colin with his memoirs. As it happened, the Constable had passed his childhood in Murricombe, and it was there that he had first conceived the idea of entering the police force. The immediate cause had been the escape of a bull called John who belonged to Lord Shepton. Now everyone in Murricombe, Constable Bottomley explained, had a great reverence for John, who had fathered several successful herds, and who was also the prize exhibit at fairs, fêtes and cattle shows. Every Christmas Eve John would be invited to the Wimpole Arms, where he would be led by his moist ringed nose to the gated side door, to be plied with pint after pint of mild. John gave no evidence of enjoying this experience, but neither did he refuse it, being as dutiful in the consumption of liquids as he was in their production. Only once had he seemed to stagger on leaving for home, but, until the fateful day of his escape, he had handled himself like a true Christian gentleman. Nobody knows why, on that Christmas Eve, John had behaved so completely out of character. Nevertheless, the long and short of it was that, after no more than five or six pints, he suddenly reared up, wrenched himself free of his guardian, and charged off through the village. Of course, there was pandemonium, and things began to look bad when John, having been cornered against the church by a group of farmhands, suddenly ran at one of them and gored him through the thigh. Soon there was complete anarchy in the village, as John cantered down street after street, smashed his way through fences, trampled gardens and lawns, and menaced with full-voiced roars every person who approached him. Bottomley watched in fear as the bull, having returned to the church, began to lean against the door behind which various children had taken refuge.

The situation had been saved by Lord Shepton. Next to John, the villagers held Lord Shepton in highest esteem, not because of his social position, but because once, during the war, when a soldier on leave had run amok, threatening the villagers with his gun, Lord Shepton had donned his officer's uniform, approached the man, and with calm authority induced him to disarm. The appearance of this hero on the scene of their new calamity reassured the villagers, and John too, hearing himself summoned in that crisp, cold voice, turned from the church door and tried his best to look nonchalant. Lord Shepton approached the bull slowly, quietly speaking to it as an army commander might address his troops. Everybody was breathless with fear and excitement, as the distance narrowed between the antagonists, but nobody had expected things to end as they did.

Bottomley answered a query brought to him by the officer in shirt-sleeves. As he did so, a handcuffed man was led in from the street, making faint shifting movements vaguely symbolic of resistance. He had peculiar dilated eyes, which avoided every glance, and when Constable Bottomley turned to greet him, saying, 'Business not so good, Jimmy,' he uttered a low howl of grief, like an abandoned puppy. Two constables hustled Jimmy slowly through the gothic door into the busy back-room of the station, and Bottomley resumed his story.

'When his lordship had approached to about four feet, and John stood looking at him a bit sheepish like, with that rope hanging from his nose and blood all over his horns, you could have heard a pin drop it was that tense. Then, without any warning, his lordship reached into his pocket, took out a pistol, and shot John right between the eyes, bang, bang, bang, three times, like that. Old John he stood there like he didn't know what had hit him. Nor did he neither. His lordship walked off, cool as a cucumber. Then a peculiar thing happened. John began to follow him, moving very slowly, staggering a bit, but like he wanted to show his obedience in the last few seconds before he died. That was the strangest sight as ever I saw, and when old John finally crumpled at the knees and went down with a great roar like an avalanche, I felt that sorry I could have cried.'

'Phew!' said Colin.

'But that was the day I felt my vocation. That was the day I saw the value of authority, and how, when there's a crisis, there's got to be someone in charge. Find the commander, and the troops obey. Lose the commander, and there's hell to pay.'

Colin confided that the girl who was coming to rescue him was none other than the daughter of Bottomley's hero. The Constable whistled and said 'well, fancy that!' and then, after a pause, 'I suppose anybody can get mixed up with anybody, can't they?' Then he continued his story, describing many crimes of drunkenness, of which John's had been the first. Bottomley had a fatherly concern both to minimise Colin's offence, and also to warn him of the dangers. He was speaking quite genially by the time that Francesca entered. She pleaded at first for Colin's release. But Bottomley was immovable. Eventually he led them to a room apart, so that they could talk in private. Colin was immediately anxious, sensing that the little bubble of peace that he had constructed in the presence of the Constable was about to be exploded.

'Why do you want me?' he asked.

His head was beginning to throb, and his hand slightly trembled. They were sitting on either side of a plywood table, which was covered in spidery patterns, etched during previous tense encounters.

'I think I can see your strategy,' she said. 'You want me to prove that I love you. But first you have to protect yourself by creating this absurd *tableau vivant* in a copshop. You want to disclaim me if I muff my part.'

Colin looked up.

'Almost as sophisticated as Sarah,' he commented. 'But unfortunately no nearer the truth.'

'Then what has happened? Why this display?'

'I'll tell you why. It's those blank years. Those years when you didn't see me.'

'When I couldn't see you.'

'When you avoided seeing me.'

'As for that,' she said, turning on him the full force of a temporary anger, 'if you don't understand by now, you never will. And why should it matter? Everything has changed.'

'Has it?'

'Yes,' she said.

He got up and went to her. She struggled for a moment, and then gave way beneath his kisses. After a while she fell limp in his arms, her eyes half closed, as though she had fainted. He called to her, shook her, and finally pulled back her head and slapped it. She opened her eyes.

'Colin,' she cried, as though astonished to see him. 'Oh dear!'

She freed herself, got up and then held her face for a long moment in her hands.

'It doesn't matter Colin. You must know that I am happy with you, happier than I have ever been. But I am sad too; terribly sad.'

He looked at her in alarm.

'Don't ask me why. I just am.'

She offered her sadness as she had offered her honesty – as an axiom that was never to be questioned, even though it rested on nothing but her own avowal.

'I don't know what you mean,' he said.

'Perhaps you're too drunk to understand.'

He shrank from her.

'I've been stupid, Francesca. The best thing is to leave me to cool off for the night. I'll be alright. Maybe I'll get off with a fine.'

She walked past him into the open office of the police station; he heard her giving instructions to Constable Bottomley. Her voice ceased, and after a moment he followed her. Bottomley was sitting at the desk, busily writing something with furrowed brow. He pressed the biro hard, channelling a blue passage slowly through official-looking paper.

'Did she bewilder you?' Colin asked.

Bottomley looked up slowly.

'Miss Wimpole? Nothing wrong with her. She's sending you a solicitor.'

'But I thought we'd agreed . . .'

'Yes. But now, you see, there's someone in charge. And like I said, there is the problem of ABH.'

Colin shared a cell with two snoring drunks and a furious red-haired Irishman, who abused the Virgin Mary in terms that were both angry and intimate. From time to time the drunks got up to fill the lavatory with their surfeits, and the Irishman undid his trousers and began slowly to masturbate, shaking the bunk which he shared with Colin and then at last falling back into quiescence, his undischarged member flaccid in his hand. Colin slept fitfully, and awoke in the early hours, his head sore, dry and feverish. When the officer came to fetch him, he said goodbye to his companions. One of the drunks said 'Huh?', and the Irishman whispered, 'Fuck off, you bleeding orange cunt,' in tones of gentle endearment.

'My name's Trenchard. Francesca asked me to come in person. I arrived early. We shall get your case heard at once.'

The neatly-groomed suit continued to utter clipped phrases, asking very little, and occasionally putting up from the shiny ring of its metallic collar a little periscopic eye which would stare unblinkingly at Colin and then lower itself again. As far as Colin could observe, a small carefully measured quantity of the best pink flesh enfolded this eye, which was crowned by thin platinum wire attached to the skin by little black stitches. There were pauses in the suit's monologue into which it seemed appropriate to insert words. Colin experimented at first with various kinds of apology such as 'I didn't know what I was doing,' or 'I hope I caused no damage.' But the solicitor continued his instructions in a sharper tone, as though such remarks constituted a breach of decorum. Eventually Colin thought that he should explain himself.

'I was pissed as a newt,' he said. 'I had very good reasons, though I can't remember them. I was completely irresponsible for my actions. I think that's about all.'

'The only question is bail,' Trenchard continued. 'Have you a record?'

'A what?'

'Convictions,' the suit croaked irritably.

'About what?'

There was a silence, and then a sigh emerged from the collar.

'Why,' said the voice in a tone of exasperation, 'does Francesca always get into these scrapes?'

Colin did not like the implications of this remark, and tried to think of ways to negate it. He was about to ask the solicitor why he referred to Miss Wimpole by her Christian name, when he realised that the interview was at an end. He was being led by a young constable through doors and corridors crowded with gothic details. Colin's attention was caught by a stone gargoyle that had slyly crept down a shaft from the ceiling, and clung to the wall, sucking a long scaly tail in its amused and big-lipped mouth. A door opened onto a courtroom, in which a small crowd of people was already assembled. Colin saw Francesca in the gallery, and blushed. His name was called, and he was guided forward to a kind of pulpit. A plump, grey-faced magistrate with a ledger, a wooden hammer, and a wig sat in front of him behind a table raised on a dais. A light oak panelling made a kind of cloth of honour, and the royal coat of arms colourfully emblazoned on the plaster of the wall shone out with unnatural gaiety across the courtroom. A policeman entered another pulpit on the left side of the bench; a clerk sat poised beneath him with a biro in his hands. A few barristers, court officials and patient observers, who had been joined by Mr Trenchard's crisply mobile suit, were bunched in attitudes of professional boredom along the facing benches. Colin could no longer see the public gallery, but its faint human rustle of anticipation drew his thoughts back to Francesca. Her face had worn an expression of total loyalty, which he knew might give way at once to another expression of total betrayal. Curiously, he counted it as a sign of her love that both these aspects were offered to him so vividly, each ready for his sign.

'Colin Ferguson,' the policeman called. 'Age twenty-four. No previous convictions.'

'Read the indictment please.'

The magistrate sounded tired; but then, looking up and catching sight of Colin, a brief flicker of interest crossed his features, and he let his soft grey eyes rest for a moment on the face of his victim.

'Your honour, the accused is brought before you charged with being drunk and disorderly, and with assault causing actual bodily harm. The facts are as follows. On February 25th at 4.15 pm, the accused, who had been drinking, was seen by several witnesses to be behaving in an uncontrolled manner on Primrose Hill. Upon meeting with Mr Joseph Ensleigh it is alleged that he deliberately collided with the said Mr Ensleigh, and then, on being reprimanded, began to assault him. Mr Ensleigh suffered cuts and abrasions, and is to be called in evidence for the prosecution. The accused seeks bail, and is represented your honour.'

The policeman passed a paper to the clerk who passed it to the magistrate. After raising his eyes again to Colin's face, the magistrate addressed the bench of professionals.

'Will the accused's representative make his submission.'

The suit straightened itself into an upright position, and emitted a slight cough.

'Your honour has seen the relevant materials. I have nothing to add, except that my client is due to begin employment tomorrow in an important post, and, while admitting the facts as alleged by the prosecution, begs to plead in mitigation certain personal misfortunes which caused him to behave in an unusual fashion.'

'What important job?' Colin asked, genuinely curious. The policeman on his left gripped his arm as though this utterance were a sign that he might there and then renew his criminal behaviour. There was a silence, followed by anticipatory shufflings from the gallery.

'I apologise to the court, your honour, that my client should speak out of order.'

'Since he has done so, however, Mr Trenchard, you may trouble yourself to answer his question. There seem to be two views about this important job to which you refer.'

The periscope withdrew within the suit, and the discourse of the court was drowned in a sea of murmurs. Colin looked round again at his surroundings. His head was beginning to clear, and the Edwardian details of the courtroom, its sparseness and high white ceiling set him on a train of introspection. He was reminded of the schoolhouse at Murricombe, and he began to recall the days of his father's illness. He remembered a conversation about politics, in which the schoolmaster had attempted, for the last time, to awaken in his son that revolutionary fervour upon which the future of mankind did or did not depend, according to the way you looked at it, or it at you, as Colin said. How angry Mr Ferguson had been, as he tried to induce assent to the great dissent by which he had lived, or failed to live, as Colin reminded him. A faint shadow of remorse passed across Colin's feelings as he rehearsed the conversation. The fact was that he could not share the schoolmaster's vast resentment. In his heart he believed in the legitimacy of institutions: he believed in law, in ceremony, in the colourful nonsense of condign punishment. He believed in the ruling class, in privilege, in heredity and customary power. He believed in the rights of Lord Shepton, of Nigel de Litham, of the spoiled and impossible Francesca. He believed in it, as Tertullian in the incarnation, because it was absurd. Through Francesca he came face to face with the madness that lies at the heart of all legitimate order – the boiling core of contradictions, upon which the volcanic crust of stability incongruously rests.

And then a strange sight caught his eye. Sitting among the figures on the professional benches was the Inspector. He was sure it was her, although the neat black jacket and clean white blouse were abnormal, dictated not by nature but by art. Of course, it was possible that she should be there. He remembered that her job had some legal aspect. She must be waiting for some later case which required her presence. She was not looking at him, and seemed to be uninterested in the proceedings. She was even cleaning her nails, taking the little balls of dirt from the nail file and laying them carefully on a blank sheet of paper on the ledge before her. Once, Colin remembered, she had picked her nose while staring at his father's dying form. The yellow balls of snot had rained on the schoolmaster's insensible forehead, and then bounced into the tunnels of the bed. When she turned away with a snort and left the room, Colin carefully straightened the sheet, hitting away all the detritus that had gathered in them. His father stirred a little, and, seeing the weak body stretched out there, its left hand clutching the side where the cancer grew, Colin had on an impulse straightened the pyjamas too, freeing the red turkey neck from its twist of cloth. He felt the roughness of the unshaven jowls, and a strange tenderness overcame him. When the schoolmaster's hand left its station and spidered towards him over the unconscious body, he did not resist its attempts to clutch and hold. He replaced the cover gently, and sat for a while with his father's strengthless hand pressed between his thumb and forefinger. And then the schoolmaster, opening his eyes, smiled at his son, before sleeping again. Colin replaced the hand, folded back the counterpane, and stared from the window at the rank garden and the distant trees. He supposed that there were theological conceptions which would enable him to feel this sudden tenderness as a reconciling, a merciful prelude to death. No one had taught him these things and in that moment he envied Francesca, whose schooldays must have been filled with priests, with holy words, with an unworldly aroma of incense, atonement and forgiveness. The garden of the Fergusons contained no ghosts except those which died with the beholder. When the schoolmaster next opened his eyes it was to utter his short bitter laugh.

Things had been said and papers passed. Apparently his interruption had been accommodated and routine responses were again permissible. It was not the Inspector, he realised, with a certain regret. He had, in that moment, felt the desire to speak to her, and to recover one or two pieces of information that seemed particularly important. What had happened, for example, to his father's brass microscope, and to the mahogany box containing slides of pickled tissue, pressed spiders, flower stamens, and other such didactic things? Where were his school trousers? And had she remembered to plant the first annuals this month? He hoped that she did not allow Archie to sleep in the schoolmaster's bedroom. That seemed to be extremely important, and as he thought about it, Colin became provisionally indignant at the abuses of his father's memory that the Inspector might be planning.

The court was moving, the periscope had again retracted, papers were being fitted into bags and folders, a policeman tugged at his arm. As he stepped down from the box he turned towards the gallery and saw Francesca. She looked as though she were about to laugh, and her eyes were brimful of interest in some person who stood in the place that was occupied by his body. He recognised the impossibility of the thing, but smiled back at her all the same, and made a move in her direction. The policeman gripped him more firmly, and he was led from the court.

After a few brief formalities, he stepped into the street. Francesca waited in blazing sunlight. She laughed and embraced him.

'You chump! You adorable chump!'

'I think I did rather well,' he said, with dignity.

'I've got some news for you.'

Colin stood back and looked at her laughing eyes and her moist mobile lips. Her hand in the nape of his neck was cool and gentle, and she let it rest there with just the faintest suggestion of a touch.

'I know,' he said. 'I've got a job at Plumptre's. Isn't it absurd?'

'No, you fool. We are going down to Bassington.'

'To Bassington? But I don't live there now.'

'Where do you live?'

'With . . . with Judith, Mrs Blakely.'

'With me, you fool. I've cleared the study for you. Henceforth it's yours.'

'Why did you do that?'

'Because I need you there.'

'That's not a good reason.'

'It's good enough for me. I don't want to lose you, ever. And look what happens to you, as soon as I let you out of my sight.'

She laughed again.

'Then why do I have to go to Bassington?'

'Because the house is empty. For two weeks. We can have a whale of a time.'

She spoke emphatically, as though maintaining her good humour by an act of will. And the laughter bore no relation to her words. It seemed to come from some other part of her. She pressed against him, and it felt as though the spirit were not quite incarnate in her body.

They drove down in her blue Morris Minor. He watched the factories slip by, their architectural messages unread. She hardly spoke, and after a while he slept fitfully against the bouncing head-rest.

It was late afternoon as they arrived, and the yellow February sun sloped behind the Hall in a dazzle of hazy light. Colin glanced quickly at the cottage, and saw a light burning downstairs. The Hall was dark, and, as Francesca switched off the engine, a great silence enveloped them. They sat for a moment in the car, until Francesca, in a whisper, said *Te Deum laudamus*, and gently got out. Her footsteps on the gravel were like the quiet breaking of waves on shingle. She walked up to the steps, and pushed open the great dark door, which moved slowly on its hinges.

'Why isn't it locked?' he asked in astonishment.

'Never is.'

He carried their bags, hers leather-edged, soft, made from an Afghan rug, his rough, torn at the corners, and made of canvas. Francesca moved fast, melting into shadows, and he followed her in silence. Soon they were in a bedroom, full of puppets. Some were luxurious, oriental, bedecked in jewels; others were two-dimensional, dragon-shaped, in flaming colours, and mounted on sticks. Still others were eyeless heaps of rag, catatonic Petrouchkas with absent souls. There was a cupboard, a chest of drawers, a washbasin, and a threequarter-size bed covered with a patchwork quilt.

Francesca pulled him towards her. She was hot and her heart beat fast and irregular beneath his hand. She tore at the belt of his trousers and at his shirt, with three or four movements stepping out of her clothes. In the fading light she was marble-white, her outline touched with highlights, her long legs disappearing into the darkness as though they did not wholly belong to her – as though they were rooted in some other sphere. She fell onto the bed suddenly, and as she pulled him to her she covered his mouth with her hand. Afterwards she cried, and kissed him a thousand times with lips that were taut and agile like the E string of a violin. Then she laughed, a shrill, eerie, theatrical laugh, which seemed like a defiance of the empty house surrounding them.

Ten

'AND THERE was something else he did, something far worse, that I've never told to anyone.'

Francesca's eyes were burning as she twirled the wine glass between her fingers. She sat in the high leather chair of the library, and he listened from his work place, a great marquetry partners' desk. Across the front of the Hall he saw a row of leafless elms, black against the winter twilight, and the long black cowl of Offlet Hill, with the faint greyish scar of pasture just visible in its lower corner. There was no view of the cottage from the library, and all day he could stare at the landscape of his childhood from a vantage point of pure dominion. A novel was taking shape in his mind – a new version of his father's autobiography, cleansed of resentment, simple, not without love. Towards four o'clock he laid down his pen, and browsed among the books: *Gil Blas*, *The Spectator*, *Lays of Ancient Rome*. When Francesca entered after an hour or so, it was usually with an open bottle of champagne. In London she drank nothing; but since arriving in Bassington she had been half drunk at every hour of the day.

'I was just back from school, after a bad term. The nuns had fought over me. Some hated with a passion that I could understand because it was clean, sharp, detached. One loved me horribly, and wrapped her fingers in my blouse whenever we were alone together. I couldn't stand the dormitories, with their whispers, their hilarious secrets, their crush of bodies and their constant touch of hands. I would have run away, if it had not been for Sarah: she smoked pot at midnight, and lay in bed reading Shelley by torchlight until dragged out by Sister Beatrice and walloped. The harder she was hit, the more erect and disdainful she became, occasionally saying 'ouch!' as though for politeness' sake, and so as to display her distance from what was happening. She was like a beautiful statue, immune, solemn, and somehow faintly humorous. It was so amusing and so awe-inspiring to be with her. When I wanted to justify my isolation, I thought always of Sarah, and took courage from her example. Sometimes too I thought of you. But I had postponed you – you were conditional on my future, and at that time I was not convinced that I had a future. When I came back – it was the vacation after you had gone – everything in the world seemed wrong to me, except for Sarah. But she had gone to Scotland to people who were not her parents (she is an orphan). She called them her "loved ones" in order to signify the fact that she was already in her heart bereaved of them. The thing that was most wrong was the Hall. Familiar objects seemed strange to me, and things that I had never seen before were totally and eerily familiar. I discovered the pond – I mean, I had been there before, but because we never used that part of the grounds, and because of something that had happened there, they kept the door locked and let the place grow wild.'

'What had happened there?'

Francesca looked up, torn from reverie.

'Oh. Something very foolish. They quarrelled in a boat. He knocked her over and she fell in. She did not get back into the boat but swam off to the shore. It was probably an accident – in any case, they made it up in the end. Piggy saw it happen, and, years later, he told me about it, and how she had walked around the kitchen afterwards, trembling and furious. But that's not the point. It's not what he did to her that matters, but what he did to me. She matters only because she did not protect me, and sometimes I hate her for that. When I came home it was with a sense of being totally cut off from everything: they were never here, or when they were, I could not speak to them, could not approach them. They were centaurs who would gallop through my life and leave only tatters. I wanted to ask them to take me from that school, to take me out of those clouds of incense and whispers, those petty sins, those long tremolandoes of guilt over nothing, that sense of nothing made big as God and then sold off in packets at the altar. It disgusted me, in particular Mother Angelica, who was my spiritual guardian, *in loco parentis* (and if she had known them, she would have realised just how *loco* that is). She spoke in a spirit of unmitigated lewdness. She had eyes like quartz – solid, immovable, unscratchable. Her voice was a kind of baritone, and everything she said sounded dirty. Even when she was telling you to remember your parents in your prayers, you felt that her real thought was an obscene one, and she was watching you from her two glass eyes to see precisely at which moment you would blush. That gave her terrible power, and a terrible repulsiveness. I tried to tell them about this. But they would change the subject, or sometimes just walk away in the middle of my lament, since there were always more urgent things to consider. Besides, they are artists – or he is at least – and regarded my religious education largely as a training for my sense of humour.

'Something strange was happening to me. I was changing from a nervous, unformed thing, into a kind of monster. I felt my new body growing all over me like a fungus – it seemed to me that everyone around me must be observing my change. They had seen it at school. Mother Angelica had seen it, and curled up her face in a knowing smile. I could not speak to them. In my desperation I tried Françoise, my mother's old nanny, who simply said, "*Faut pas balbuiter de ça.*" I tried my mother. Some mysterious process of feeling, not in the least inspired by the *stella maris* that we had been taught to revere in our nunnish ways at school, persuaded me that you should talk to a mother about these things. It was then, as I tried to communicate my distress, that I realised that in everything save the bare minimum required for procreation, she was not related to me. Everything in her was indifferent to my survival. I was a mistake which she had once made, an embarrassing encumbrance which hampered her on the road to social triumph. She had a deep personal interest in depriving me of clues, in abandoning me on the slopes of the *Venusberg* like an infant left to the mercy of the gods. Her remarks were cold, fixing me in an icy cage of virginity from which I was to emerge by my own efforts or not at all.

'Then one day I came down for breakfast, shaking with fright. I had decided to experiment with the idea of womanhood, to discipline this new body so that at least it had the appearance of being mind. I had put on the canary yellow frock which still just fitted me, and which always made me think of you. Wearing it gave me a kind of courage, because you belonged to the future into which I was trying to launch myself. He was sitting there in his dressing gown, speaking loudly in French about someone they knew. He had a cigarette in his hand, and kept waving it in the air as he spoke, which was always a sign of aggression. I remember he was describing this person as a *petite friponne* and for a moment I wondered whether it was me that he meant. Then he saw me and stopped in mid-sentence. There was something about the way he looked me up and down which totally penetrated me: something I shall never forget. It wasn't just that he lingered over every detail that betrayed a weakness: that was his normal manner. It was something that had perhaps always been there but which became suddenly vivid to me at that moment, a kind of systematic negation of my existence. It was neither warm nor cold, neither hostile nor sympathetic: it was simply his way of recognising and dismissing the attempt that I had made. He made no remark at first; instead he asked me to ring for my breakfast. Normally I would have got my own breakfast; in asking me to ring, he was daring me to make a gesture that they had reserved for the adult world – daring me to play at being a centaur, so that I would lame myself incurably. I said I could manage, and went over to the hot plate where the coffee was. She went out and I was left alone with him; he continued to look at me in that horrible way and I felt hot and confused. I tried to drink my coffee, and spilt it over the front of my frock. I didn't dare to wipe it for fear of drawing attention to my body, so I left for my room, wanting to cry until my flesh had melted into tears.

'I had trouble with my back at the time, and the doctor had advised against riding. However, thinking I would feel better in the company of an animal, I went round the park on Arthur, my old pony. Arthur was too small for me, and his friendly jogging – always half way between a walk and a trot, or a trot and a canter – sent me bouncing up and down until the pain in my breasts was unbearable. I felt this pain as a foreboding, a warning, a sign that my body could be joined to me in no other way.

'Pain and shame prevented sleep. In the middle of the night I crept down here to the library. I don't know why I did so: maybe I was drawn by some hidden force. Maybe I was half asleep, consciously unconscious. It was quite out of character, and a further sign of how disturbed I had become. A friend of my parents was staying – a doctor called Kiss. (That was how I pronounced it, though it is a Hungarian name and rhymes with dish.) Reaching the door of the library I heard voices. Daddy and Dr Kiss were deep in conversation, and I could just see through the crack to where they sat across from each other, haloed by tobacco smoke.

'At first I didn't understand what they were talking about – it concerned a female, "she", whose body was an object of considerable interest. Then I saw in a flash that "she" was me. And I understood that I was being possessed in words, made into a thing. I was a subject for experiment, a curious torso to be pried apart scientifically. Their conversation was in that cryptic, manly idiom from which girls are by nature excluded. But a strange atmosphere of desecration arose from it, and I was gripped by fear – fear of something they were planning. And then an unfortunate thing happened. Whether I had been standing too long, or whether I could no longer bear the inner pressure, my back suddenly gave way, and I sprang like a jack-in-the box against the door. The men fell instantly silent, while I stood in the doorway, white with pain, and no doubt looking as dreadful as I felt. Dr Kiss had peculiar leathery skin, and hooded eyes like an eagle. When he looked at you it was as though he were searching for something – something which he sought in every woman, but which no woman could provide. I don't know how to express it, except in drastic terms: it was not just sex he wanted, but death. And sex and death for him were one.

'I gripped the night-gown closely, pulling it across my aching breasts, and trying to stand firm, despite my back. I even managed to apologise for intruding. Then Daddy spoke. He said they would see me through, that I would have a full life as a woman, and that I should not be afraid. He laid a peculiar emphasis on the word "woman", and I was reminded of Mother Angelica. His eyes and face seemed for an instant as hard and glossy as hers. I am not sure what happened next. I think one or other of them – maybe it was Dr Kiss – got up and came forward. Perhaps he tried to touch me. In any case I screamed. "Leave me alone," I said. I backed away as best I could, and hobbled down the corridor, shouting at them, and taking evasive action at every turn. Eventually I lost them. I found myself then in a little room which had once been part of the nursery. A child's bed stood against the wall, sprinkled with cuddly toys. I curled up there, trembling like a fugitive. Gradually the pain in my body subsided, and a kind of fitful dozing supervened, punctuated by nightmares.

'I longed then to have an older sister, sitting with me in that secret room, in whose eyes I could find blood sympathy and the concrete evidence of survival. My brother didn't count, and in any case he was always away, swanning in some villa in Barbados or trading polo ponies in the

Argentine. My mother counted even less: I couldn't look her in the eyes now. It wasn't just strength and support that I needed: I wanted proof of my existence. I carried round the letter you had written to me at school, because sometimes, looked at in a favourable light, it seemed to address me as though I were real. Every day for a year I meant to reply to it. But I believed that, until I was sure of my existence, I would only spoil everything, and make myself ridiculous in your eyes. Besides, it was already beginning to be a principle with me, that I would get through all this without you.

'The next morning I sneaked out of the house and went down to the cottage: it was absurd, because I knew you were in London and I knew that I couldn't hope to explain to you, if I saw you, these things that I couldn't explain to myself. No one answered my knocking, and I remember standing there, staring at the little garden with its neat rows of cord and stakes where things had been planted, its odds and ends of winter vegetables with methodical gaps where they had been harvested, the brown, soft, weedless earth, the little path of crazy paving. It seemed so neat, orderly, self-contained. Of course, I know more now about the dark side of your life there. But then you were a dream to me, and I couldn't imagine any suffering attached to that place. It was perfect, simple, a picture of economy. I hated the abundance of the Hall, the waste; it symbolised his inexhaustible power and his self-bestowed licence to transgress every boundary.'

Francesca got up, and walked slowly back and forth. Colin watched her in silence; that she was confiding in him, that she was totally alive for him, filling with her words the hollows of her past, that she was casting herself completely in the role of his companion – these things caused him such joy, that he was thankful for her suffering. Nor did he concern himself over-much about her story, drastic and dream-like though it was. Perhaps none of it had really happened; or perhaps it had happened in a quite different way. He did not know even whether it was love or hatred, desire or fear, which prompted her descriptions.

She sat down, poured more wine into her glass, and fell still, her chiaroscuro made visionary by the polished bindings of the books and the warm glowing leather of the armchair. Her legs stretched in front of her, touching a rug which she nervously shuffled with the soles of her running shoes. She was wound up like a spring, concentrated; the various parts of her touched at last, and in her pain she was entire. Her eyes rested on him; then on the desk, and finally on her wine glass as she extinguished her expression in its depths.

'I left your front door, trembling. I walked along the road, following the wall. It was almost impossible to believe that the park and the Hall were behind there, quietly sitting in their places. I did not really know the wall from that side: you expected it to contain mobile things – an army camp, a herd of wild animals, something terrible that had to be contained. The journey along that wall was one of the most terrifying of my life. Simply to know that they were on the other side of it, that I was compelled to go in there, and that all the same I was not compelled at all, walking in the free clear winter air of the village, where you and your father walked, towards the Post Office and the church, towards the alms houses, towards the innocent-seeming telephone boxes in which people telephoned their grandmothers or called for ambulances, towards the bus-stop where I could stand like an ordinary person and take a bus to Dunsbury – to know all this was to experience the real humiliation, the real enslavement into which they had trapped me. It was not possible for a Wimpole to run away. It was not possible for a Wimpole to take flight in the face of the ordained experiences. I had to enter at the gate, to shuffle up the gravel path, and to sit down to lunch at the stroke of one. Then, as I got to the end of the path, a strange thing happened, something that I should perhaps describe in religious terms – and which therefore I cannot properly describe, having lost my faith in the arms of Sarah. I can't speak of sin, penance, grace or redemption: nothing in those words captures either the littleness of my experience, or the sheer unaccustomed terror of it. Religious experience, however awesome, unites you with the world, calls you back into normality. What I saw then, as I walked towards the Hall, was the opposite: it divided me completely and utterly from everything that was human, from my past and future, from them, from Sarah, from you. It was like falling into a ravine, falling and falling like Alice but without the jars of marmalade. There were shelves alright: they carried bones, decaying flesh, bundled-up bodies of martyrs stowed in catacombs, with the smell of fear and burning still on their skin. The sensation passed: or rather, I fell on my feet exactly where I had been. But things were subtly different. A tree in front of me stood out. It seemed not to belong – to have intruded its presence from another dimension. Then I noticed another tree, standing away from things, refusing to be joined. Then the house, then each window of the house, the porch, each little stone. The world slowly atomised before my eyes. The metaphysical glue was dissolving, and I felt instinctively that it was I who had dissolved it. I was the solvent which destroyed everything. I annihilated the world with my poison, and now it was going to annihilate me: all those fragments were piling up around me and would crush me to death. I closed my eyes and rushed forwards: I tripped and fell; the sensation vanished. Everything was back in place again. But I had changed. I had glimpsed hell and nothingness and seen myself a part of it. Trembling like a leaf I went indoors and ran to my room.

'Lying on the bed I tried to feel safe. There were all kinds of things I could do to make me feel safe. For example, one of the puppets, called Rhadamurtha, had a soothing expression and could be spoken to. His face greeted what you said with a kind of knowing tolerance, a serene familiarity with every human fault. But this time his expression was strange, transfigured: he too seemed to have noticed my new body, and to be looking at it with distaste. I put him away, and said the *Ave Maria*, time and time again, but I was too sceptical to take comfort in those words. There was a clock on the mantelpiece of my room, and I watched the time tick away as I tried to find some meaning in my prayers. The clock frightened me; it had something to tell me, something urgent, oppressive, terrible. Then the door opened with a quiet click, and Dr Kiss stood before me, wearing a dressing gown, his legs naked beneath it. His bird eyes targeted me, and his body was possessed by need. He seemed to fall from a vast height towards the bed. I jumped back, and he said "Why be frightened?" again and again. He went on speaking, I couldn't tell about what, except that he offered some vast excuse for everything. What was happening, he implied, had been dictated by forces outside our control. We were both victims, puppets, bits of mechanism. My body seemed explicable in those terms. It was no longer a human body, it did not have desires, fears, graces, awkwardness. It was just a thrown-away thing. I had jettisoned it. Somewhere in the corner of that room my spirit coiled in a fit of renunciation. I observed his body and mine like two battling insects in an insect world, impersonal, grotesque, scraping things which had been pushed into contact by the dispassionate scientist who governs all.'

Francesca passed her hand across her brow, looked at him, and quickly looked away. Colin's chest constricted in fear at what she was about to say.

'He took off his dressing gown. That's the wrong way of describing it. The dressing gown was taken from him by an invisible hand. "Oh God": those were his words, which he spoke in a thin, scraping voice, like an insect. It was exactly as Kafka describes the voice of the transformed Gregor Samsa. And then suddenly he was on top of me, tearing, scratching, his rough cheek on mine, his tobacco-smelling breath everywhere like the searing breath of a dragon. My clothes betrayed me. I saw the dress, your yellow dress, torn and dismembered on the rug. My neck chain broke apart, and my mouth opened to let out a scream. I had no idea what this scream would sound like, because it wasn't mine. It was the scream of a doll, the scream of a speechless thing that could no longer keep silence. I think this scream had been preparing itself for years, ever since the body was first assembled. It wanted to warn him, to tell him that he was observed. A snake was coiled in that room with its poison boiling for him and for my father whose agent he was. Most of all he had to be careful not to remove those new little bits of cloth that had been stuck all over me by the commanding scientist. But his hands became larger; they absorbed everything into themselves. He only had to touch my clothes and they melted into his palms – suddenly the broken doll was naked and shapeless on the bed. And then the scream emerged.'

She paused, and the tears ran down her cheeks. She was not crying, but simply displaying to him the constant drip of penance in her soul. Colin made to get up, but she forbad him with a look.

'It was horrible. The scream emerged, took shape, became a word, and the word was "yes". It was not my word, nor was it anyone's. It was not an affirmation or an offer. It contained no acceptance, no thought of past or future. It meant that there was nothing, that the body was empty, that the soul had fled. But then his hand stifled it, and my body went limp under his weight as he forced himself into it, shaking like a dying animal. I remember nothing after that, except his form standing in the window, clad once again in its dressing gown. He was looking away from me, saying "Now you are mine," not in the tone of command or supplication, but as though stating a fact. Then he turned round and with the uncanniest touch of gentleness, covered me with the bed clothes before going out onto the stairs.

'I lay still. My mind was blank. Then the feeling came back, that had assailed me in the park. Nothing was related. Every object, every part of every object, stood in isolation. The world wasn't holding together, and I knew it was my fault. I had spread the poison of my body everywhere. I began to feel panic. The little nugget of fear inside me expanded until it filled the whole room, the whole house, the whole world. I took a shirt and some jeans and ran along the corridor to the bathroom. I washed and washed myself, thinking that water would take away the original sin of my non-existence. It was a crazy baptism, and futile, since it was not my body but the whole world that stood in need of it. Suddenly I heard my father moving in the corridor – I was sure it was him, because of the determined movement of his feet, that sense of a giant passing, indifferent to the things beneath his feet. A terrible desire to hurt him rose up in me, and it focused on the scissors that were lying there above the sink. I had the half-crazed idea that it was my father who had set Dr Kiss to do this thing, that he had chosen this method to drag me into the adult world, while remaining aloof and disdainful, knowing what I suffered. I went out in pursuit of him, the scissors jammed into the back pocket of my jeans, longing for their target. Only this act of violence could assuage my injury: only this, I imagined, could undo the desecration which had been wrought in me, and which had cut me off forever from the life which I had wanted. I saw him, turning a corner at the head of the stairs, and I ran towards him. I was pregnant with revenge, I would have killed then, I really would have done it. Only the most unfortunate thing occurred – the most miserable thing . . .'

Francesca looked up; her eyes seemed to retreat from each other, spreading themselves like nacreous pools across her temples. Colin went over to her. But her body was inert and lifeless, and he was afraid to draw attention to the arms which he placed around her shoulders.

'My back gave out again, I slipped and fell on the stairs. The scissors had been longing for flesh, and they found it at last. But it was my flesh, and I felt the sharp point of them go bumping along my spine. The last thing I saw was Daddy, stooping over me, with a look on his face of such concern that I felt I must surely be condemned for ever for having wished to murder him.'

How strange her story was; yet, even as he doubted it, he knew that it was true – not true in all its details, which were perhaps no more than symbols of the terror which had ruined her. But true nevertheless, with the truth of sacred texts, dredged up from the eternal residue of fear and suffering, given place, time and flesh like the human soul. It was a story from *Genesis*, which must be literally believed, if its unliteral truth is to penetrate our understanding. Colin kissed her brow, overcome by tenderness.

'And what happened to you?'

'Happened to me?'

Francesca looked up in surprise.

'After this, after your . . . after your hurting yourself so.'

'They patched me up of course, and it was agreed that we should agree not to speak about it. I was a prostrate form to be whispered over, the body of a holy nun miraculously covered in layers of gauze. He came, she came, the doctor came – not Dr Kiss, who disappeared, but another more abstract doctor, of the kind you get from telephone directories. And they all made polite ghastly noises, like people praying who have lost the habit. I was a nothing, a corpse. I liked the role, and could even stare through them with a glazed expression that forbad them to exist.'

Colin relinquished her shoulder, and paced about the room. He was full of hatred for the Sheptons, a joyous, exuberant hatred, made real and vital by Francesca's oneness. Beside his hatred the schoolmaster's resentment was nothing, a banner thrown down by a fleeing soldier. Colin would do great deeds, possessing her through his vengeance.

'It's a miracle you've come through,' he said. 'A miracle.'

And even as he spoke, he knew that he could not justify the hatred which excited him.

'But I didn't come through, don't you see? That's just an hypothesis of yours, one that you ask me each day to confirm. Oh I grant you that the corpse eventually raised itself from the sheets, that I gingerly unwrapped the white thing from its bandages and promised to treat it as a human body. It took some zombie-like steps towards the outer world. It even looked for you.'

'What do you mean?'

'It appeared each day at the empty cottage, and uttered lugubrious cries. But of course you were in London, and I had known that ever since receiving your letter. And then someone told me that your father too had moved, to the schoolhouse in Murricombe. Another letter came from you, forwarded from the school. I couldn't make sense of it. You seemed to reproach me for something and I could not tell what it was. I thought that perhaps you were not really in London, but had contrived to send the letter from there, so that you could meet me by surprise and restore the reality of things. I read the letter several times, treasuring all the signs that these little details of a squalid London life were really imagined, or taken from books. You see how mad my thoughts had become. I could not write to you. I just walked about the park, and the kitchen garden, and the pond, day after day.

'Until suddenly my body woke up. It became crazy with anger and hatred. It declared war on men. A resolution was made to trap them and destroy them. Only you were to be exempt. I began with Piggy. It was easy. I just had to follow him about, watch him, stand close to him, and then, within two days, I saw that he was *épris*; he would step with me just so soon as I made the gesture into the little bower that I had prepared for him. When he did it, his face became sad, and his eyes rolled upwards into his skull. There was immense satisfaction in that, seeing his face become a blank under the influence of my body. I wanted to draw a blind over every male face in just that way, to replace will and desire by a featureless screen. I made sure that Daddy discovered, and Piggy was sacked. At once I began to hunt again, with no thought at all for the consequences of my actions. All men were to be victims to me. All except you. Daddy was watching me through narrow eyes. He was sarcastic, denigratory, utterly without visible wounds. But I knew how deeply I was hurting him. His permissive ribaldries were for the sake of form only, and for the sake of form I even matched them, accompanying myself with a hollow laugh, which came from an empty and desolated heart. So it went on for a whole summer. I invaded my brother's parties – he used to come home often then – and exacted revenge at each of them, on some nameless creature who had no idea how I despised, hated and rejected him in the so-called act of love. Now you know a horrible fact about me. Colin. Have I ruined everything yet, or should I go on?'

The question hung in the air, and he did not know how to snatch it down. To say no would be to breach their imagined agreement; to say yes would be to invite the truth whereby that fiction would be destroyed. All the same, he was sick with jealousy, as though a great hand had reached inside and emptied him. But then, he reflected, perhaps this coda to the story was no more literally true than anything else she had recounted. Perhaps it too had the force of legend.

Francesca got up and embraced him.

'I couldn't live without you,' she said. 'Don't let me ruin everything.'

'You haven't and you won't. But you must forget those days.'

'I can't. All my confusion has its origins there.'

'Can't you exclude them from your life?'

'Exclude whom?'

'Your parents. The Hall. The people who torment you.'

'Do I need that kind of power?'

'Yes, you do.'

'Over you too?'

'No, not over me. I am weaponless.'

'Over Sarah?'

'What does she matter?'

'Because she rescued me from that muddle. We were together always in the next year, sitting in forbidden places, smoking forbidden things, reading to each other from forbidden books, and sometimes engaged in forbidden acts. Then it was genuine, exciting, an act of love. Except that I was overcome by it. I felt that I had filled my hollowness, but only by filling it with her. My existence was not proven, but simply negated in a new and more interesting way. So as soon as I was with her I wanted to be without her; sometimes I wanted so badly to be without her that I would even have returned to the terror of that day in the park. I have been with her and without her ever since.'

'And will you be with me and without me too?'

She did not answer but sat in silence, drinking from her glass, constantly refilling, until the bottle was empty and she was drunk. 'I am doomed,' she said, with a disclaiming giggle, as he carried her to bed.

During the days which followed, Francesca paraded her world before him. Sometimes her face would clench with anxiety; sometimes she was serene, insouciant, like a child at play. They ransacked every chest and wardrobe, dressing like children in the robes of the dead. The Hall stood back from them, observed with astonishment as they explored its undefended recesses. Why, he asked, are all these precious things so vacant, so strengthless, so dead?

'No one lives here. The Hall is kept as a monument to the Wimpoles, a family tomb. It is the proof of our non-existence.'

'But why do you come back to it? And why are we happy here?'

'Because we are ghosts among ghosts.'

She took him boating on the pond. The water shook with uncertain sunlight. Solemn clouds moved in its depths, and mud-bubbles rose fluttering through them to the surface. A breeze shook the dry branches of holly, and the sporadic sound was like a voice distantly calling. Francesca lay in the boat and looked at him, her coat wrapped tightly about her. For two hours they remained there in silence, without exchanging a smile. When he approached her there was a strange music in her body. But it came from some unconscious region, and its voice was not hers.

Each day brought some new fragment of the puzzle that surrounded her. Pondering her story as they lay together, he gently searched her body, and discovered a scar, old and almost vanished, at the base of her spine. He marvelled that he had not come across it earlier. If this blemish proved the truth of her narrative, however, it also showed how unadventurous their caresses had been. Troubled by such thoughts, he made and unmade theories, settling at last for the simplest one, which was that Francesca had been entombed by her family. Their idea of her stood like a monument above her body, preventing life and growth. He would cast it down, and coax her forth with love. The theory, which marked out such an important role for himself, was too pleasant to be easily abandoned. And he found confirmation for it in the fact that her family had ear-marked Jonathan Burridge as Francesca's future husband. Even now they were pressing her to accept an offer which the young man had made. Together they laughed at the idea; and it seemed to him that he had never been so happy as in this mockery of Jonathan Burridge.

Clinging to his theory, he felt the pain of jealousy subside. Even when Francesca revealed to him that a certain John Paluto had exhausted himself in the attempt to live with her, giving up every moment that his job as a script-writer did not take from him, in order to guide and reassure, and earning nothing in exchange besides a sour resentment, Colin's faith remained unshaken. Those earlier efforts, she assured him, were doomed from the start. It was with Colin that she was to look for her true consolation, and if she had postponed things, it was only in order to be more ready for his love. This new twist to their fairy-tale was at once confirmed as doctrine, and they alluded to it often, in order to remind it to be true. It made him, if not indispensable – since after all she might continue to believe that she had no future – at least as real to her as the possibility that she might herself be real. In this way they achieved what seemed to him to be a happy compromise. Their life together took on a form that gave sense equally to the lightest kisses and to the most solemn hesitations. They were part of each other, and if there was anything that she took from him he was glad, and saw it disappear into the darkness of her being with the cheerfulness of a mother who waves her child on its way to school.

Colin had some money; Francesca had more. They were able to buy the luxuries of Bassington Post Office, and to combine them with the meat, eggs and vegetables which appeared mysteriously each morning on the kitchen table. The trip to the Post Office was not without hazards. At one point they were clearly visible from the cottage, and although Colin never turned round, he was fairly certain that the Inspector had once been standing at the downstairs window, observing their passage and making a mental note of it. There were also acquaintances who, although they belonged to a different order of existence, and stood before them wondrously decorated in this fact, had an aspect of menacing recognition. The world might wake up to the fact that they had contracted out of it. The dissident premises of their fairy-tale would not be tolerated for long.

One day there were telephone calls; he heard her voice in distant lobbies, muffled, and intimate. At dinner she sat silent and withdrawn. He had prepared a duck, crammed full with garlic: one of the Inspector's boldest recipes. But she would not eat it, and every attempt at conversation ended fumblingly. Her hands crawled on the table-cloth like wounded animals, and her shoulders shook slightly, as though shrugging off an offence. After a long silence, she said,

'My brother is coming.'
'Your brother – why?'
'No particular reason. He wants to give a party.'
'A party!'
It seemed like the grossest outrage, a violation of their

privacy, an insult to the Hall.

'Yes. On Friday. When is that? Tomorrow? I forget.'

She was not looking at him. He noticed an uncanny detail. On her embroidered blouse, scarcely hidden by the blue chiffon which covered her neck, was the brooch of a pig in pink enamel. He had not seen this ornament since their first encounter, and the sight of it destroyed his confidence immediately. She was telling him that nothing had changed since those days, that she was still the property of the Hall, obedient to its iron imperatives, just as he was excluded from their jurisdiction.

'Tomorrow,' he said. 'But why?'

'I had forgotten. We always make a splash at this time of year.'

'We? You mean you and your brother?'

'I mean the Wimpoles. Only generally the guests are mine.'

'Are your parents coming?'

He made the question huge and accusing, but she did not answer it. In any case, the fault was his. He had neglected festivals, just as he had refused every routine outside himself. Suddenly he was appalled by the self-absorption of his love. Whoever provides custom and law, he knew, also offers permanence. And in this, as in everything, he could not live by his knowledge.

'We cannot see them! Surely we cannot see them!'

'Oh but yes and yes and yes, you fool. Do you think I'm going to enjoy it?'

She took his hand. He contemplated the pale white wrist, and then transferred his gaze to the other hand. Her little bones moved under the skin, gently displacing the bluish veins. At these times of misunderstanding he felt so much awe of her body that her touch disturbed him. She was like an exquisite mechanism, the creation of infinite patience and concentrated thought, and although somewhere in that mechanism a vital part had been wrenched out of order, to handle her was a privilege to which he was not really entitled.

She freed her hand and raised it to her face.

'Colin,' she whispered, 'it is bound to catch up with me from time to time. But it passes on. You know what I feel about them, and about the life they made me lead. I have had to live at a speed that was not my own. Whether I was propelled at maximum velocity across continents or whether I was stuck under close observation at home, it was all the same: I was trapped in a time that was not mine. It was like being separated by an epoch from everything around. I would go into my garden in order to watch things move and grow at the speed that was natural to them. Something of their rhythm rubbed off onto me. I felt myself joined to the world at last, a necessary link in the chain of cause and effect. That is the feeling I have with you, and if I can go on having it, even in the midst of them, won't that be a triumph?'

'But what of me? What am *I* to feel?'

'It's true, I am afraid for you.'

Colin went drunk to bed. He lay awake, breathing the peculiar smell of the Hall – a smell of beeswax polish, soap and emptiness – and waiting for her to come to him. But she was off in some distant corner and the next morning he awoke to find himself alone, his head aching. He had a vague memory of Francesca's form, as it hovered in the darkness. He lay for a while in bed, aware that the Hall had changed. In place of the dream-like void, he sensed a plenitude of life, hidden, busy and malevolent. There were movements, and voices; things were being shifted and rearranged, like scenery. A man was giving instructions, softly and confidently, while something heavy, soft and cornerless was dragged from room to room. Outside a car swished on the gravel and pulled up sharply with a creak of the brake.

Colin stood listening at the canvas-covered door of the room. A malign spirit, driven away by their days of love, had seized some unguarded moment and rushed back to its rightful dwelling place. He looked at the unmade bed, on which a patchwork quilt lay crumpled like a woman raped. From an oval portrait stared the face of a French marquise:

her smile, which had ten times welcomed him to bed, now seemed sharp and supercilious, sparked into acid vigilance. He stared at her and she, cold, contemptuous and invulnerable, looked back in mockery. He went into the corridor with a sheepish tremor of the legs, as though expecting her to laugh.

The first person he came across, as he made his way through the great downstairs, was Sarah. She was dressed from top to toe in glistering pink, with a pink ribbon in her hair, a pair of pink leather boots, strapped by pink laces which continued criss-crossing the pink stockings on her thighs, to the point where a shirt of pink satin barely concealed their juncture.

'The eternal husband,' she said, and gave him a pink kiss from her sticky lips.

She walked on casually, and, reaching a door, turned to address him.

'There's a letter for you. Recorded delivery. A summons, I suppose. I didn't bring it.'

Colin went into the park, towards Francesca's garden. The little gate was locked, and he walked along the wall, letting his hand hit from time to time against its surface, and trailing his feet through the long grass that clumped at its base, where the motor mower had conceded the ground to nature. The wall turned at one point, and seemed to break ranks, stuttering in irregular steps towards a hollow where it was lost in trees. Further on it rose again, towards the crest of a sheep-studded hillock, to join the outer wall of the estate. That wall, which he had seen from the other side in childhood, and which had then seemed like the permissive guardian of the most precious treasures, appeared now as the bastion of a prison. The Hall had turned against them. They had been discovered, and their fairy-tale was blown: the proof of his existence, like the proof of hers, now lacked the essential premises.

Colin looked down into the hollow, and watched for a

while the sideways shifting of a raven in the top of a denuded beech tree. Saxon furrows striated the little hillock, and hedgerows crossed at the corner, where two neighbouring tithe-lands must once have been joined. The rush-fingered patch in the hollow would be the mark of a former watering place. Looking at the landscape with the schoolmaster's possessive intellect, he could make out the history which accused the Wimpoles of their usurpation, and he was glad now to blame them as he turned back to the house.

Behind the wall, he heard voices – soft, quick and in conclave. They seemed to come from Francesca's garden, darting bird-like over the wall and back again before he could catch a meaning. Then they were gone and the air was still. Approaching the gate he heard them again, nearer now. He stopped in his tracks; the key turned in the lock and the hinges of the gate began to squeal.

'But how long has it been going on?'

It was a man's voice, polished and languid.

'Not long,' Francesca replied. 'In a sense. But – oh!'

Colin looked at her; her eyes met his and seemed to falter. Here was the boundary between their worlds, the impassable wall of steel. He had been hoping to find her on his side of the barrier, but if she discussed him with her family, that was because she still belonged with them.

Her brother was tall, broad, older than both of them by a few years. His hair was thinning at the temples, and there played about his greenish eyes the same slightly sarcastic look that Colin remembered in Lord Shepton. He did not smile until Francesca introduced them, as Colin Ferguson and my brother Bob. The limp hand permitted Colin's grip, and then instantly withdrew. Colin fell in step beside them. There was a silence, during which he debated with himself whether to call Francesca's brother Robert or Bob. This debate was entirely futile because he realised in time that Robert or Bob would give him no opportunity to call him either. He continued talking in a monotone to Francesca, about securities, investment premiums, and the need to press ahead with the development of Offlet Hill, leaving her no space for a reply and conducting the conversation as though for the benefit of a meeting of shareholders among which she alone was without a vote. Colin walked uneasily beside them, until at last her brother addressed him, staring above Colin's head at a celestial event which it was Bob's or Robert's exclusive privilege to observe.

'You are a writer.'

The statement was irrefutable. Any further information that Colin might care to offer would be considered for inclusion, but there was no doubt that the dossier was already more or less complete.

'Yes. A righter of wrongs.'

There was a silence, and Colin, agitated by Francesca's gaze, tripped over the outgrowing root of a beech tree. He tottered, and then pulled himself back into marching position.

'Yes,' he continued, 'the habit was instilled into me at an early age. Everything that gave me pleasure as a youth was small, vulnerable and – judged from your point of view – rather depressing. The care for such things was urged on me by my father. When you were talking about me just then, probably Francesca mentioned my father. For him the smallest things were the most real. If you looked at the public world, at politics, society, establishment, then you no longer saw the truth of things – such was his view. He had the conviction, absurd in its way, that there was more history, more humanity, more real legitimate power contained in a properly made paving stone than in the Bank of England, the stock exchange and Lloyds all wrapped together. Curious. And so to him, there was a deep injustice in the heart of things. I wrote about this in his autobiography, with the intention of turning the world, in his eyes, the right way up again. I don't know if you understand what I am saying?'

'Not much,' said Bob or Robert rudely. Colin laughed and they walked on in silence. Entering the house, Colin stepped aside from the scullery door to let them pass;

Francesca looked enigmatically back at him, and then disappeared.

For the rest of the morning Colin hid from her, in the sparsely furnished bedroom next to the one now haunted by the marquise. He heard her go in there once, and move around, as though looking for something. He kept still, like a hunted animal. But he knew that she sensed his presence, and when the gong sounded for lunch, and there was a gentle tap at his door, he was surprised to hear her voice, whispering in the corridor.

'We assemble in the drawing room,' she said. 'In two minutes.'

He went to the door, but she had already disappeared, taking the back stairs into the unknowable regions from which he was excluded.

In the drawing room he was greeted by Harold Plumptre, who clapped a large red hand on his shoulder.

'Watcher old sport. Rather thought I'd be seeing you here. Missed you at the office. Looking forward to your trial and subsequent imprisonment. I have a friend doing time at the moment – a regular, upgrade sort of chap. I'll give you a letter of introduction. Food's not up to much, but they allow books to be sent in. You can even read for an external degree.'

Lady Shepton approached, bearing a small poised head beneath her trim grey hair. She expressed the hope that Colin had enjoyed the silence of her husband's ancestors. On the whole he had; she spoke to him about something which he had written and which had interested her. Her grey eyes fixed him with a firm, gracious, private look, and when she made her way daintily away into the throng, he was left with the impression that, despite being Francesca's secret enemy, she was also his dear protective friend. Lady Shepton seemed to talk to everyone with an easy assumption of equality. Her manner implied that each guest had some distinction or talent, and that it was this, rather than any relation to Francesca, which defined and justified the gathering. Her passing allusion to his writings was a reminder that he need not explain himself; his credentials had been noted and henceforth he could behave as he pleased.

Sarah came to speak to him. Nigel de Litham passed by, and scrutinised him sardonically through the empty frame of a monocle. Other dimly remembered figures appeared, and then disappeared, emerging before him like painted figures on a scroll. Jonathan Burridge was there, squeezing the arms and kissing the cheeks of pretty girls; so too was the architectural historian, who nosed about in a distant corner, as though in pursuit of evidence. People who had come and gone in Francesca's house were now assembled, facing each other from animated faces, and dancing in and out of the throng. Francesca came, was kissed hungrily by everyone – and ran out again, her face wilfully animated. He followed her into the dining room, where she was moving in an agitated way around the enormous table, picking up place cards, and leaning them against the episcopal napkins which sat in judgement before every chair.

'Just think,' she said without looking at him, 'they wanted me to sit next to that awful Nigel de Litham, and you were going to be stuck with Candy Carter on one side and Dr Angela Meadowes on the other. But I want you next to me.'

Lord Shepton entered, and stood for a moment beneath the broken pediment of the door, watching his daughter blankly. She continued to arrange the cards, then, looking up, said,

'Daddy, this is Colin. You have met before.'

Lord Shepton rolled his eyes briefly in Colin's direction, then back to Francesca. Pivoting slowly on his heels, he left the room.

'Stay here,' Francesca whispered. But Colin broke free of her feeble grip and walked to the door. He could not see Lord Shepton, and his wanderings in the corridor, among silent duchesses and bold upstanding imps with buckled swords, became increasingly aimless. What he had noticed, he concluded, was not Lord Shepton, but a ghost, conjured by

Francesca's fear of it.

He found himself in a small room, which must have been an annexe to the library. Disintegrating books covered the walls, and were stacked in heaps on the floor. The only light entered through a small leaded window and fell in a grey lozenge at the centre of the room, where a figure stooped over a Davenport, turning the pages of a folio volume. It was Francesca's brother, who look up slowly. Less handsome than his father, but with the same imperious stare, and flared, contemptuous nostrils, he struck a pose of provisional anger.

'Come in, and close the door,' he said, after a moment.

Startled into obedience, Colin closed the door and stood to attention.

'I'm glad I've caught you,' Robert went on, as though they met by some effort of his own. 'There is something I want to say to you.'

'I'm expected for lunch,' Colin answered.

'It can wait. God knows why Francesca arranged this do.'

'I was told you had a part in it.'

'In that case you have been misinformed. Do I look as though I belong with my sister's courtiers?'

Robert's eyes were fixed ahead of him, staring over Colin's head.

'Didn't you come here for the party?' Colin asked.

'I came here to prevent it. Or at least, to minimise the damage.'

Colin stared hard into Robert's face.

'And is that why your father came?'

'My father moves in mysterious ways. He arrived several days ago.'

'Impossible!' said Colin 'I would have heard.'

He remembered, however, that Francesca had kept him away from the West Wing of the house.

'My father's presence is never detected against his will.'

Colin suspected Robert of playing with him, seeking to undermine his last scrap of confidence. But his steady unnerving stare, and the cool indifference conveyed by his every word, at last persuaded Colin that Robert meant what he said. A group of people ran past in the corridor, and the sound of their laughter was like a sudden crash of breaking glass.

'So you have been staying here?'

Robert's tone seemed more resigned than accusing.

'Yes. As Francesca's guest.'

'A rather special guest.'

'I like to think so,' said Colin angrily.

'I imagine you do. And I imagine you look at Sarah Germ and Harold Plumptre and Nigel de Litham and all the other dwarfs and cripples and you say to yourself "Thank God I'm something special. Thank God I'm not one of them." But the fact is, she collected you just as she collected them.'

'Perhaps you are bound to collect rubbish if you have lived with it from birth.'

Robert smiled grimly.

'As a matter of fact I agree with you. We are rubbish. With the exception of my mother, the Wimpoles are a breed of selfish neurotics.'

'Speak for yourself,' said Colin, who summoned in his memory the little occasions when Francesca had favoured him with some generous gesture. He had to admit that they were not many.

'I do speak for myself,' Robert continued. 'That's why I know what Francesca's going through.'

'What do you mean?'

'My sister is very unhappy. I suppose you realise that.'

Robert looked down at the folio volume and began slowly to turn the pages. With his tweedy clothes and rigid demeanour, he seemed strangely Edwardian, like the illustration from some *Boy's Own* morality. And yet his words were cynical, undeceived and modern: words of a spirit which knows nothing sacred, and to which nothing in the world had been denied.

'Francesca's fine,' Colin said, 'so long as she's allowed to be.'

'That's exactly what I think,' said Robert. 'I am therefore prepared to make you an offer.'

'An offer?'

'Yes. A generous offer, though I know you would be doing us a favour in accepting it.'

Colin felt a hot rush of anticipated injury, and at once the schoolmaster was beside him in his thoughts, rehearsing the grievance of the Fergusons and inciting him to join the ancient cause.

'Are you talking of money?'

'I'm talking, to be precise, of a thousand pounds.'

'And what am I to do for this thousand pounds?'

'That's up to you. Provided you do it with someone else.'

'You mean,' said Colin, after a moment's thought, 'that I am to get out of Francesca's life?'

'I didn't wish to put it so crudely,' said Robert, who continued to turn over the pages of the book, as though they contained official memoranda which would justify, were he to bother to refer to them, his naturally insolent manner.

'I don't see how you could put it any other way.'

Robert closed the book at last, and took a long, tired breath.

'The offer stands, in any case. Needless to say, I have not discussed this with Francesca.'

'How very decent of you. What a superhuman measure of respect for her that shows. I shall always be grateful to you.'

He tried to imitate a contemptuous laugh, but managed only a hoarse, breathless cackle, which reminded him of the schoolmaster. Somewhere in the corridor the cackle was repeated more timidly. Colin felt a weight on his chest, and began to struggle for breath. He groped behind him for the door-handle and was startled to touch something cold, smooth and flesh-like – hard but polished like Francesca's hand. With a gasp he turned, expecting to find her. The door was veneered with leather bindings, and it was one of these that his fingers touched.

Colin gripped the handle and turned back to Robert.

'As a matter of fact,' he said, 'I have other plans.'

'No doubt,' said Robert unperturbed. 'You wish to remove her from *our* influence. But you will not succeed. And as I say, the offer stands.'

Colin found his way to the luncheon room. Francesca waited at the door, her face lined and knitted like the face of a cone.

'Thank God you're back,' she whispered. She raised a hand to touch his lips, and the tender gesture arrested him.

All the guests were assembled, most of them were drunk. Lord Shepton was not among them, nor was his wife. An old priest, in antique canonicals, wearing gaiters and spats on his tottering legs, recited a Latin grace, turning to one of the empty chairs as though addressing the invisible presence of God himself.

Deus est caritas, et qui manet in caritate in Deo manet, sic Deus in nobis, et nos maneamus in Ipso.

'Amen,' said Nigel de Litham, to muted applause. Francesca pulled Colin into the room, and sat him down at her side. She looked down at her plate in silent meditation. Colin tried to talk to his other neighbour – a young girl who wore a safety-pin through her alabaster ear, and who replied to everything he said with a single word, pitched now high, now low, and which sounded like 'freegs'. Across from them Sarah was uttering a spirited defence of her homosexuality. Lesbian love, she argued, enables narcissism to flourish in an atmosphere of domesticity, and so leads to a truly mutual emotion, subject and object being one and the same. As she spoke her eyes danced with the joy of intellectual triumph, and the worldly old priest shook his finger in mock reprobation. Nigel de Litham sat silently, wearing the unchanging snarl of Pongo, who had nestled somewhere beneath the table, indifferent to the world. Harold Plumptre feigned sleep, leaning his head on Sarah's shoulder.

The food was served by two ancient women in aprons. Approaching Francesca, one of them suddenly put her plate of meat on the table. Leaning forward, she gave a squeeze to Francesca's shoulder, and shook it a little in a comradely way. Without raising her eyes, Francesca placed her hand on the servant's hand and held it there.

'Lovely to see you, darling,' said the woman.

'And you, Mrs Mowbey.'

'The language of *Faust*,' said Harold, who was awake now and putting up his hand as though requesting an audience, 'is the language of Heine, and Meine, and Keine, and Reiner and Steiner, of Leine and Weiner, and of kleine, feine Beine.'

He roared with laughter, and collapsed again on Sarah's shoulder.

Sarah looked pointedly at Colin.

'Has Robert button-holed you yet?' she asked. 'Told you that we are all dwarfs?'

'Not exactly,' Colin began, and then stopped in confusion.

'I object, in any case,' Sarah went on. 'I am no dwarf but a moral cripple, and it's wrong to make remarks about cripples.'

'Freegs!'

Colin's neighbour caught Sarah's attention for the first time.

'Yummee!' she said, and, pushing Harold from her shoulder, leaned across the table to kiss the girl's mouth.

Francesca began to speak in a rapid undertone.

'My brother's right,' she said. 'They are dwarfs. And I'm the same. The Germans have a word for it: *Maskenfreiheit*. It's the only freedom I achieve. Except that, with you I have no mask – you know that, don't you? With you therefore, I am not free. You should do as he says. Get out of this, while you can.'

'Do you want me to?'

Francesca replied by describing her days with Paluto, days

of squalor, lassitude and wasted time: futile days, which had left only a legacy of hatred. She spoke softly, rapidly, and without expression; Colin could hardly hear what she said through the riot that surrounded them. He could not stop his ears to a speech of Harold's on the contrasting versions of *Walpurgisnacht*, nor to another from Sarah on the sexual life of cripples. It was as though Francesca required this explosion of surrounding nonsense, in order to negate the meaning of her words.

Robert appeared in the doorway, and glanced at the guests as would a farmer at a barn-full of pigs. A look passed between him and Francesca, who suddenly rose from the table in mid-sentence and streaked from the room. Robert extended an arm to guide her through the doorway, and then left in tweedy good order. Stupefied, Colin fixed his eyes on Harold, who eased the yellow waistcoat which belted his stomach, and administered a pinch of goodwill to Sarah.

'Does temptation require a tempter?' he asked, to no one in particular, 'or misleading a misleader? I put it to you, dear girl,' he added, turning to his neighbour on the other side – a wan, blank beauty in a lichen-green concoction which flowed over table, chair and carpet, melting everywhere into its surroundings like a bank of moss. Feeling Harold's pinch, the dress rustled slightly, and then settled again.

'Haven't seen you in print of late,' Harold went on, leaning across to Colin.

'No.'

'Working on something big?'

'No.'

'I see. Other things on your mind.'

Harold looked thoughtful.

'Declare ye in Egypt,' said Sarah, 'and publish in Migdol, and publish in Noph and in Tahpanes, and in Faber and Faber, saying, stand fast and prepare thee, for the sword shall devour round about thee.'

'Impressive,' said Harold, as he stroked his chin, and 'Freegs!' added Colin's neighbour.

'But what lesson in it for Ferguson, I ask?' Sarah blinked theatrically. Her pink-smeared eyelids draped across her eyes like naughty knickers in a window.

'There's one way to survive what you're going through,' said Harold. 'Observe it and write it down.'

'He's bang right, old man,' added Sarah.

'You take my advice. Sarah, Nigel, Jonathan, Pongo, Harold, Francesca – we're all fictions; characters in search of an author. So you go quietly up to that library, gather your papers into a neat little bundle, and out you go on tiptoe, through the marble vestibule, onto the portico steps and away down the ribbon of gravel, to some lonely attic far away.'

Harold looked at him with melancholy eyes.

'Maybe you're right,' said Colin, and a chill feeling of despair ran through him. Harold promptly resumed his monologue, in strident competition with Sarah.

Colin rose and wandered in the corridor. At one point he came across Lord Shepton, standing in a shaft of sunlight. Colin hurried past to the library. His papers had been disturbed, and he could not find the last page of his father's autobiography. He left the house through the scullery, following the path along the windows of the luncheon room. The voice of Sarah rang out on the air, bell-like and serene.

'Hear, oh earth: behold, I will bring evil upon this people, even the fruit of their thoughts, because they have not hearkened unto my words, nor to my law, but rejected it.'

The cottage glowed in the last sunlight, its slate roof glistening with melted frost. A figure stood in the garden, bent, troubled and alone. Colin hurried towards him, home after many years.

Eleven

THE GARDEN of the cottage had been paved over; a new fence of white palings divided it from the road. Lace curtains disgraced the upper window, and the window-frames were freshly painted. Colin stood outside himself, watching the creature who knocked. It was Archie who came round from the garden. His astonishment gave way to an awkward deference, as he showed Colin into the kitchen. There were signs of a new domestic order: linoleum of grey and black squares covered the floor, and one of the Inspector's watercolours hung above the table. It showed Archie's cart strangely discomposed into black cubes, and surmounted by a Guernica horse in a screaming orange. Archie filled the enamel kettle and placed it on the Aga. He pointed Colin to an empty windsor chair.

'Change a bit since you last bin.'

He look unhappily at Colin, so as to convey the thought that it was none of his doing. Colin nodded.

'Is my father's room still empty?'

Archie rubbed his nose pensively.

'I don't know as she has any definite use for it.'

He began to spoon quantities of black powdery tea into the pot.

'How is she?' Colin asked. Through the window he contemplated the wall of the estate, and the tips of the cedar branches moving quietly above it.

'Ain't too bad. Likes the work. Often wonders what you're up to.'

Archie sat down, and returned to his normal posture, with head down, and large red hands hanging into his lap out of the ravelled sleeves of an old tweed jacket.

'No good is the simple answer.'

Archie nodded as though this were a perfectly acceptable instance of known permutations.

'Actually, she was wondering whether you would be coming back.'

'I am back.'

'I mean to stay like. It being your father's house and that . . .'

Archie petered out in embarrassment. If there were a way back to his father now, then he would take it. And if there were a way not to see Francesca – in particular a way which would ensure that every now and then he might see her against his will – then he would take that too.

'Do you think she would mind if I stayed tonight, in my father's room?'

'Don't matter, do it, if she mind or if she don't mind. The place is yourn.'

Archie glanced at Colin; his grey eyes for a moment lit up with the recognition of a moral truth. And then he subsided into the position that was naturally his.

'I don't want to intrude.'

Colin asked himself whether this elaborate courtesy towards Archie were feigned or real. He decided that it was real. A satisfying theory of his own integrity lay at the heart of this decision, and he clung to it, unwilling to examine the premises. Archie merely looked at him and let his hands move along the greasy cloth of his trousers.

'You see, maybe you live here now. And maybe I'm upsetting the arrangements.'

Archie turned to the window.

'Naw. Got me cart still. Only Flossie got took ill, an' she 'ad 'er put down.'

'*She* did?'

'Said she can't bear to see nothing suffer, be it man or

'orse. Carting was my hoccupation. So there we are. I'm done with it. Retired. Out to grass.'

'But where?'

'They let me to keep the cart up on Offlet's. There's a bit of ground as was marked up for 'ouses, only 'slordship changed 'is mind. They'd already brought the water, and it ain't far from the road. I comes down 'ere though, most days.'

Archie finished his speech and nodded, several times, so as to confirm it. The Aga let out a little puff of smoke from a cracked joint in the flue, and the smell of burning coal filled the kitchen. Colin sat for a while in silence.

'You need to repair that flue,' he said at last.

'Yes, only she likes the smell of smoke.'

'Does she now,' said Colin.

'Yes,' said Archie, benignly, 'reminds her of childhood. So she says.'

They sat for a while without speaking. And then Colin enquired what Archie thought about Offlet Hill. The enquiry led to another, and to another, until the whole question of political order was raised. Archie felt that there was too much power in the hands of those with houses, and not enough in the hands of roving folk. Some people thought it was a crime to be on the move. But someone had to collect things from those that didn't want them, and to make them available at a reasonable price to those that did. Colin listened amiably, his attention only half engaged. He concurred with Archie's sentiments, was particularly scathing of the power wielded by Lord Shepton, and after a while they settled down to a cup of tea on the understanding that they agreed about all matters of consequence in their common search for a just political order.

When the Inspector came, she greeted Colin calmly as though he had never left.

'Bugger,' she said. 'I shall have to go down to the shop.'

Colin noticed the absence of the dog. He learned that it too had died, so that Archie's loss was matched by Harriet's and their union was without impediment. Over their evening meal of cauliflower cheese and bottled beer, the Inspector and Archie settled into a trance of complicitous solipsism, and Colin sat apart also, in his own impenetrable sphere of solitude. A kind of peace attached to this negation of love. Here was a kingdom without commitments, established in his father's lost domains. The Inspector offered Colin a small cigar, and suggested that there was no insuperable objection to his staying overnight in his father's room. She threw some cleanish-looking sheets through the door onto the bed, and took a quick distracted look around the room.

'Needs a sweep,' she said.

Colin's body lay on the bed where it had been conceived with all the cool fortitude of St Lawrence on his grid. Like the saint, he turned only once, and with an irony calculated to impress his tormentors with the true significance of their actions. He stared about him with the lordly composure of the martyr, and his father's world wriggled uncomfortably. The wallpaper struggled to avoid his gaze, and even the maps experimented with alien shapes, appearing sometimes as books, sometimes as model towers or squat cathedrals; and through all this metamorphosis he, god-like, pursued them with impartial justice. Only one place escaped his attention – the engraving of Bassington Hall which hung above the bed. When his eyes strayed in its direction he ordered them back into line, and conjured some image of his childhood through which to control them. It was while he was engaged in one of these elaborate diversions, isolated and unhappy on the football pitch at school, the teacher blowing a brass whistle to summon him and a horrible wetness streaming over face and neck, that the door opened and Francesca stepped in.

'You *are* here,' she said, her voice soft but purposeful.

The energy of her presence terrified him.

'No I'm not,' he tried. He considered running to the window and jumping into the cabbages. This absurd image stayed with him for a while; he asked himself whether the window were wide enough, whether he should stay to grab his slippers and dressing gown, whether he might even have time to hurl a few books down in front of him, whether the cabbage patch still existed beneath his father's window, or whether it too had been paved over by the Inspector. His mind became dizzy with irrelevances and his will to resist dissolved. Francesca knelt astride his body and gripped him by the shoulders. He detached her hands but they grappled with his, and stayed locked in his fingers. The softness of her flesh excited him, and he opened his eyes. There was blood on her lips.

'What have you done?' he asked, and touched her mouth at the corner.

'I bit my tongue. In a temper.'

'With me?'

'With myself, of course. And with them.'

There was a silence, during which she rocked back and forth above him, her hands locked in his.

'I'm not seeing you again,' he said at last. 'I mean I don't want to.'

'I wonder about that.'

She tried to kiss him, and he pushed her away. She wept a little, and he wept too. She fell onto his breast, and he pushed her away. She fell again, and he lay still, frozen, avoiding signs of life.

'We must go,' she whispered.

'You go. I'm staying. I like it here. This is my home.'

He chuckled, and the sound remained him of the schoolmaster.

'No Colin. I have decided. You will forgive me, I know you will. I believe in you, more than you know, more than I can say. We'll go away somewhere. We'll settle down. You'll forgive me. I've got it all worked out.'

He shifted slightly beneath her weight.

'You frighten me Francesca.'

'I know. I frighten myself.'

An owl hooted across the park, and another, more distant, answered it with a fluttering call.

'Do you hear them? They are the furies. Our family curse. No good can come of me, you see, unless I stay with you. You know that.'

'But what about me? Have you ever thought of that? How am I to live?'

'With me. Happily. And we start tonight. I've got Daddy's car downstairs – I borrowed it. We can go now.'

'Where?'

'Back home. To London. I've got it worked out. You'll see.'

She rose up and tried to lift him bodily from the bed. He feigned death, and finally she let go of him.

She knelt by the bed and hid her face in the blankets. He stroked her hair, and she looked up at him imploringly.

'Please, please, Colin, come with me. I can't order you. But I have no hope if you leave me. I shall prove to you that I love you. I shall do everything – everything.'

She got up quickly and stood in the centre of the room, her legs slightly apart, rocking back and forth in her running shoes as though gathering energy for their journey. Colin studied her with amazement. He felt that he had seen four or five people that day in Francesca's body, each portrayed with histrionic brilliance by a single actor, and if he said yes to the present one he was not at all clear whether his answer would also bind him to the others. There seemed to be nothing to do, however, except to follow her. He got up from the bed and began to dress. His mouth was dry, and he went over to the sink in the corner. The single brass tap no longer turned, and the sink was full of cobwebs.

'There's a bottle of champagne in the car. Also I loaded your things into it. I couldn't find your papers. Harold said you must have collected them yourself.'

'But how will we live?'

'That's easy. I've got some money.'

'Your father's money.'

'No! My *own* money.'

She went to the window and pulled back the lace curtains. She was humming quietly, and stared out across the park with a look that was almost serene.

The great black car whispered along the lanes, fitting itself between the high hedges like the calm hand of a surgeon. The moonlit trees fanned out before them, the little glitter of their frosty branches like a dance of spirits in the air above. Francesca drove in silence, her hands firmly attached to the wheel. He watched her face, expressionless, responding to the road as though guided by an unseen puppet-master. His feelings came together in a sustained discord of dread.

Colin left his desk. Every word that he had brushed against had fled from him. For weeks now he had been sitting before blank sheets of paper, turning the pages of books which he no longer fathomed. The afternoons at the College of Law were some relief, and he concentrated well as he sat in the crammed lecture hall, between Nigel the fishmonger and Jennifer the teacher of Greek, his thoughts focused on his future independence. But for the present he had nothing of his own, besides the small honorarium with which Harold Plumptre rewarded his weekly attendance at Plumptre's of Threadneedle Street. There he would impose, in the panelled office of the deputy manager (exports), logical and grammatical discipline upon the thoughts of the deputy manager (exports). Harold's thoughts ranged widely, from marginalist economics and the history of the joint stock company to sexual comportment, Baudelaire's prose poems, and the dialectic of Hegel. However, all themes were held together by the single one of *Faust*, from which quotations would be drawn, ideas lifted, and a general aura of literary distinction and imaginative power distilled, in the interests of the Plumptre persona. The thoughts came to Colin on a recorded tape, interspersed with pauses longer than themselves, and occasionally punctuated by burps, farts and gurgles, as Harold's overworked digestion heaved them to the surface of his being. As Colin transcribed and embellished them, he looked out from the Edwardian room at the sprawling badlands of the city, where skyscrapers of steely glass were beginning to make their appearance. Harold and he shared a common destiny, a common isolation from the new world that was springing up everywhere in the ruins of England. If Francesca had a meaning, it was because she had come to him from that other world – the old world of class, country, and inheritance in which the schoolmaster had dug out his little nest of comfortable resentments. And Francesca was no more able than was Colin to translate her being into this new, ethereal, order – this harlequinade of aspects in which change alone was permanent.

Colin walked twice about the room which had been designated as his. His trunk lay open on the floor, exposing the rumpled clothes and the books which were his sole authentic possessions. From the window he could see Francesca's garden. They had returned here six weeks before, after crashing Lord Shepton's Rolls in Ealing, and riding a minicab through the sick green light of a suburban dawn. She had told him that all would be well, that every detail had been meticulously rehearsed, and that he could not be happier, or more creative, than with her. For a few hours they had slept in the cocoon of this new delusion.

Colin pushed the unwritten pages together and threw them into the trunk. He hesitated before going out, uncertain as to what his next move should be. In truth he was without plans, and was carried along with the flotsam of Francesca's entourage knowing only that the lifeline, when it was thrown, would not be thrown for him. The stairs of the house were always haunted now by voices, and often a broken glass, or a dead bunch of flowers, lay crushed on one of the steps. In the living room Francesca was sitting in a black leather armchair. Another form, its features hidden in billowing folds of crêpe de chine, was spread on the couch, blowing smoke rings towards the ceiling.

'Six miles beneath the surface of the sea,' Sarah

murmured, picking up a wine glass from the floor and twirling it above her face in a fit of meditation, 'nothing has eyes. Yet everything crawls about much as we do, eating and being eaten, attacking and being attacked, and making, or receiving, love. Without eyes all this seems futile. Yet several of the blind people who appear from time to time on the surface of the earth testify to pleasures of the flesh, and locate the meaning of love in the nose and the fingertips, through which the recipient is sniffed and palpated like a piece of dough.'

Francesca stared towards the window, and Colin moved vaguely about in front of her, hoping that she would notice him and speak. The new cat was lying upside down on the chest of drawers. Someone – perhaps the street poet who had appeared and disappeared the night before – had written *fuck me* in red marker ink on its milky stomach. The cat purred as loudly as Sarah.

'Why don't we wash that cat?' he asked.

Nobody answered. Suddenly the thought of washing a cat revolted him. He imagined it squealing and scratching in the bowl, throwing up soap-flakes in his eyes, its wild unseeingness everywhere.

'In the stratosphere,' Sarah continued, 'the organs of sense are further reduced. In a state of weightlessness all touch is without significance and felt only after the event and when it is not to be remedied. Nothing presents an obstacle, so nothing can be overcome. The delights of pursuit, evasion, modesty and rape – all are unknown. Eating is hazardous and slithery. Each time you close your teeth on your victim the impact sends him quietly on his way, moving in a straight line until impeded by some other force, such as contact with a victim of his own. Destruction must inevitably proceed by the smallest gradations, and most creatures move with parts of their bums and shoulders bitten off, the process of their ingestion unfinished. Love-making has yet to be attempted.'

'I am going out,' he said.

Francesca's eyes turned slowly in his direction, and then remained fixed on some point beyond him, rendering him transparent, a diagram of veins and nerves.

'I won't be back till late,' he added.

'Time is not, as some think, a constant,' said Sarah. 'On the contrary, it varies from person to person and from place to place. There is the time of gardens on a summer afternoon, slowly, sadly turning back on itself, becoming murky and coagulated after tea. There is the time of the pensioner, ticking obtrusively on the mantelpiece, and marching jerkily between post and tote. There is the time of the lover, slithering in the tunnel that leads to the womb, working against the current, always defeated, always striving to return. There is the time . . .'

'My trial is tomorrow. Is anyone thinking of turning up for it?'

Francesca's eyes suddenly focused on him.

'Of course,' she whispered, her lips barely moving. Could it be that she hated him?

'Super idea,' said Sarah, interrupting herself in a tone of businesslike preoccupation. 'Yes. The time of the engineer – the most coruscated, the boniest, the brittlest time of all . . .'

Colin's visits to Cynthia were regular now. He rang her from a call box, and found that she was free. Her evangelism had been supplemented by bodily comforts, and she bubbled at the door, enclosing his thin mouth in the fleshy purse of her lips.

'You just come in and lemme give you power to fight de battle an' speed to run de race. I bin thinking all day of you trial, and dat judge going to let you off sure as I'm a first-order sinner. Because you going dere wid all contrition and meekness of heart, and you be making clear to him just what state you was in on dat accursed day dey took you.'

She told him to look smart, blameless, herald of a spotless future. She poured Spanish burgundy from the bottle that he had brought with him, into two of her best glasses of rainbow-coloured crystal, and they drank to his acquittal. In the corner the new television showed a jiving, jiggering Elvis, with the sound turned off. Its cold blue light flickered across their bodies, as they wrestled on the couch. Colin felt, as he always did with Cynthia, a strange glamour of remoteness, an exotic sense of being elsewhere and unaccountable. Her powerful body scent, and rough, ample flesh welcomed him like a nomad's tent. He crept into their protection with all the desert wanderer's sense of hospitality offered unconditionally and at the brink of doom. Cynthia seemed to welcome his embraces: Colin was not another driving post, but a protégé whom she enfolded. He lay outside the norms of business, and their transaction was understood as part of a larger, more ambitious union, in which they both acted justified and touching parts.

Colin found a strange comfort too in Cynthia's surroundings. The objects which, viewed in isolation, had the aspect of powerless deities, together seemed to distil from themselves a spirit of victory over day-to-day vexations. His anxiety became self-imposed, even comic, in the presence of these cheerful baubles, whose insouciant disregard for all aesthetic measure gave to them a war-time air of chins up and carry on. He particularly liked the Venetian glass rabbits which Cynthia had gathered on the long window-sill, and which could collect the red light of the sun at six, dribbling it in diluted colours onto the wall. He felt no impulse to stare beyond the windows, despite the view of the city and St Paul's, and, from the other side, of the desolate docklands with their retreating margins of life-engendering slums. Those things, which had first scintillated in his imagination, were now held back by sentinels of bric-à-brac. His vision strayed from one appendage of Cynthia to another, and whether it be the elephant-textured skin of her buttocks, or a wispy frippery of glass, it resounded with the same sense of achievement, the same lack of pettiness, that he discerned in her dull admonitions and in her generous openings of love.

Cynthia was not allowed to speak of Francesca, but Colin knew what she thought. He read in her eyes the same mixture of deference and condemnation with which she had greeted his original attempt to describe his sorrows. For Cynthia, Francesca was comprehensible only on account of the Roman Catholic faith, which had turned so many people from the ways of the Lord. All Cynthia's morality was concentrated on illustrating the ways of Popery, and although names were never mentioned, Colin had learned to close his ears when reference was made to the idols of Canaan or to the daughter of Herodias. This time, however, he unburdened himself. He began slowly, softly, as Cynthia handed him her post-coital basketful of breasts. He described the recklessness of his existence, whirled from catastrophe to catastrophe, and now unable to obtain an answer even to the most urgent question. He had asked Francesca whether he should leave, and now tried to describe to Cynthia the peculiar pained expression with which she withheld her reply. He remembered that the air had seemed to thicken about her head, becoming grey, lightless, like a halo of lead. He had not been able to look at those eyes. Cynthia held his head and pressed it down onto her lips, drinking with unaffected relish from the little rivulets of tears. He described beastly evenings, in which overdressed phantoms danced on his grave. He imitated the well-bred insinuations of de Litham, the Hooray Henrying of Burridge, the whimsical affectation of Sarah. Cynthia understood nothing of this, but indicated that her breasts were ample compensation for the strain of living among freaks. Colin experienced an enormous relief in unburdening himself, and left Cynthia's flat with a sense that he would not, after all, go under, and that Francesca had lost some part of her authority.

As he walked back towards the Bank, he rang the Inspector from a phone box. The line had been cut off. So as not to lose the impulse, he scribbled a note to her, asking her to prepare his father's room. He placed the note in his wallet and walked on.

The house was empty on his return. She fell beside him in the middle of the night, her body raw, feverish and radiating pain, like the body of the dying Mrs Ferguson, as the schoolmaster had described it. Colin lay sleepless beside it, afraid to move lest he should make contact with its excruciated surface. In the morning he did not waken her; he preferred to enhance his resentment, going alone to his trial.

Colin stood between two policemen on a raised podium and took oaths. A large red man, dressed as a barrister, referred to him as 'my client' and gave an impassioned, though in Colin's view highly inaccurate, account of the scene on Primrose Hill. Colin learned that he had quarrelled with a girlfriend, who had jilted him that day. As a result of this, and of the realisation that he was failing as a writer, Colin had suffered an acute fit of something quaintly called melancholia. This in turn had led to the consumption of a bottle of whisky. Evidence was brought: the empty whisky bottle; a policeman who had taken Colin into custody; details of the failed writings. Colin was surprised to learn that he had written a play, entitled *The Desirable Gorgon*, which had been repeatedly rejected by fringe theatres all over London. A monograph on Goethe's *Faust* was mentioned: it had sold five copies. His failure as a writer was magnificent and covered many genres: poetry, essays, novels, stories, dramatic works of every description. He had even failed as a librettist, and a neurasthenic youth in a red shirt and luminous green tie came forward impersonating an avant-garde composer, and testifying volubly to Colin's incompetence. The spectacle of so great an ambition, and so great a disaster, fascinated Colin. There but for the grace of God, he thought. Of course, there was no reason why such a man should be forgiven. But in comparison with the evidence for the prosecution, which consisted in an illiterate summary uttered by a constable, and a single witness, a scruffy man in his mid-forties who wore for effect a few patches of sticking plaster about his forehead, the story had drama, humanity, and even sex-appeal. The girlfriend was brought in. Colin was surprised to see Judith Blakely. Not looking at him, she recited in a monotone how she had, through no fault of Colin's, decided on that afternoon to ask him to leave. For some time their relationship had been in disarray, Colin's depression over his writing created an ever greater strain between them, and the two children made impossible demands on her. The commonplace narrative redeemed its hero. Here was a perfectly normal, unassuming failure, a harmless vacuum in the lives of others, into which some chose to empty their energies, and from which others impatiently turned. This was not the stuff of a jailbird, and there was no surprise in the court when the judge, accepting the plea in mitigation, gave a suspended sentence. The thousand pounds compensation seemed a bit steep, but Colin supposed that whoever had paid for this performance would pay for that as well.

Sarah stood outside the courtroom and bundled him at once into a waiting taxi.

'We're off to the Afro,' she announced, turning to wave from the taxi window, and smiling cosmetically like the Queen.

The Afro Dizzy was a private club in Soho: only jet setters belonged to it, and they, or at least the younger group of them, could be seen leaning in their loud shirts against the chromium bar at every hour of the day and night, contemplating themselves in the room-length mirror which stretched behind the hermaphroditic barmen. The cocktails had bizarre names like 'fleeting fantasy' (in which grappa, champagne and green peppercorns competed for attention), 'French kiss' (a concoction of several liquers with iced Beaujolais and carrot juice) and 'friendly armpits' (an amalgam of Cointreau, garlic and goat's milk). Sarah poured champagne, as she described in detail the latest and most fashionable perversion, involving specially trained dogs, and dildoes flavoured with aniseed.

Colin fell almost instantly asleep. He awoke to the sound of music. At least, it might have been music. An insipid scuttering on bass and drums accompanied casual chords, placed on a black piano by ring-obliterated fingers. The pianist, a fat hermaphrodite in a sequin dress, addressed the room with staring, heroin eyes. People cried 'yeah!', and clapped once or twice languorously.

A girl sat imprisoned by drums, eyes half closed, thick fair hair cut long but boyishly, thighs apart. In her hands the drumsticks buzzed and fluttered like birds, brushing here, striking there, her foot moving independently like a preying creature trying to catch the rhythm of those entrancing wings. Colin watched her for a while; and then he became aware that Francesca was beside him, drinking a chocolate cocktail and staring at a man who sat opposite, dressed in a crocodile-skin coat.

She took Colin's arm and squeezed it.

'You're awake. And a free man. How lovely. I'm really sorry – not waking up in time. I didn't feel too good. This is David Ansell, one of my lecturers.'

The crocodile coat lifted itself and cracked open, to reveal a naked, smiling belly.

'Hello,' said Colin, 'make yourself at home.'

Sarah was now sitting with the drummer, staring into her face like a patient heron by a fishpond. Colin noticed that David Ansell, whose face was taut, lined and distracted, wore a Mickey Mouse watch.

'You must have children,' he commented, pointing to it.

Ansell looked at Colin with interest.

'Not at all,' he said. 'I searched for this watch for a long time. My friend – our friend – Cranmoor Bunce, found it for me. Francesca knows him of old: he is someone who shares my profound and moving passion for Mickey Mouse. I am what you call a Mickey Mouse nut. It's very serious. I think I actually love Mickey Mouse. The trouble began when I was a child. I had a Mickey Mouse doll that I used to fondle night and day. It got dirty in the process; in fact, to be frank, it began to smell. One day, when I was at school, my mother consulted a neighbour, who was an amateur psychiatrist, and particularly apprehensive of fetishism in children who were poised between the oral and the genital. The two bitches decided to throw the doll in the dustbin. When I came home I was told that Mickey Mouse had run away. I was inconsolable. Ever since then I have been like one of those creatures in What's-his-name's speech in *The Symposium*, wandering the earth in search of my other half, and consoling myself with images. I've just acquired a Mickey Mouse camera. A friend in New York has discovered some of the original Mickey Mouse costumes in a Disney memorabilia shop. Only five hundred dollars for a complete Mickey Mouse suit! As worn by little Janie Mason in the first Broadway performances. The trouble is, they are also bringing out a Mickey Mouse telephone, and I am hard up. I cannot decide between them. I simply *must* have both. What am I to do? Instead of being a man and deciding one way or the other, I throw away what little I earn on champagne and fripperies. And the result is that I shan't be able to afford either the suit or the telephone. My life is in ruins.'

'I'll buy you the suit,' said Francesca jubilantly, detaching her arm from Colin's. Ansell spread his hands in a reposeful gesture.

'You are an angel. You see Colin,' he went on, leaning forward confidentially, 'this is a serious matter. Women understand that. They understand that my sexual identity is involved. That's what the termagant who calls herself my mother discovered: she and the other hag saw a way to emasculate me. Naturally, I don't pretend that any of these objects come into the category of high art. But for me they are something far more important: they are part of myself. They are me. This is useful not only for David Ansell, but for his friends and acquaintances too. I have an identity: I can be acknowledged, grasped, loved, worshipped, without any fear of deception. My students give me Mickey Mouse tea-cloths, Mickey Mouse plates and cups, Mickey Mouse knickers, and Mickey Mouse bibelots; and they know that their gesture will go straight to my heart. In fact Colin,' he continued glancing sideways at Francesca, 'you cannot imagine how much more simple and orderly life becomes, just so long as the channels of passion are unobstructed. Until this recent conflict about the suit and the telephone I was one of the most tranquil people I know. I was on the point of compensating for that primal loss, which for me was a symbolic one, and therefore capable of restoration. Had I attached those sublime feelings, God forbid, to a father or a mother, where would I be now, with both the bastards dead, and no one but myself to water their graves? A mess, an embarrassment, an emotional vagrant. As it is, I have only to extend my arms and my first love rushes again towards them in a thousand forms, always the same, yet always surprising and delighting me with his new disguises. On the whole I think I have been beautifully served by my obsession. In fact, I would go so far as to say that it is the only part of me that is truly noble.'

Colin got up, Francesca put out a hand to restrain him, but her gesture was irresolute, and he walked past her to the door. As he left she looked at him, a strange, sad, defiant expression on her face. The music was louder, but Ansell was still talking rapidly, and had even taken Francesca's hand, which lay unresisting across the table.

Colin was compelled by a force stronger than himself to remain in Francesca's house. He rifled her cupboards, and spread her colourful costumes on the floor. He dabbed himself with her perfume, washed his hair in her honey-thick shampoo, which smelt of boiled sweets and hazel nuts. He went through her books and records, German classics, Beethoven, Gershwin. Her red and white woollen socks excited him, and he assembled them on the bed together with a pair of jeans and an unworn tee-shirt printed with the Wimpole motto: *Fertig Sey*. He contemplated this arrangement for three days, creeping carefully into the bed beside it so that it should not be disturbed.

During this time the house was silent. It did not surprise him that neither Francesca nor Sarah had returned from the Afro Dizzy. He imagined Francesca with Ansell, and Sarah with the electric drummer-girl, each couple clinging together in some pose of factitious ecstasy. He gathered up his clothes and papers, and dragged the trunk into the hall. Then he began to wash the cat, feeling as he did so that the drowning desperate creature was really himself. As he held it by the collar and splashed soapy water on its reddened belly, he began to mutter angrily. It seemed to him that there was no creature more stupid, more futile, more deserving of punishment at that moment than the cat. In a fit of bitterness he held its panicking head below the water, forcing it down with both hands until it had ceased to move. Afterwards it floated lopsidedly, with two stiffening legs emerging from the suds.

On the third day he discovered Francesca's journal. At the bottom of one of the cupboards, hidden beneath some Chinese curtains that had been stored there, were five large exercise books. He opened one of them, and then quickly closed it. For three hours he walked around the house in a state of abstraction, trying to remove from his mind the thought of secret things. To occupy himself, he fished the stiff catflesh from the kitchen sink and buried it in the garden. He felt pleasure in the task, as though he were doing someone a favour for which he would eventually be rewarded. To mark the spot he left one stiff black paw protruding from the earth.

He found himself resolved to read the journal. By chance the volume that he picked up related to the months of their happiness. He recognised the dates over several pages as corresponding to particular incidents – a picnic in a country churchyard, a visit to the opera, the first days alone at Bassington Hall. He felt certain that here, at least, he could find some real testimonial to her love for him. He chose the entry for October 3rd, the day of the picnic in the little churchyard overlooking the chill bright vale of Oxford. He remembered the soft bones of her wrist as they moved beneath his fingers, and her intent, serious expression as she taught him to say the *Confiteor* and the *Ave Maria*.

'Oh C., why must you speak all the time of love? Why must you place this electric halo round the world, just because you look at it and look at me, and so wrongly and unjustly connect us? If only you knew, if only you knew what I have hidden from you – this Thing which possesses me and which excludes every rival. It is a jealous god, the Thing. It will destroy you as it destroyed the others – J., F., Mr. X. Here C. – I offer you a poem. Should I send it to you, leave it for you? That would be like speaking from the heart. So I shall write it in this book, where you will never see it. My imitation heart stands proxy for the real one, and the real one was given forever to the Thing. Remember that C.! Remember it!

CFW

> A baby – is it you? Is it me?
> A refugee – you? Or me?
>
> Someone wants, someone holds –
> Is it you? Is it me?
> Someone strays, someone scolds –
> Me in you? You in me?
>
> An orphan – who will take it in,
> Wash it clean of your, my sin?
> Nobody? Nobody?
>
> This dark encampment,
> Borderland,
> This mark, this stamp, meant
> For you, or me
> In murderland;
>
> 'Me-in-you,' 'You-in-me' –
> Little label,
> Pre-Babel,

          Rational,
          International –
          'Refugee'.

          Orphan branded,
          Held and handed
          Me to thee, and thee to me –
          Is it you? Is it me?
          Me in you, you in me?

          The Officials to not say,
          Cannot stay,
          Other murders on today,
          But 'Stay
          Put, don't stray,
          Not worth it anyway.'

          Poor orphelin,
          They've locked you in,
          Landed, branded,
          Stamped and clamped –

          Who'll manage your identity?
          Will nobody? Nobody?

Where did that come from, C.? From deep down, from the place where the Thing resides and reigns eternally, silently. Heed it, and beware!'

Colin closed the journal with trembling hands. Of course he had been deceived – not by her, since she had hinted that some other thing possessed her. She had even explicitly warned him of it, in the allegory of Dr Kiss. No, he had been deceived by himself, and by this world they had created together, with such bitter-sweet complicity. He replaced the journal, and rose to go.

Francesca was standing in the door of the room, watching him. Her expression – pinched and twisted like a tortured thing – was so far removed from her repertoire that it was a moment before he recognised her.

'Please go.'

She spoke softly, but her face did not change. The outraged pupils swamped her picasso eyes, and her features seemed to twist round on themselves cubistically, front and sides visible together like a pinned dissected creature.

He tried to speak, but his throat was dry. She moved back a pace, and he walked onto the landing. There was a noise in the street, and then as he descended the stairs the front door opened violently. Sarah came in, leading a dance of death in which everyone had been included. Harold Plumptre smiled at Colin, but the others were grim and taciturn as they passed into the drawing room. They rolled up the carpets and began to rattle like bones, tapping their heels on the floorboards.

Colin went into the garden. He wanted a last look at the house; at Francesca's window; at the little patch of grass and the herbal border where the cat was buried, its paw still signalling from the lower world. He wished for tears, but they would not come. Everything real was buried now, a lifeless paw the only sign of his former passion.

In the living room Sarah was standing among a troupe of admirers, blowing smoke rings and chanting. The drummer-girl hung on Sarah's arm, murmuring quietly and occasionally kissing her neck. Harold Plumptre got up from a giggle of groupies on the sofa, stepped towards him, and said:

'You'd be better off out of this, old man.'

'I think you're right.'

'I know I'm right. A mistake to haunt the scene of failure.'

'A mistake I always make.'

'Ah, so do I, old man,' said Harold agreeably. 'So do I. But then, in my case, there are no other scenes to haunt.'

Sarah had ambled to the telephone, leaving the drummer-girl draped like a shawl over Francesca's armchair. Dialling a number, she chattered in an American accent about a black man's penis which had been displayed to the cognoscenti that afternoon; the girl cooed and chortled softly, and then, with a sudden cough, poured a stream of wine-dark vomit onto the cushions. Colin snatched the telephone and slammed it down. Sarah watched him distractedly. 'My, what muscles!' she said, and sauntered over to Harold, who was manhandling the pale form of the drummer-girl to the bathroom.

As he left the house, Colin came across Francesca, standing alone in the hallway.

'You are crying,' she said, as though she were answering a question.

Twelve

IT WAS early November, and Colin sat alone at his desk. The mist had risen; a chill sunlight cast long shadows across the park, and poured over his desk, where it whitened the paper, and mocked his emptiness. A horn sounded and suddenly the hunt was passing, hounds in full cry, the tarmac ringing from the hooves of horses, as they leaped the wall by the cottage. One man – a dandy in pink with rolling eyes – rode diagonally at the jump. His delicate chestnut refused, slipped, tried vainly to collect itself, and was rammed from behind. The crack seemed to split the day apart, discarding every fact except this moment. The chestnut sank to the ground, threw its rider sideways and then, its white eyes starting from their sockets, struggled to its feet, a broken hindleg shrivelled to a ham-shaped wad of agony. Thrice the horse rose to stagger after its fellows; thrice it keeled over, touched the road with its shattered hock, and squealed to its gods for mercy. The blood rushed to Colin's heart; his mouth went dry, his throat tightened, and he dropped his pen to the floor.

The sympathy we feel for speechless things is a homage to their innocence; why, we ask, must they suffer, who are incapable of wrong? Colin bounded to the stairs, breathing rapidly. He would repair the fault of creation, adjust with words and guns and medicines all the fibres of commiseration, so that this horse be saved. The neighing was desperate now, calling to him from realms of wildest terror. Colin cantered along the hallway. His nostrils flared, his eyes rolled, and his head filled with plans. He would fetch the vet; he would hold the horse and coax it home; he would ease its leg into a splint, spend all his savings on a miraculous cure. With patience, he had read, even the most shattered leg could be re-set. He reached the door and opened it.

The doorframe jammed against a letter. Colin bent down impatiently. Then he noticed Francesca's handwriting. There it was: his name, flamboyant and italicised. How long had it been lying there? He did not know, for the letter bore no stamp.

There was another curious detail: the address was typed, as though she had dictated it. Colin relinquished the doorknob and hobbled back to his father's room. Outside a shot rang out, but he scarcely noticed. It occurred in another space and another time, in a world that he could never enter.

> Dear Colin, [he read] much has happened since I saw you. I sincerely hope that you are well and happy, as I am. Tomorrow I am getting married to Jonathan Burridge. The freaks have taken leave of my senses, and stepped out of my life through doors that I never dreamed could be opened. You were right to dislike those people, Colin, and I am glad that I finished with them. Now I can begin again, and I am looking forward to it so much! When we meet we will be as good friends as ever, won't we? Meanwhile, look after yourself. With love from F.

Colin could think of no reply to this letter. In the failing light he walked by the river under Offlet Hill. Life had sunk to its depths, and winter sifted the water with slow chill fingers of frost. Mist was gathering again beneath the trees, like tears under eyelashes, and everywhere came the same quiet dripping sound, comfortless and chill. Entering the horse-sick pasture where they should have met, he saw two ponies standing together for warmth, their alert ears following his movement as he criss-crossed towards them through the mist. He stroked the mane of the friendly skewbald; and then its neighbour, with a sudden jerk of the head, reared away. They went galloping over the rise, their long tails flowing behind them, catching the last glimmer of light, goodbye, goodbye.

The Hall shone yellow and unreal beneath him. Francesca had been claimed by it, and the windows blazed in celebration. Shafts of light were staked across the gravel, and a large black Daimler flicked through their lines, turning in a circle by the porch. Through the still air came the sound of a car door slamming – a sound of wealth and power, of indifference and domination. One day he would be revenged on the Wimpoles, for his own sake, for his father's sake, and for the sake of all who suffered from this pestilence of power.

It was not easy to begin his retribution. Bitterness encased his heart; and as winter wore on and the colour drained from the countryside, he became ever more secretive and still. The Inspector hovered, and Archie visited. But Colin barely noticed them. He was elsewhere, in an element where heat and light did not pass. He sat among books which he could not read, and sheets of paper on which he could not write, and planned his unforgiving actions. He would complete the course at the College of Law, become a barrister, and take legal action for the defence of Offlet Hill. He would apply to the training college in Dunsbury, and be a teacher like his father, injecting anger and rebellion into the hearts of the young. He would write unceasingly, become a famous journalist, biting, controversial, a champion of the underdog against the faceless world of power. He would travel abroad, join forbidden armies, return hardened and violent, with a hand of steel; he would be a politician, an evangelist, a murderer. And as the senseless schemes formed and unformed in his mind like clouds blown by the wind, he crouched at the desk, his eyes fixed on the wall where the chestnut horse had fallen.

Sometimes he would regain the sense of reality, and stand over and above himself like an artist or a god. At these moments he would take his pen and begin to write – poems, paragraphs of meditation, and once a letter to his father, recounting the story of Francesca in terse, cryptic phrases. Then, in the middle of a sentence, he would lose track of his thoughts and stare into the park, his mind awash with useless images.

His trance was broken by Cynthia. It was a day late in February, unnaturally warm, and full of the startled creaking of awakened things. The soggy sun, drunk with mist, rolled along the horizon, trailing its lazy ribbons in the soup of life. On such a day, with the mould of nature lying broken and scattered, a ghost can speak from the field or the sky, as well as from the telephone. For a moment Colin imagined that Cynthia was merely haunting him, as Francesca and the schoolmaster haunted him. For he had become a hauntee, a creature who has no contact with the living. The cascade of Cynthia-sound was like a conversation in a dream, its meaning imprecise and atmospheric. Then suddenly she spoke the word 'Francesca'.

'Who gave you my number?' he asked.

'She did.'

'Who? What the hell are you saying?'

'Francesca, she give your nummer, like I said. You listen baby?'

'I don't understand.'

'Dis urgen' Colin. You come see me now.'

'Where?'

'Like I said, de Hospice of de Sacred Heart.'

The Hospice of the Sacred Heart stands on a hill above the valley of the Thames, at the point where the last fragments of London lie broken in the fields, and the first beechwoods begin to intervene along the river banks. At the foot of the hill an old Norman abbey lies ruined among immaculate red houses, its graves and cloisters rolled over by neatly tonsured lawns. Those who can afford it send their more alarming relatives to Sacred Heart, where they are cared for in genteel captivity. And when the padded Rolls has whispered fruitlessly from door to door in Harley Street, they come here themselves to die. No expense is spared in adding charm and modesty to death's demeanour, and in forging those links with the world beyond which make us insensible of the final transition. Here patients move with whatever limbs and powers remain to them in a peculiar no-man's-land, a place seized from death's vast kingdom and planted with statuary and flowers. Nothing at Sacred Heart is ordinary; and nothing extraordinary either. Life is sliced so thin you can see to the other side; yet it retains its traditional pattern. Breakfast, lunch, tea and dinner; reading, writing, conversing, walking and listening; and even the newspapers each morning, coming marked with your name to the breakfast table.

Cynthia was standing behind wrought-iron gates with armorial crestings. Her plump figure had been pressed by a starchy uniform into square blocks of blue and white. Behind her stood a Regency villa with gothic windows, battlements and crenellated turrets, from one of which a figure was frantically beckoning. Colin passed through the gates, and a man stepped across his path. He was neatly dressed, the top pocket of his jacket crammed full of expensive pens. His features were taut and lined with age, and his bloodless lips moved rapidly and soundlessly as he clutched at Colin's sleeve. Colin could never rid himself of the impression that urgent people should be taken at their own evaluation: frequently they come from God, with personal messages it would be folly to ignore. 'Out with it,' he cried, 'out with it!' Then Cynthia too laid an arm on his sleeve and brushed the supplicant away.

'Mr Windeatt, you leave de visitor alone. You stop you naughtinesses or I shall smite thee so that thou shalt not stand.'

The old man retreated a pace or two and then stared in awe at Cynthia, who took Colin's arm and began to lead him away.

'Well darlin', dis de strangest meetin' we ever have an' I reel sorry.'

'I don't understand. Tell me everything. Tell me first what *you* are doing here?'

'De ole man, he left for Sain' Vincen' like he said he would. You know I never suit dat udder trade, but what I do wid my qualicashuns? Well, de good Lord He provide, and dey 'ployed me here on speck. Only it's a strange, sad place Colin – and dey be Papishes runnin' it, and so many dese people Moabites and idolators, I give dem no en' of a stick, you bet. Dere.'

Cynthia, who could not contemplate her own grievances for long, brightened sympathetically at the thought of his trouble.

'Dat poor kid,' she continued. 'Ain't nuttin' dey can do for her.'

Mr Windeatt stepped between them and glanced at Colin from grey dismal eyes, moving his lips disconsolately. Suddenly Cynthia began to shout.

'Mr Windeatt, you go long now and eat you jelly! O terrible voice of mos' jus' judgemen', which shall be pronounce upon dem, when it shall be said unto dem, Go, ye cursed, into de fire everlastin' . . .'

Before Cynthia could finish her commination, Mr Windeatt had scurried back across the lawn towards the hospice, and begun to pack himself in agitation through a small lancet window. Cynthia breathed deeply and turned back to Colin.

'Some dese people dey right out o' dere heads. Dat's where I come in, for de strong-arm stuff. No qualicashuns needed for shoutin'.'

She led him behind a cluster of evergreen oaks, out of sight of the house. There she recounted her strange and terrible discovery. As junior nurse in the geriatric wing, Cynthia's days were far from gay. Nothing is more grievous to the sight than senile decay, in which the body staggers about the world, its soul already petering out, dwindling by degrees like an indecisive guest who dreads his next appointment. Worn down with peevish demands, Cynthia was in the habit of absenting herself, knowing that neither her presence nor her absence could change the air of stagnant exasperation in which her patients moved. She preferred the wing where the youngest patients were housed, and where she had a special friend called Mirabelle, a nurse from Rhodesia. Here, in sunlit rooms, the doomed children of the upper classes passed away in style, enjoying pleasant views, and spacious halls where they could talk and congregate. They smiled mirthlessly but often, from thin, stoical faces, each bearing a personal badge of death like a noble decoration. Some were in wheelchairs, some were blanched and cheesy from chemotherapy or radium; some lay motionless on banks of cushions, like pleasure-boats rotting in the mud. Yet all did what they could to make a success of the party, and the nurses and doctors joined in the solemn transactions like shy tourists, pressingly invited to some heathen ceremony. A few residents, however, were too ill to take part in the corporate life – which was a corporate death – of Sacred Heart. And one of them was Francesca.

Cynthia and Mirabelle often visited the upper corridor, where the worst cases were stored in private rooms. Four weeks before a young and pretty girl had been moved here, after a hunting accident on her husband's estate in Leicestershire. It was not the accident – a trivial fall against a fence – which brought her to Sacred Heart, but the spinal tumour which it triggered, the recurrence, apparently, of a former ailment, now rampaging out of control. Mirabelle had learned these facts from the confidential files which were her favourite reading. Now Francesca lay in one of the airy upper rooms, gripped by a paralysing hand, hardly speaking. A neat busy lady visited and gave instructions, and once a gentleman, large, slow-eyed and authoritative, stood severely in the doorway, tried various forms of words, and departed in disarray. As for the husband, there had been no sign of him.

'Lord what discovries I come on Colin. An' how bad I judge you know, when I go forgettin' all our righteousnesses are as filthy rags, and us needin' His mercy one an' all. For she bin sick dis many year, an' hidin' it like somethin' shameful, mebbie for famlie reasons. Famlie reasons de mos' importan' reasons in Sacred Heart.'

Cynthia put out her two pink palms to him, and he held them a moment. Two large and undemanding tears formed in her sooty eyes, and he watched them, as they detached themselves and dribbled onto her chin.

'Den you know Colin I take a shine to her: she so pretty an' quiet an' never complainin'. An' I don' min' de cross roun' her neck, nor de pries' comin' an' goin'. So I speak to her offen, an' I read de Holy Book, an' tell stories of my wickedness: I see in her eyes she enjoy dem and mebbie feel she not so bad and ready to be goin' 'cross to glory. She smile sometime, like an angel. An' wid de injeckshuns, de pain go sudden down, an' she speak to me, so kine an' gentle, while she can. Den dis mornin' she ask to see you, an' for de firs' time I think, mebbie I know dis girl, mebbie I bin travellin' quiet alongside her many a year. Course dere some few people in de worl' call' Colin Ferguson, an' I never knewed your nummer. But when she say it muss be seecrit, an' dey mussn' know, den' I have no doubt of it. So dere, I come straight to dat phone, an I soun' through like de voice of judgemen'. An' I grieve for you Colin, I grieve reel sore, tinkin' mebbie you don' wanna know, mebbie I do bad in tellin' you . . .'

'You did right,' he said. And in his desolation he found space for gratitude towards Cynthia, the only generous creature in his life, the only comforter.

She took his arm, led him in silence across the lawn, and pushed him through the gothic arch of the door. A woman's face raised its eyes towards them from behind a marquetry desk, and then lowered them to the pages of a paperback. A huge chandelier of brass lit up the entrance hall, and above it a vaulted ceiling fanned out in eight directions to boldly painted octagonal walls of gold and ultramarine.

'We go dis way,' said Cynthia, pointing to the sign marked 'Geriatric'. 'Dey won' suspeck where we aimin' for.'

A large panelled door stood open, and through it, cushioned by the no-noise of the Hospice, ruined ancient figures moved back and forth. Inside the room others were engaged in a slow circuitous ballet, carefully preserving their limbs from all contact with each other. Elegant furniture had unaccountably been placed there, and they brushed against it curiously, like fish against the gorgeous wreck of an ocean liner. Cynthia led him along a corridor. Other figures passed them, retreating to the wall as Cynthia approached, and growling quietly.

They climbed some stairs into a passage, which was long, silent, and carpeted thickly in green. The patients were younger now, gaunt, sallow and with an air of resignation in their eyes. Colin noticed a series of numbered doors. Beyond was a frosted glass panel, and Cynthia pointed to it, saying, 'Dat Mirabelle's awfice; when you finish, you see me dere.' Pushing open one of the doors, she poked her head around it, said, in a chirrupy voice, 'Colin here darlin',' and quickly withdrew, squeezing his hand.

The room was bright, comfortable, with antique furniture and a carpet of thick blue pile. The lancet windows looked out over the garden, and the coverlet of the bed was printed with a gay sunny pattern of yellow and green. One of her puppets was propped on a low chest of drawers, together with a bottle of lotion. The room smelled faintly of Francesca, but he could not see her. Maybe they had taken her away for examination; maybe they were treating her in some other place, where they pried her unconscious body on a table.

Then he caught sight of her pale hair, spread on the pillow like a fan. So thin had she become that the bedclothes lay flat upon her and her face was hidden by the counterpane. A hand gradually crept from the bedclothes and faintly stirred in his direction. He stood above the drained white face; her grey eyes rested on him, and her lips began to quiver. With the greatest effort, she lifted a hand in his direction, and there lingered on her face that still, solemn expression which he had seen when first they met.

'Francesca.'

Her fingers were cold, rigid, and bent over his hand like hooks.

'Francesca.'

He looked for some hint of a smile, so that he could catch it, magnify its glimmer, and reflect back the promise of health. Waves of tenderness swept over him, and he caressed her fingers, feeling certain that he could warm them into life. But they remained cold, tightly gripping. She made an effort to uncoil her locked body, and move her head towards him. But she succeeded only in rocking a little, while shadows of pain ran across her cheeks and temples. He reached out to touch her mouth: it was damp, cold, and the lips quivered against him.

'You,' she said.

Her voice was stifled, barely audible. Her hand moved to his wrist, and fixed itself there, like a scaly claw on a perch. A thousand images of her coursed through his mind, all condensed at last into this broken doll which trembled before him. For some minutes they did not move. Colin looked from the window: a spring breeze fanned the trees in the garden. Beyond them he could just make out the silver gleam of the river as it caught the sunlight between two wooded hills.

He had the impression that he sat in the cottage in Bassington, and that the thing which he guarded was not Francesca but some memorial of her, as though she were already dead. And when the door opened he imagined that it was the Inspector entering to sniff the air. He turned to find Lord Shepton, who stood in the doorway, his strange pale eyes resting motionless on Colin. Francesca closed her eyes. Her stillness transmitted itself through the room, to

Colin, and to her father, who looked down on the scene with no trace of feeling. It was as though their three lives, meeting at last in a single point, were locked immovably. Time stopped in that light-filled room, and her breathing, which barely lifted the air, was like the faint pulse of a clock whose hands are tied.

Then Lord Shepton beckoned to him, mouthing silently. As Colin reached the door, the baronial arm came down behind him, sweeping him across the threshold and out of her life. The passage to Francesca was closed.

'Goodbye,' he said softly, 'goodbye Francesca.'

Lord Shepton turned, making a wall across the doorway. Burnished arrows of windowlight sped along his cheek and flecked his sparse hair with flame. With one hand behind him he nudged Colin away, and his gesture, as he softly closed the door, had something indefinable of family. It announced an exclusive claim, beyond affection and immune to compromise. A Wimpole, it said, belongs with other Wimpoles, is obliged to them and obscurely watched over by them, lives only by virtue of their intricate permissions, and joins them at last in a place where no lesser kind can enter, and where explanations are not required. The door clicked gently shut on her, with metal perfection. And it was as though he closed already the door of her tomb.

The Rolls had never recovered from its maltreatment in Ealing, and now led a withdrawn existence, like a dowager who had been beaten by teenage thugs. Lord Shepton did not expressly mention the fact, but let it be known nevertheless as they sped in the failing light to Bassington. He apologised for the Daimler, in which they travelled separated from the uniformed driver by a screen of glass; and he recalled this or that advantage of his former conveyance, in the anxious tone of one who reaches in his weariness for a familiar support and finds that it has vanished.

A strange transformation had overcome Lord Shepton's features, since they appeared (it was outside the gates of

Sacred Heart) in the rear window of the whispering limousine. Colin's first instinct had been to refuse the invitation. Only five minutes before he had been weeping on Cynthia's neck, and condemning Lord Shepton as the true cause of all this suffering – though how Francesca's illness could have been avoided by a wiser choice of parent neither he nor Cynthia could say. However, he was struck by something urgent and vulnerable in her father's tone. If he entered the Daimler, he told himself, it was not for the convenience of a lift to Bassington (though the journey that morning by bus and train had taken the best part of three hours), but in order to take advantage of this opportunity, speeding in a capsule from which there was no escape, to secure his retribution.

The extraordinary thing, however, was that Lord Shepton began at once to apologise. Colin, he said, had done right to visit Francesca, had done right to stand by her, to watch over her, to struggle, however fruitlessly, against a family bent on driving her down paths which were not hers. Whereas they, the Wimpoles, had done grievous wrong, in striving to bring her back to them, in pushing her little by little and uncommitted, into a marriage with a crass buffoon, in trying to hide from the world, as they hid from themselves, and had hidden for ten weary years, the illness which ought to have ruled out the very possibility of such ersatz solutions.

Colin had seen Lord Shepton once, caught in a shaft of sunlight in the corridor of the Hall. He had looked then as he did now, distracted, heavy, his wattles trembling with subdued emotion, and his eyes rolled heavenwards, as though testifying to a vestigial belief in a being higher than himself. Pain spread over his countenance in a kind of oily luminescence, so that the face approximated ever more closely to his daughter's: the same stationary eyes, the same slow turning of the neck in response, the same half-open lips on which a question seemed always to be forming. At one point he even raised his left hand to his eyes, so that Colin's role as prosecutor was no longer possible. Soon nothing remained of Colin's accusations, save charges which Lord

Shepton had already levelled – and with a pre-emptive bid for exculpation – at himself.

'You see Colin, we have lived for many years in the knowledge that this would happen. The specialist who treated her is an old friend of the family. He was frank with us, and we were grateful. It was only a matter of time, he said, before it would strike again, and the second blow is fatal. Unfortunately Francesca knew it too. She overheard a certain conversation, and it affected her badly. She began to hate us, to hate me in particular, to run from the dreadful fact that life and love were now beyond all hoping for. She escaped into a world of her own, a world of fantasy. And seeing this, we copied her. We each found our way to hide the truth. Hers was to mix with frivolous people, to canter through the air amid broomsticks and nightmares. Ours was to make stupid plans for her, to lay out the contours of a normal country life, complete with servants, farm, husband and even children. Her own lie didn't deceive her, so at last she adopted ours. *Enfin bref* – this hunting accident, what was it, in the end, but a self-willed confrontation with the truth, a challenge to her fate to step out at last and show itself?'

Colin clasped his hands together, to prevent them from shaking.

'This specialist,' he said. 'Was his name Kiss?'

'Kish. How did you know?'

Colin recounted Francesca's story. He felt her beside him, summoning his loyalty, asking him for the last time to speak for her and vindicate her suffering. But his words were hesitant and full of doubt, and his voice became muffled, as though in shame at what he was saying. Lord Shepton leaned against the leather seat and hid his face in his hands.

For a long while the only sound was the swish of tyres on the road, and the occasional clatter of branches against the roof of the car. As they swept over the rise into the vale of Bassington, the last light lingered on Offlet Hill. Beyond was Murricombe, and the Victorian barn where the schoolmaster had died, believing to the last that the broken figure, which still clutched its face in the corner of the Daimler, was his implacable enemy and the cause of all catastrophes.

'Poor girl,' Lord Shepton said at last.

There was a light in the kitchen window of the cottage. Lord Shepton signalled to the driver and the Daimler began to lose speed with a faint, smooth, rhythmical sound like the noise of someone polishing.

'I hope you will go on living here,' he said, as Colin descended. 'There were plans to widen the road, but we must stop that. It was a stupid idea of my son's to build on Offlet Hill. Thank God your father made such a fuss.'

He extended his hand, and Colin gripped it uncertainly.

'Goodbye,' said Lord Shepton, quietly and coldly, instantly withdrawing his hand. He rolled his eyes away and, as the car began to move, sank back into the corner, his left hand shielding his face.

After two days a letter was handed into the schoolmaster's room. The Inspector grunted 'You', and closed the door on the darkness which had reigned since Colin's return from Sacred Heart. The envelope was addressed in a childish hand. Opening it, Colin found another, inscribed with his name in Francesca's bold italics. A note read: 'Cynthia said to send you this, Mrs Burridge what we look after being desirus of it, yours faithfully, Mirabelle Nkoto.'

Colin drew the curtain violently: his mother's lalique vase fell and splintered. Out in the park sunlight striped the damp meadows, and the trees glistened with dew. His first instinct was to throw away the letter. It would be only one more concoction, one more enigma, one more allegory for facts that he could not comprehend. But how could she have written it, she who was hardly conscious? A great astonishment came over him: astonishment at Francesca's soul, which invaded and possessed him in so many transmutations, and which still found the way to him even at the edge of life. He sat down at the desk, and opened the letter; it dated from six weeks before, and was addressed from a farm in Leicestershire.

Dearest Colin,
Perhaps this will be my last communication to you. Yesterday I hurt my back, and I fear that something is happening to me – something that will cut me off from you for ever. I must tell you what I have always wanted to tell you, before it is too late, and knowing that we may never meet again.

The truth that I hid from you I called by many names: Dr Kiss was only one of them; another was the Thing. Yet could you not guess what it was and how it tortured me? It is death that has made such a mockery of life for me, and such a mockery of our love. How crabbed and cruel and coldhearted I became under death's instructions. Even to the point of marrying at last, where I could not love. Yet it was not the cruel Thing which acted through my body. Not really, not when the masks were down.

I've been thinking all morning of the hell that I contrived for you over these years, contrived because I wanted you so much, wanted to be a part of you, and to make you share in the chaos which is mine. When I came back home that day last summer, and saw you reading my diary, and saw the terrible sadness in your face, believe me, I wasn't angry with you. I wanted to throw myself at your feet and ask forgiveness. I wanted to take your hands, your cold, nervous hands, and press them to my lips, and tell you that what you were reading was not the truth, that the truth was here, on its knees, before you. Now the time has passed for that; I cannot see you to say to your dear face how much beyond words I have loved and wanted you. Not just now and recently, but for years. And yet I told you to go. Can you forgive me? Please Colin, you must try to forgive me, for those words, and for all the other words that have hurt you. They were not meant. No, they were meant. A whole part of me spoke through them, and I hardly knew this part or understood its purposes until it was too late.

Dear Colin, it is strange to think that I was born for this, just to come into the world in order to love you and destroy you. But it is true. Whenever the Thing lets me alone, and my soul is there shaken but living in my body, I pray for you. And in these moments of respite I see everything with a new clarity: the clouds open and all the past lies before me, etched with light. One episode comes back to me, and now I must tell you, although I have kept it hidden for so long. I did not love you at first; not even after 1.2 meetings. It happened a year later, one day when I was alone at the Hall. One of your letters had arrived, with its strange accounts of pimps and vagabonds, and its peculiar language to which I would never reply – though once or twice I tried. I knew you had the secret of loneliness. I wanted to learn from you, so as to bear the solitude of being me. Your letter filled me with anticipation; but it also warned me away. I went into the park; everything had a hollow look. Nothing belonged, nothing touched or hung together; the sunlight poured through the world like water through a sieve, washing its solidity away, and leaving only a mesh of holes. I sat down on the bench – the bench where you had sat, bending forward in that funny way and telling me about Bassington and the countryside and all those things around me which I'd never noticed, except to label them as 'ours'. A figure appeared at the gateway to the drive. It seemed to catch sight of me; then it hesitated a moment and walked on. I don't know why, but I caught my breath as it passed. There was a kind of doom in its movements. As I looked at the space between the gate-posts, it reappeared and stood for a moment, watching me. Then it came slowly down the drive in my direction, drifting from side to side like something borne on the wind. I wanted to run, but my legs lost their strength, and I had no protection, except to close my eyes. When I looked out again, a man stood before me, small, thin, with a wiry neck and an Adam's apple that went up and down like a ping-pong ball in a fountain. His eyes were deeply set and staring, and his cheeks were iron-grey and lifeless, like the cheeks of a corpse. He told me my name, just as you had done, and introduced himself as 'Colin's father'. My heart jumped into my mouth, and I could not answer. What a miserable, wheedling tale he told, of you and him. Did you not see how much he cared for you? He could not understand the world's ingratitude. He could not understand why he suffered so much. He seemed to know that you had written to me. He wanted news of you: where were you, what doing, and with whom? I stayed silent, and his eyes accused me.

'Very well,' he said, 'you will not speak to me. But perhaps you'd do me a favour.'

He stood for a moment in a premeditated trance, his hands twisted together, and his eyes all aglow.

'Perhaps you'll let him know that I exist. That's all. Just that I exist.'

And he laughed, an uncanny sound which seemed to come from somewhere else. He withdrew from me backwards, fixing me with those dreadful eyes, and vanishing slowly like a ghost.

'No you don't exist,' I said to myself, 'you don't exist.' And I felt a kind of triumph. All of a sudden my love for you was born: love for someone determined, despite their efforts, just to be. That was the image I cherished, and I wanted to be true to it: not to see you or touch you but just to know that you stood in solitude, denying them. I understood you then, Colin, and understood that you were me. What a strange secret this was, and how hard to keep from you: that my love was your father's doing.

There is a park here, but ironed out and sad. I look from the window at the treeless meadows, and I long for Offlet Hill, where we should have met. I remember the pond at home, the shadows of trees beneath it, and those things that I named in honour of you. If I can fight off the Thing, if I can be whole and alive and free from dread, then I shall come home there, home to Bassington, to the cottage, and to you. We shall walk everywhere on Offlet Hill and the vale, and around Murricombe and horrid, sprawling Dunsbury, and I will listen to the things you know about Bassington, and the country, and my family, and about how important and wicked we have always been. And I shall laugh and think how very unimportant we are beside you. Perhaps you could write our history, and triumph over us. And even I could have a place in it – a place in what you write. As I was looking across the garden, the gardener came leading a child by the hand. I thought how strange it was that I should be watching them. I remembered you leading me everywhere by the hand, and I felt the touch of your fingers on my wrist. Then I began to cry because I shall not see you again.

If I get well again I would never maltreat you Colin. I cry now when I think of what you have suffered because of me. I wish I could walk every step that you walked, touch every corner of every room that you lived in and say 'I was here, I was there, because he was.' But it is too late now. My life was an experiment. I thought that by loving you I would be real. But instead you were included in my fate and I dragged you down.

I must say goodbye Colin. Forgive me, and pray for me.

F.

P.S. If I ever dare to send this letter, you must keep it to yourself forever. And please don't get in touch with me.
F.

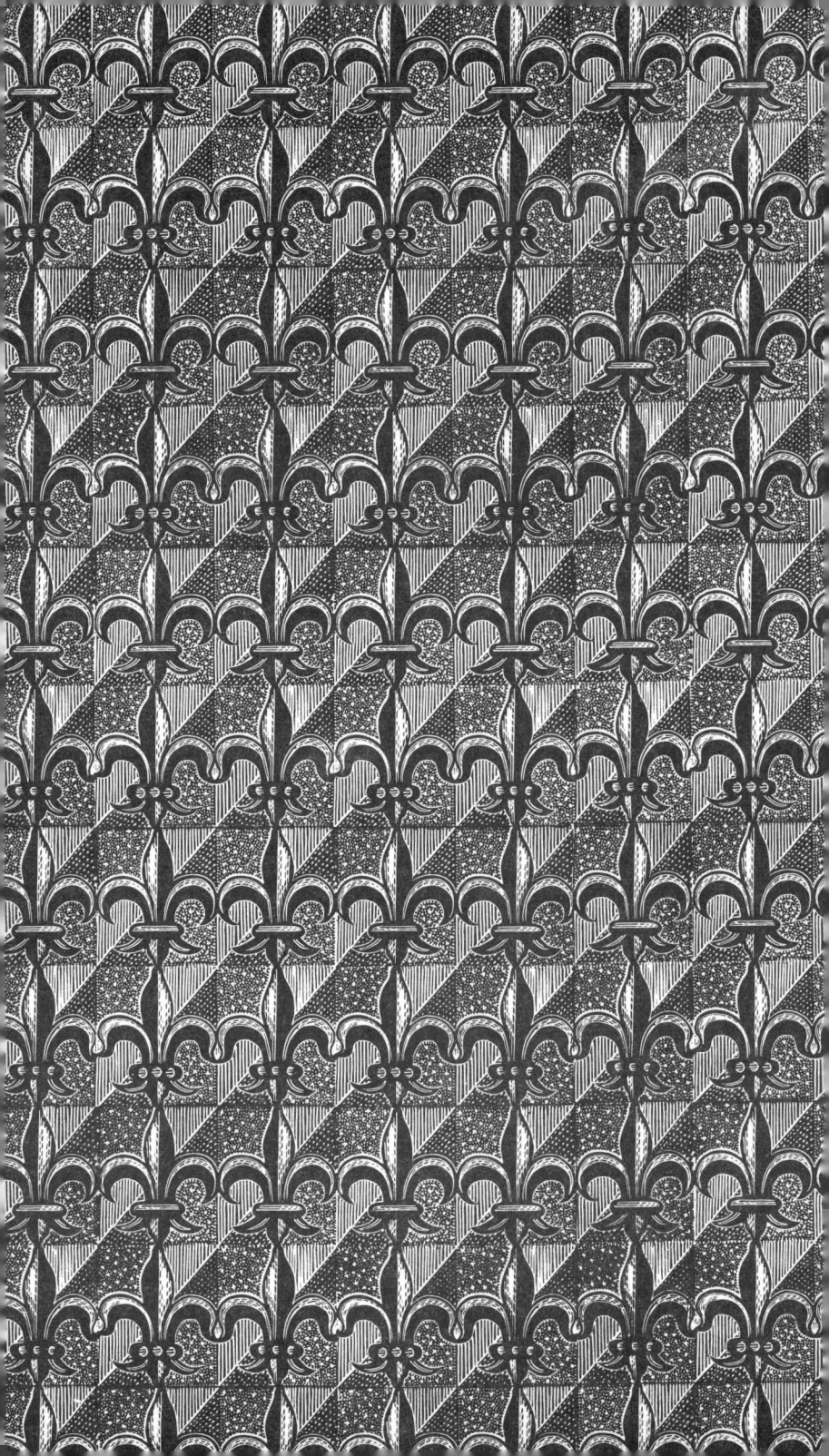